A SUITABLE BRIDE

FENELLA J MILLER

B

Boldwood

First published in 2016. This edition published in Great Britain in 2025 by Boldwood Books Ltd.

Cover Design by Colin Thomas

Cover Images: Colin Thomas and Shutterstock

A CIP catalogue record for this book is available from the British Library.

Paperback ISBN 978-1-83678-294-0

Large Print ISBN 978-1-83678-295-7

Hardback ISBN 978-1-83678-293-3

Ebook ISBN 978-1-83678-296-4

Kindle ISBN 978-1-83678-297-1

Audio CD ISBN 978-1-83678-288-9

MP3 CD ISBN 978-1-83678-289-6

Digital audio download ISBN 978-1-83678-292-6

This book is printed on certified sustainable paper. Boldwood Books is dedicated to putting sustainability at the heart of our business. For more information please visit https://www.boldwoodbooks.com/about-us/sustainability/

Boldwood Books Ltd, 23 Bowerdean Street, London, SW6 3TN

www.boldwoodbooks.com

1

SILCHESTER COURT, HERTFORDSHIRE

Beaumont Edward Peregrine Sheldon, seventh Duke of Silchester, had known from his birth that he would one day take over the position of head of the family, so becoming a duke was not a shock to him. However, finding the family coffers almost empty was another matter entirely.

His father had been in his fifties and one might have expected him to live for another twenty years at least, but he'd taken a tumble down the stairs when in his cups and broken his neck. The drinking had become an issue since Mama had died from the influenza five years ago and it was a miracle the duke hadn't met a similar end before this.

Beau shuffled the pile of papers in front of him and put them down with a sigh. His siblings would be horrified when he told them the parlous state of the Silchester finances. He couldn't put it off any longer – they would be together in the butterfly drawing room, so-called because of the hand-painted wallpaper, and he had no option but to give them the bad news.

There was no need for him to take the documents with him – the miserable contents were etched on his brain. He strode from the study, down the long corridor that bisected the house, and headed for the chamber in which his family were waiting. Bennett, who had now become heir to the dukedom, would be sitting with the twins, Aubrey and Peregrine. His sisters, Madeline and Giselle, would no doubt be perusing the latest fashion plates from London.

There were no footmen lurking about ready to open and close doors at Silchester, as he preferred to stand on as little ceremony as possible when only the family was in residence. He stopped in the doorway and surveyed the room.

Bennett, at eight and twenty, was two years his junior. His brother was staring morosely out of the window no doubt regretting that he couldn't return to his regiment. They looked around, but none of them smiled. Despite his decline into a drunk, they had been fond of Papa and his loss was still deeply felt.

'I've had time to go through the documents that arrived from London yesterday. I need to tell you what I discovered.'

The girls put down their journals, the twins put down their cards and Bennett turned and strolled over to join the group in front of the fire. 'Well, tell us the worst. From your expression I gather the news isn't good.'

'Bennett, your assessment is correct. The estates are returning sufficient to keep Silchester Court running smoothly; however, unless we get a large input of cash from somewhere I'll not be able to open the London house for the Season next year.'

'The anniversary of our father's death is not until December – we can't come out of mourning until then anyway,' Madeline said. 'I'm in no hurry to be paraded like a horse in front of suitable husbands. What about you, Giselle?'

The younger girl smiled. 'I prefer to be in the country as you know, so the longer it is until my debut the happier I shall be.'

Bennett laughed. 'There you are, Beau, nobody wants to go to London. As for a large injection of cash, I can think of only one way that would be acceptable.'

His brother had their full attention now. 'Well, enlighten us,' Peregrine said whilst attempting to take a surreptitious look at his brother's hand. Without looking in his direction Aubrey snatched his cards away.

'I shall find myself an heiress – one of us must become leg-shackled and start filling their nursery. As I've been obliged to resign my commission, I'll be the one to sacrifice himself. I'm sure there are plenty of debutantes who would be delighted to marry into such an illustrious family.'

'A noble thought, brother, but not necessary. Mama was most insistent that we all married for love, that duty must come second,' Beau said.

'You're practically in your dotage, Beau, and have still not met the girl of your dreams – neither have Perry, Aubrey nor I. Devil take it, man, you're one and thirty next anniversary and most men in your position would already have an heir or two to secure the succession.' Bennett looked at each one of them in turn before continuing. 'Therefore, I'll bite the bullet for you. There's no need to open Silchester House as I'll take lodgings in Albemarle Street.'

There was nothing any of them could say to dissuade him from his course. Beau came up with an alternative solution to his brother attending the London season on his own.

'I shall host a house party this summer. I'm sure between us we can come up with a dozen or so families with eligible daughters and we shall invite them all here. It will be perfectly acceptable to entertain at home so don't raise your eyebrows at me, Madeline.'

'I shall bow to your superior knowledge, sir, but whatever anyone else does, I shall not go into colours but wear lavender and lilac.'

Giselle giggled. 'You only want to do that so you can order a new wardrobe. I'm quite happy to continue to wear whatever my maid puts out for me each day. I require no new clothes.'

He left them amiably bickering and drew Bennett to one side where they could speak without being overheard. 'I'm not happy with your decision, but accept I cannot change your mind. However, you must give me your word you'll not offer for a young lady who will bore you within a month. You are a military man, used to giving orders and making life-and-death decisions...'

'You're telling me something I already know – what is this to do with finding myself a suitable bride?'

'If you must marry then you have to select an intelligent girl, someone who can be your companion, share your interests.'

'If you can find me a young lady who loves to ride, prefers to be outside and has no wish to attend balls and parties and also has a magnificent dowry – then I'll marry her immediately.'

'She must also have an impeccable pedigree and not be bracket-faced.'

His brother smiled. 'I shall go at once to the study and draw up my list of requirements. I'm sure your man of affairs will be able to root out all the girls on the market this season.'

Madeline strolled over to join them and overheard this last remark. 'There's one snag to your brilliant scheme, brothers – the most eligible debutantes will already be spoken for and those who are left will not be diamonds of the first water.'

Bennett shrugged. 'Even better. Those who have been overlooked will be all the more eager to accept an offer from me. My estate brings in more than sufficient revenue to provide for a wife and family. I don't consider myself a wealthy man, but my income combined with my title should be enough to find me what I want.'

* * *

Miss Grace DuPont was up to her knees in muck when her erstwhile governess, now companion and dearest friend, Miss Newcomb appeared at the gate.

'My dear, you must come in at once. Mr DuPont has come back from Town and is demanding to see you.'

Grace emptied the last of the hay from the handcart and then carefully picked her way across the field. The very last thing she wanted to do was speak to her papa. He had not quite forgiven her for catching the chickenpox and being unable to make her debut, and so her come-out ball had had to be cancelled.

'Please don't be cross with me. I know we've plenty of outside men to feed my horses but I like to do it myself.'

'That's as may be, my dear, but you're a woman grown, no longer in the schoolroom, and should behave appropriately. Your father is beside himself with excitement and whatever the news, you must look pleased.'

They reached the rear of the house and Grace stopped to hook off her boots before padding through the door. She could hardly speak to her father dressed as she was because he disapproved of her wearing men's attire, even though it was only within the confines of their own estate.

Annie, her abigail, would be waiting with hot water and clean clothes. All she had to do was slip up the backstairs and into her apartment without being seen. Mama was too indolent to make a fuss about anything of matter, so there were no fears of being reprimanded from that source.

If only she had siblings then Papa would not be in such a pother to marry her off to somebody in the *ton*. He was quite determined to raise his own status by acquiring an aristocratic son-in-law and thus gain entry to the drawing rooms of society that were now closed to him. Grandpa had made a fortune with the East India Company and had returned to England as rich as Croesus.

'There you are at last, miss – there's ever such a fuss going on downstairs. You've no time to take a nice bath, but I've got plenty of hot water waiting.' Her maid had everything ready and Grace was clean and freshly attired in one of her new, fashionable, high-waisted gowns in no time at all.

'There, you look ever so pretty, miss. That russet wool is perfect with your colouring.'

'Thank you, I couldn't keep myself respectable without your help.'

She hurried down the spacious corridor and then picked up her skirts to run lightly down the staircase and across the vast, echoing entrance hall. Her footsteps announced her arrival to her parents who were in the drawing room. Her father appeared in the doorway and for once he greeted her with affection.

'My dear girl, how pretty you look today. Doesn't she look well, Mrs DuPont?' He turned and waved in the general direction of her mother who was, as usual, stretched out on a daybed eating sweetmeats and looking at the latest fashion plates from London.

'Very nice, Grace, but that colour clashes with your hair. I cannot think why I wanted it for you. You'd do better to stick to pastel shades in future.' Mama returned to her reading, no doubt unaware that yet again she'd made her daughter only too aware of her shortcomings.

'Come with me, my dear, I must talk to you in private.'

She followed without protest to the far end of the room where there was a third cluster of furniture and a second fireplace. 'I'm sorry if I kept you waiting, sir, but I came as soon as I knew you'd returned. What is it that you wish to tell me?'

He waited until they were both settled before speaking. 'I've had the most amazing luck. Word's out that Lord Sheldon, brother to the Duke of Silchester, is looking for a suitable bride. He's done with soldiering and has decided to set up his nursery. The old duke gambled away the family fortune and Lord Sheldon needs an heiress to restore the funds.'

Grace attempted to keep her smile from slipping and swallowed the lump in her throat. 'I'm sorry, but I don't see how this is of any matter to us. We don't move in his circles and, however big my dowry, I'm not of his class.'

His eyes darkened and she braced herself to receive another set-down but this time he held on to his temper. 'Lord Peabody, a second cousin to the duke, owes me a substantial amount of money. I've offered to cancel his debt if he gets us an invitation to Silchester Court this summer. There's to be a grand house party and all the suitable girls and their families are to be invited. I intend for us to be included on the list.'

A wave of relief almost overwhelmed her. 'Papa, however much money Lord Peabody owes you, you'll not be able to achieve your objective. People of our class don't get invited to the house parties of the high and mighty. Lord Sheldon would have to be destitute before he'd look in my direction.' She was warming to her theme. 'Lud, the family are not reduced to scratching about for their last penny; they'll still be far wealthier than the majority of the population.' She stood up, for once grateful she was almost as tall as he and could look him in the eye.

'Even if you could somehow obtain an invitation, I refuse to go. I would be as welcome there as a carthorse would be at Newmarket Races. I don't want to be humiliated and ridiculed.'

This time his temper broke and he was on his feet, his face red and his fists clenched. 'You will do as I say. You will go to that house party or I'll have your dogs and horses shot.'

For a moment she couldn't believe what he'd said, then she stepped away from him. 'I don't believe you would do anything so appalling even to get your own way. Please excuse me, sir, I'm going to my room.'

She turned to go but he moved with remarkable speed for a man of his bulk and he grabbed her elbow, his fingers biting painfully into her arm. 'Don't you dare to turn your back on me, young lady. I've allowed you too much freedom. It's time you learned to do as you're told. I'll not be gainsaid and you'll do well to obey if you don't want to suffer the consequences.'

She bit her lip and turned her head away so he couldn't see her tears. 'I'll not go to Silchester Court and I can't believe that you would carry out such a dreadful threat in order to force me to go.'

He released her and she dashed away. Her mother didn't look up, but Grace hadn't expected her to. Neither of her parents held her in high regard – indeed the only affection she'd ever received had come from her governess.

She would change and ride over to visit Charlotte, her bosom bow, who lived at the Rectory in the village three miles away. Not for the first time she wished she'd been born into a happy family like Charlotte's. They had little money to spare at the end of each quarter, but never complained and were always ready to share with those less fortunate than themselves.

Her stallion, Rufus, so named for his bright chestnut coat, was as eager as she to get away from DuPont Manor. She galloped him over the fields, revelling in the feeling of power beneath her, enjoying every hedge and ditch that they flew over. Although she preferred to ride astride she wouldn't dream of doing so anywhere but on her own estate.

'Good boy, good fellow, we must slow down now, for I don't intend to arrive in the village at such speed.' She applied a gentle pressure on the reins and transferred her weight to the rear of the saddle and instantly the animal responded. He might be a stallion, and more than sixteen hands in height, but he was a gentle giant – at least he was with her.

She trotted through the woods and turned into the lane that led to the village street. She was well known here and was greeted by several people on her way to the Rectory. By the time she arrived, her horse was cool and she could hand him over to the ancient groom knowing he would come to no harm in her absence.

'Good afternoon, miss, good to see you. Will you be staying long? Shall I remove his saddle?'

'Yes, if you don't mind, Tom. I'll need him ready at four o'clock.'

That gave her more than two hours to spend here, and even if Charlotte was out delivering food parcels or some such worthy pastime she would be content to spend time with the Rutherford family, for she loved them all.

Her friend was indeed absent and so Grace had no opportunity to discuss what had taken place between her and her father. After a pleasant visit she returned to the stable and scrambled back into the saddle. Tom was far too ancient to offer her any assistance.

She returned at a more decorous pace and arrived in a better humour than she'd departed. On reflection she realised she'd overreacted, that it would have been better to agree with her father's preposterous suggestion as he was never going to obtain them an invitation anyway.

When they met for dinner at six o'clock she would apologise and say she'd had time to reconsider and would agree to his proposal should an invitation be forthcoming. For all his bluster he wasn't an unkind man and surely would never carry out his horrible threat to kill her beloved animals?

Although not especially interested in horseflesh he was an astute businessman and well aware that the stud she'd set up was already bringing in a satisfactory return. Obviously she couldn't legally own this business venture, but so far he had allowed her free rein and was content to sign whatever papers she put in front of him. To shoot any of her livestock didn't make economic sense.

But what about her dogs? He wasn't fond of them and they were of no monetary value. She kicked Rufus into a canter and arrived in the stable yard at such speed that an unfortunate boy tripped over his pitchfork and fell head first into a pile of manure.

2

Grace tumbled from the saddle and dropped to her knees to greet her three dogs who were waiting patiently for her. She apologised to the stable boy and tossed him the reins; her stallion would behave now he'd had his exercise for the day.

This time she didn't go upstairs to change before searching out her father. He was, as usual, in his study going through various business documents and papers. He looked up, his expression unfriendly, when she stepped in.

'What do you want now, miss? Have you come to your senses?'

She curtsied politely. 'I've come to apologise, Papa, and tell you that I agree to attend this house party if an invitation can be obtained for us to go. Can you tell me when this event is likely to take place?'

Immediately he was all smiles and *bonhomie*. 'Good girl, I knew you would see sense. I shall write at once to Lord Peabody and set things in motion. The house party is to take place in three months' time in June, and we shall be there for several weeks. Your mother must send for the modiste and have your wardrobes replenished. I'll not have you looking dowdy – I want you both to look as fine as any of the toffs.'

'I shall go at once and give her the message. We have ample time to get ready, which is a relief.'

Mama roused herself sufficiently to listen to this news. 'A completely new wardrobe each? How delightful! Sit down, daughter, and look through these fashion plates, which arrived only yesterday from Town. We shall have gowns, spencers, new bonnets and parasols to match – we shall spare no expense. Imagine being invited to such a prestigious event and to be mingling with a duke and his family – I've never been so excited in my life.'

Her mother swung her legs to the carpet and stood up. 'I'll send a man by post to London and have Madam Ducray return with him.' She bustled off with more speed than Grace had seen since the new carriage had arrived three years ago.

* * *

Several days later the interminable measuring and selection of fabrics was over and Madame Ducray had departed, promising the gowns would be delivered within the allotted time. 'If you don't mind, Mama, I'm going to the stables. We have a new filly just born and I want to ensure she's well.'

Her mother waved a hand. 'Run along, Grace, but remember your papa is returning today and will expect you to be here to greet him at four.'

'Yes, Mama, I'll not be long. The men we employ are more than capable of taking care of things, but I like to see for myself how matters are progressing.'

Her mother sniffed. 'I warn you, my girl, that all this nonsense will stop once you're betrothed to Lord Sheldon. Young ladies shouldn't spend so much time in the stables; they should be doing embroidery, playing the pianoforte or painting pretty watercolours.'

'Yes, Mama, I'll bear that in mind.'

The mare and the new filly were doing well and Grace returned to the house in good time to change and be downstairs in order to greet her father. He was going to be in a foul mood because he would have now discovered what she already knew: that members of the *ton* did not invite lesser mortals such as themselves, however wealthy, to attend their house parties. She would shake her head and commiserate with him, and promise to do her best to find herself an aristocratic husband next year when she had her delayed debut in London.

Two of the three things her mother had mentioned as being essential if a young lady was to find herself an eligible husband were things she was hopeless at. Her stitching was worse than that of a five-year-old and she could no more paint a picture than fly in the air like a bird. Perhaps being an excellent pianist would be enough to compensate for her lack of the other two skills? What she could do was run a stud farm, manage an estate and ride and train any horse that came her way.

She smiled to herself. These qualities were hardly likely to endear her to any prospective husband, so she would remain a spinster and take care of her parents when they became infirm. This prospect wasn't something she was looking forward to, but it was preferable to becoming trapped in a marriage with a man who viewed her as no more than a mother for his children and mistress for his house.

Correctly attired and no longer smelling of the stable, she duly appeared in the drawing room at the appointed hour to find a mother in tears and no sign of her father.

'Mama, what's wrong? Has there been an accident?' Grace ran across and dropped down beside her parent and tried to offer what comfort she could.

'I'm devastated. I've never been so unhappy in my life.' Mama gulped and tried to stem the flow of tears with a small handkerchief.

'Has Papa done something to overset you? Please tell me how I can help.'

'It's all very well for you. You can go; he's arranged for his precious daughter to attend the duke's house party. But we're to be excluded – not good enough for the likes of them.'

Grace was horrified. Never for a moment had she thought the invitation would be issued – she'd never have agreed to go otherwise. 'Where is he? I'm going to see him right away and tell him that unless we can all go, I shan't be going either.'

Her pronouncement did nothing to improve the situation as her mother redoubled her sobs. 'You silly girl, don't you understand? Your father's depending on you to gain him entry into society by marrying Lord Sheldon. If you don't succeed I don't know what he'll do.'

Her father was in his study making heavy inroads into a decanter of brandy. She hesitated in the doorway, knowing he would be even more unpleasant if he was bosky. Unfortunately he spotted her.

'You've heard then? Stupid woman – she should be grateful you can go and stop her snivelling.'

'I don't understand, sir, how I've been invited when you haven't.'

He glared at her. 'Peabody has agreed to take you with his party. He's going to introduce you as Lady Peabody's goddaughter so you'll have to be very careful not to reveal your background.'

The more she heard the worse it sounded. 'How can I attract the attention of a suitable husband if no one knows who I am? Even if I did, as soon as my true status is revealed I will be ejected from the house. People like that don't associate with people like us, however rich we might be.'

This remark did not improve the situation. He slammed his hands on the desk, sending his half-full glass flying and covering the documents he was looking at with brandy. He swore and surged to his feet. Grace fled, not wishing to be on the receiving end of his rage.

She had given her word she would go if she received an invitation and could not renege on this promise. At least her mother would get a wardrobe full of new gowns even if she couldn't accompany her to Silchester Court. Whatever her father might expect, she would do her best to remain in the shadows and make sure that no one, especially Lord Sheldon, could possibly think of her as a suitable bride.

* * *

Bennett scrutinised the list of candidates trying to summon up enthusiasm for this project. Restoring the family fortunes was down to him; Beau had more than enough to do running the many estates and being head of the Silchester clan. The twins at two and twenty were far too young to contemplate matrimony; indeed, they appeared to have little interest in anything apart from cards and horses.

He had no choice in the matter. He must do his duty in the same way he'd served King and Country these past ten years. Although he had a profitable estate no more than twenty miles away, he preferred to live here with his siblings. He'd spent so much time apart from them when soldiering on the Continent that he scarcely knew his sisters or his younger brothers. He'd always been close to Beau and thought the world of him. He didn't envy him one bit being the eldest and having to shoulder the responsibility of the dukedom.

'Seen anyone on your list that you think might be a possible candidate?' His older brother had wandered into the study to find him and was reading over his shoulder.

'None of the names mean anything to me. I've been so long out of society I can't recall any of the names or titles mentioned here. Why don't you ask everyone on this list? God knows there's more than enough room in this vast building to house a hundred extra people and their staff.'

'I recognise most of the names, but there are one or two unknown to me. Peabody? That rings a bell – isn't he a distant relative of some sort?' He pointed to the name. '*Lord and Lady Peabody, Miss Peabody and Miss DuPont.* I suppose this other girl's a niece of some sort – I can't say I've ever heard the name DuPont mentioned anywhere. One must assume the girl's acceptable if she's being sponsored by Peabody.'

'I see there are almost as many gentlemen coming as there are young ladies. Is Madeline planning the entertainment? We can shoot, ride and play billiards but what will the ladies do during the day?'

His brother laughed. 'I expect they'll need all day to get ready for the evenings – don't forget they will all be outdoing each other to impress you.'

Bennett tossed the paper aside. 'Don't forget the twins will be here too and they are equally eligible. I shall be close to slitting my throat if I'm obliged to spend four weeks talking to simpering debutantes and their doting mothers.'

Madeline had overheard his remark as she arrived in the study. 'We must have a garden party and invite the neighbours, also a ball and perhaps a musical evening as well.'

He groaned and covered his face with his hands in mock despair. 'Heaven help us!' He recovered as he thought of a way he could make things more bearable. 'In which case I insist that we have horse races, plus a village event to which all our tenants and workers can come, and a treasure hunt we can all be involved in.'

His sister clapped her hands. 'What fun! I'll leave you to organise your suggestions and Giselle and I will take care of the rest. There's ample time to send out invitations and get everything prepared before our guests arrive.' She counted on her fingers. 'It's exactly nine weeks to the house party. The lake will have warmed up splendidly by then, the rose garden will be in full bloom...'

'Are you intending we should swim, Madeline?' Beau asked.

'I expect that some of the gentlemen might do so, but it wouldn't be acceptable for the ladies to join them in this pastime. No, I was thinking of having a variety of water-related events – we could have rowing, sailing, fishing and even a picnic.'

'What about cricket matches? That's something ladies and gentlemen can do together.' Bennett was now becoming enthusiastic. It had been many years since he'd been able to enjoy such frivolity, and if there was so much of interest going on the search for his future wife might become bearable. One thing was for certain, he'd rule out immediately any young lady who had no interest in participating in the outdoor events.

* * *

Grace continued to run her stud and her parents, satisfied they'd achieved their objective, left her to it. She was obliged to go in to be fitted when her gowns and other items arrived, but apart from that she spent as much time outside as she could.

'Look at you, young lady, you look like a girl from the village. Your face is unpleasantly brown and you will stand out from the others in a most unflattering way. I cannot imagine how Mr DuPont and I managed to produce a child like you. You must be a throwback, for it's certain you don't take after either of us.'

'I shall wear a bonnet and gloves when I go out into the grounds of Silchester Court, Mama, and am putting on milk of roses every night as you instructed.'

'Do you want to be a figure of fun, Grace? You'll be ostracised by all the well-bred girls; they will think you a common person because your complexion is no longer pale like theirs.'

'Then they will be correct as I will be a fish out of water. I know I had the best education money can buy, that my wardrobe will be second to none, that my dowry will be three times bigger than most, but to them I am unacceptable. I wish you wouldn't make me go. It will end in disaster, I'll be found out and sent packing in ignominy and that'll do nothing for Papa's good name.'

No sooner had she spoken than she wished the words unsaid. She had merely stated the truth, but her mother was averse to hearing anything that didn't fit in with her wishes. Grace wasn't surprised when her parent succumbed to loud sobbing. There was no point trying to comfort her mama as she'd been the cause of her distress.

Instead she sent a footman to fetch her mother's dresser and decided to make good her escape. However, the noise attracted her father and he roared at her to return and explain what all the noise was about. She ignored his command and scurried up the staircase and ran to her apartment. She slammed her sitting room door and turned the key, then raced into her bedchamber to make sure the external door was also locked.

When he heard what she'd said he would be incandescent with anger and she hoped she wouldn't be on the receiving end of a beating. He was a strict disciplinarian and had used a birch on her many times when she was a child. Fortunately she'd learned to control her wayward tongue and avoided further chastisement – until now.

Annie was elsewhere and there was no time to send for her. Perhaps Miss Newcomb was in her rooms and would be prepared to stand beside her and prevent her father from attacking her. There had been no birching since her governess had joined the household and this must mean she would be safe in her company.

If she took the servants' staircase she wouldn't need to go out of her apartment and risk coming face to face with her father. As she dashed into the dressing room there was a thunderous hammering on her sitting room door, and this added wings to her feet. She wouldn't be surprised if her parent kicked in her door – she'd never heard him so enraged before.

She emerged on the floor above and burst into Miss Newcomb's sitting room without knocking. 'Good heavens, Miss DuPont, whatever's wrong? You're as white as a sheet.'

'My father wishes to do me harm for something I said to my mother. I don't think he'll attack me if I'm with you.' Her knees were trembling and cold perspiration trickled between her shoulder blades. She'd hoped never to feel this way again, that such terror was a thing of the past.

'Sit down, my dear. I promise nothing untoward will take place whilst you're with me. Mr DuPont is well aware that I am still in contact with my previous employers, Sir John and Lady Roberts. He'll not wish me to blacken his name.'

Grace collapsed into the nearest chair and clasped her hands in her lap and attempted to calm herself. She could do no more than nod her thanks; the ability to speak appeared to have deserted her. She flinched as heavy footsteps could be heard approaching in the passageway outside.

Miss Newcomb moved smoothly towards the door and placed herself squarely in front of it. When it flew open she remained where she was, rigid with disapproval at such a rude entrance.

'This is my domain, sir. You've no right to enter it without my permission. Kindly remove yourself.'

Her father, red-faced and spluttering, pushed her roughly aside. 'Get out of my way, woman. I'll not be gainsaid by the likes of you. You can pack your trunks and leave here today. You'll have no references from me.'

Suddenly Grace was on her feet, her fear gone – now she was as angry as he. 'You're despicable. How dare you treat Miss Newcomb with such disrespect? I'll be happy to go to Silchester Court and you may be very sure that I'll find myself a husband so that I have no need to ever return here.' She helped her governess to her feet. 'You shall come with me, Miss Newcomb. I'll do better with you there to guide me.'

Her father deflated, his choler gone as quickly as it came. He rubbed his eyes and his shoulders slumped. He looked bewildered, as if he didn't know how he found himself in a place he'd no right to be. 'I beg your pardon for intruding, Miss Newcomb. I'd be most appreciative if you would accompany my daughter to Silchester in three weeks' time. You'll need to replenish your wardrobe – I'll not have you showing up my daughter in your drab clothes.'

This was hardly the conciliatory speech one might have expected from someone who'd so patently misbehaved, but in the circumstances it would have to do.

'Go away, sir, you have caused enough upset for today. I'll not be dining downstairs again. In future Miss Newcomb and I will dine together in my apartment.' Grace stared at him and he muttered something unintelligible and slunk away.

As soon as he'd gone Miss Newcomb flopped onto a chair. 'My dear, how absolutely dreadful. I'd no idea Mr DuPont was such a violent man. If I'd known I should never have taken the position...' Her voice trailed away as she realised what she was saying.

Grace dropped to her knees beside her and took her hands. 'I'm very glad that you did. I don't know where I'd be without you. I wasn't looking forward to going to this house party, but with you to guide me I believe I might carry off my masquerade.'

3

The atmosphere at DuPont Manor was decidedly chilly after Grace's confrontation with her parents. Fortunately the house was so vast it was perfectly possible to avoid seeing either of them. A week passed in which Miss Newcomb selected a number of gowns that Madame Ducray vowed would be ready the following week.

'Are you quite sure Mr DuPont will pay for all these items, my dear?'

'He will; he has so much money he'd scarcely notice if we bought a thousand gowns. By the by, I've written to Lady Peabody explaining that I shall be bringing my companion as well as my personal maid and am awaiting a reply.'

'I've also made enquiries about the Duke of Silchester and received a note from a dear friend this morning. Word has it that Lord Sheldon is looking for an heiress to restore the family fortunes which means, far from being ostracised, I believe you will be a favourite candidate.'

'I should think it highly unlikely that the duke would allow his brother to make an alliance with anyone not from the top drawer of society, however much money they might bring with them.' Grace had thought about this a great deal in the past few days. 'I'm not aiming to ensnare Lord Sheldon, but am hoping there will be lesser mortals attending this house party who might consider me a catch.'

Miss Newcomb seemed unsurprised by this comment. 'In which case, my dear, might not your father refuse to release your dowry? Indeed, would he not refuse his permission altogether?'

'He could, that's true, but my trust fund was set up by my grandfather and will become the property of my husband the moment the marriage certificate is signed.'

'In which case, your scheme might well be successful. I remember hearing about a similar case some years ago. The young lady in question moved in with her future in-laws until she was legally able to wed. It would be unusual to have so long an engagement, but not unheard of.'

The weather had improved and was more like summer today. 'Shall we take a stroll around the gardens before our supper arrives? My parents have gone out to dinner so there's no likelihood of an unexpected meeting.'

Grace put on her bonnet and tied the ribbons under her chin. She tilted her head and smiled at her reflection, satisfied that despite her unfashionably brown skin she wasn't an antidote. She had two of the three necessary requisites to make a good marriage – money and appearance – however she rather thought that her lack of the third – pedigree – might prove to be more important than possessing the other two.

Her three dogs joined them on their walk and she decided to extend their promenade to the ornamental lake so she could throw sticks for the animals to fetch. Miss Newcomb remained at a safe distance as this activity was taking place.

'I'm soaked to my petticoats but the weather's so warm I'll be dry before we reach the house.' She sighed as she called the trio to follow. 'I've been thinking about my dogs and my horses and have decided that I'll take Rufus and these three with me. I don't trust my father not to dispose of my pets in my absence.'

Miss Newcomb looked aghast. 'You cannot take these animals with you. Such a thing is just not done in society. Children and pets remain at home – it's the way things are done in the *ton*.'

'Fiddlesticks to that! Silchester Court must have dozens of dogs running about the place, and an extra horse will hardly make any difference at all. After all there will be our four carriage horses to accommodate as well.'

Her governess raised her hands in surrender. 'I see that whatever I say you'll go your own way, so I must accept your decision. I sincerely hope it's not one you live to regret.'

Miss Newcomb had no interest in visiting the stables so made her way inside, leaving Grace to ponder on her decisions. She could hardly take the dozen broodmares, the half a dozen yearlings and four new foals with her, but she was equally determined her father would not sell them off; therefore alternative arrangements must be made.

The head groom, Collins, greeted her with a smile. 'I reckon the grey mare will foal tonight, Miss DuPont. Have you come to see how she does?'

'No, I've come about something far more important.' She explained her dilemma and then made her outrageous suggestion. 'I shall be leaving here next week and have no intention of ever returning. The night before I go, you must remove from here and take them all to Mr Rankin's farm. He has more than adequate stabling and plenty of good pastureland and is more than happy to accommodate you all until I can make other arrangements.'

He slapped his thigh. 'I know the place well. It's a grand idea, but don't you think Mr DuPont will look for us? He'll not be happy to find these valuable beasts have vanished.'

'I doubt he'll be bothered, at least not at first. In fact as he rarely comes down here he might not even notice. It's fortunate that the stabling for his horses is elsewhere. I have sufficient gold to tide you over and will send you more if necessary.'

The matter settled satisfactorily she returned to the house and just had time to change before Miss Newcomb and the supper trays arrived. Over their meal she made another radical suggestion.

'I wish you to call me by my given name in future. I consider you my friend. I've no idea what your first name is – would you be prepared to allow me to address you informally as well?'

'My name is Sarah, and I'd be honoured if you choose to call me that. However, Grace my dear, it might be better if you call me Aunt Sarah –

what do you think? We have no wish to raise any more eyebrows than we have to.'

'Aunt Sarah it shall be. I hope you'll stay with me whatever happens next. Although the bulk of my dowry will go to my husband, whoever he might be, I shall have an annuity of £2000 to spend as I please. If you have no wish to remain in my new household then I'll buy you a cottage nearby and give you a pension so you may live in comfort.' She reached out and clasped her hand. 'Whatever you decide to do, dear Aunt Sarah, I wish you to remain part of my life as you are the only family I have now.'

* * *

Bennett was delighted with the arrangements for the house party. Everything he'd suggested had been put into place and he couldn't remember there ever being such excitement at Silchester Court. His older brother strolled into the billiard room.

'There you are. Madeline is searching for you, waving another paper. I don't blame you for hiding.'

'Despite the vast size of your establishment, Beau, this is the only place that's not been invaded by staff wishing to primp and plump everything in their path.' He pointed out of the window towards the newly refurbished boathouse. 'Even that has been attacked. I much preferred it in its faded state – I just hope I manage to find myself a bride after all this conspicuous expenditure.'

'It's been so long since we had a function of this size that standards had been allowed to slip. We stand on no ceremony amongst ourselves, but we must keep up appearances when we have house guests.'

He was about to reply when his sister burst in, still waving the letter Beau had mentioned earlier. 'At last. I've just heard from Great-Aunt Agatha – it's an unmitigated disaster.' She pushed the paper into his hands and he saw at once it was a letter and not a list.

He quickly scanned the contents. 'Damnation! How in the name of Hades did word get round that I'm looking to marry for money?'

Beau reached out and flicked the paper from his hand. 'Not ideal, admittedly, but not an unmitigated disaster. There might well be a few polite cancellations from those who wish their daughter to not only marry an aristocrat but a *wealthy* aristocrat.'

'We've only invited girls with substantial dowries, so I don't see why anyone will refuse to come on that account. I'm irritated that somebody close to the family has been gossiping.'

Madeline retrieved her letter. 'It can't be because of the invitation list – I was very careful not to invite just heiresses, but a mix of suitable candidates. Anyway, there's nothing we can do about it now. I also came to tell you both that a diligence has just arrived piled high with a miscellany of punts, rowing boats and sailing dinghies. Our neighbours have been very generous. I thought you might like to oversee their storage, Bennett, as it's your idea to have activities involving them.'

'Excellent, Madeline, I'll come with you now. I can't work out what sort of races to organise until I know what crafts are available.'

He spent a pleasant afternoon helping the labourers unload and his younger brothers joined him. 'We've got three punts, five rowing boats and the same number of sailing dinghies. There are also a couple of coracles – God knows where they came from.' Aubrey was wearing only his breeches and he was plastered with green weed and mud from fooling about in the lake.

Perry, the more circumspect of the two, had removed his boots and stockings but kept on his shirt. 'I've counted the poles and the oars and we're one short of the latter. The dinghies all have a sail of some sort so there's no problem with them. Not sure what we need to propel the coracles along.'

'Some sort of paddle – I saw two in the bottom of the cart and put them in with the punt poles. Let's see who can go the furthest before we fall in.' Aubrey tossed one of the coracles into the water and then jumped in after it, sending a cascade of water over both his brothers.

Bennett was still in his boots and was not amused. 'You're a nincompoop, little brother, and if you were not already in the lake I'd toss you in myself. Perry, are you going to take him up on his challenge? You're so wet you might as well. I need to see how stable those things are before I include them in the aquatic events.'

Perry carefully lowered the second coracle into the lake and, holding steady with one hand, gingerly stepped in. The vessel rocked wildly for a moment and then stabilised. 'I say, this is rather fun. Come on, Aubrey, I'll race you to the island.'

Each of them had a paddle and used it vigorously. Initially the boats spun but then they worked out how to move forward and they were off. They were excellent swimmers so if they did fall in there would be no problem, especially as the lake was only deep around the island.

He tossed a coin to each of the labourers and the cart driver and wandered off to see if the magnificent maze was now ready to be used by the guests. The six-feet-tall yew hedges had been clipped back and the pathways cleared of brambles and weeds. He could hear his sisters laughing from somewhere in the depths.

'Girls, did you remember to take in your flags? You could be lost in there for days if you didn't,' he called out cheerfully.

'We've always been able to find our way out, Bennett, as you very well know. We've just placed the last clue for the treasure hunt at the centre.'

'I wish you hadn't told me that. I intend to participate in this event myself with one of our guests – now I shall have an unfair advantage. I could go directly to the centre of the maze and miss out all the other clues and thus win.'

The girls appeared at the exit flushed and happy. 'That would do you no good, brother, as you need all the clues in order to solve the conundrum and reach the prize,' Madeline said.

'Excellent. I was dreading this house party but now I'm actually looking forward to it. Apart from the odd village fête when Mama was alive there's never been anything like this. I was down in the village yesterday collecting a few items from the smithy and was stopped by a dozen or more people who could talk of nothing else. Not only are we going to enjoy ourselves, but we've also brought extra work and income to our tenants and the villagers.'

'Strangely enough the entire staff is as excited as we are to be having so many extra visitors. We have eighteen families coming, which will mean almost seventy sitting down to dine. Peebles is worried we won't fit everyone around the table and is considering using the small dining room as well as the grand.'

'Please don't burden me with these details, Madeline. I've no interest in domesticity, as you know.' He smiled and gave each sister a brotherly hug before continuing on his way to the stables. He was reassured by the head groom that they could accommodate the extra horses by turning most of them out into the paddocks. A dozen extra men had been employed to help for the month.

He wandered along the open loose boxes, patting equine noses and pulling silky ears – even here the festive atmosphere had spread. He stopped at the end box, the one that contained his own mount, Lucifer, a magnificent black stallion.

'Good afternoon, my boy, I see you're eager to be turned out for the evening. I hope you won't let me down when we have the races as I've staked my reputation and a good deal of my blunt on you winning.'

The horse dropped his head and slobbered over his shirt. A groom had overheard his remark and popped his head over the half-door of the adjacent box.

'There's not a horse in the country who can better Lucifer, my lord. He'll win every race right enough.'

Here the servants were treated well and the relationship between family and staff was relaxed. 'I sincerely hope you're right, but several of our guests are bringing their own riding horses and there will be fierce competition.'

* * *

The journey from Surrey to Hertfordshire was not overtaxing and didn't necessitate an overnight stay. Grace had everything planned and although Lady Peabody, in her latest missive, had said that they were not expected until Tuesday or Wednesday, her ladyship intended to arrive on the latter. Grace decided she would leave on the Tuesday and thus avoid having to say insincere farewells to her parents who had naturally read Lady Peabody's letter for themselves.

Collins had spirited away all the horses from the stud during the night, and had twenty guineas to pay for his and the horses' expenses. Her parents had entertained the night before and not retired until the small hours, which meant they were unlikely to be up before noon.

'I'll not be sanguine until we're a distance from here, Aunt Sarah. I keep thinking my father will appear and prevent me from leaving.'

'Annie is already outside waiting for us. I'm glad the journey is no more than five hours, for I fear that travelling in this warm weather with your dogs inside with us might be rather unpleasant.'

'The boys will be on their best behaviour, and I told Peterson not to feed them this morning. We are stopping at a hostelry for refreshments at midday and they can...'

'Please, my dear, I've no wish to hear any more about those animals of yours. I cannot imagine why you wished to keep them after you found them abandoned in that ditch two years ago. You could have given them away quite easily, for despite their unpleasant habits they are all handsome animals.'

'Ginger, Buster and Toby must have spaniel and terrier in their ancestry. They have a spaniel's coat and a terrier's build, and I think they are the most beautiful dogs in the county. Not the best-behaved, admittedly, but certainly intelligent and affectionate.'

Her team of matched greys had never looked better and the unfortunate groom who was riding Rufus was having difficulty staying in the saddle. Immediately Grace went over and took the stallion's bit. 'That's quite enough of that, my boy – you'll have plenty of opportunity to stretch your legs later. If you don't behave yourself I'll leave you behind.' The horse calmed at her touch and the groom touched his cap and grinned his thanks.

The three men who were coming with her knew they were unlikely to return to DuPont Manor but were all happy to accompany her on this adventure – none of them had ties to the neighbourhood and were eager to be employed by her future husband, whoever he might be.

It was no secret that she was going in search of a partner. The staff she was bringing with her were totally loyal and would not gossip and reveal her lack of pedigree.

The journey to Silchester Court was accomplished without mishap and a little after three o'clock they turned between massive granite gateposts and onto an immaculate, weed-free drive.

Grace hung out of the window hoping to catch a glimpse of the place she was to live for the next few weeks, but the drive was more than a mile long and the house hidden from view.

'It has occurred to me, Grace, that by coming a day before your sponsor you'll draw attention to yourself. With hindsight I think it might have been better to have stayed overnight somewhere and arrived at the same time as Lady Peabody – after all, she is supposed to be your godmother.'

'Far too late to worry about that as we're in view of the house now and I swear I've never seen anything so palatial in my life. I thought that DuPont Manor was big, but this is twice the size. We shall need a map to find our way about the place.'

The dogs, who had been curled up in the well of the carriage sleeping peacefully, woke up and began to wag their tails and sniff excitedly at the door. Despite their lack of manners, they knew better than to jump onto the squabs.

The carriage swung in a slow circle and rattled to a halt in front of an impressive portico. There were several immaculate footmen in dark green livery and demi-wigs waiting to attend to them. The dogs were becoming frantic, scratching at the door and whining.

'Very well, I shall let you out, but don't get lost.' Grace opened the carriage door and the animals shot through. She watched in horror as they flung themselves at the gentleman who had come to greet them. He lost his balance and tumbled backwards. This was not an auspicious start to her visit.

4

Bennett was returning from the stables when he saw a smart carriage turn into the drive. He scarcely looked at that; what caught his attention was a magnificent chestnut following along behind. Who the hell was this? He could hardly greet the newcomers smelling of the stable. He ran through the list of today's expected guests and, as far as he was concerned, everybody on that list had already arrived – so whoever this was they weren't expected today. His curiosity was piqued and he decided to remain despite his appearance.

It took a further fifteen minutes for the cavalcade to arrive and in this time he'd had ample opportunity to study the stallion in detail. There was no doubt about it, this horse, if ridden by a competent person, might well beat Lucifer.

He strode forward, waving the footmen away, intending to open the door of the carriage himself. At the precise moment he was leaning forward to grasp the handle the door flew back and three dogs hurtled out, sending him sprawling backwards.

Not content with knocking him over the wretched animals then proceeded to jump all over him and cover his face with their wet, pink tongues. As he lay there a girl jumped from the carriage and attempted to remove the dogs from his chest.

'Get off, you stupid animals. The gentleman wishes to get up.' As fast as she removed them they returned, obviously thinking this was part of the game.

He'd had quite enough of this. 'Off. Now.' His sharp command did the trick and the three instantly removed themselves and, not waiting for further scolding, they raced towards the shrubbery where a cacophony of bird call followed as they put up a small flock of pheasants.

He sprung to his feet and brushed the dirt from his clothes. The young lady was watching him nervously, and well she might.

'I do beg your pardon – my dogs are usually very well mannered.'

Her voice was well modulated and pleasant, and if he hadn't been so angry he might have been more conciliatory. He stared at her and her hopeful smile faded. 'I am Lord Sheldon. Who, might I ask, are you? Have you missed your way as I don't believe you are expected here?'

'I am Miss DuPont. Lady Peabody is my godmother. I apologise for arriving a day earlier than my sponsor.' She met him glare for glare and this didn't improve his temper.

He didn't bow – far too late for the civilities. 'Then I suppose you had better come in, Miss DuPont. However, your animals may not.' This was not only uncivil, it was downright rude and he was about to apologise when she closed the gap between them. To his astonishment she poked him in the chest and he almost lost his balance a second time.

'If you are Lord Sheldon then I'm not surprised you've been unable to find yourself a suitable bride and have had to resort to inviting all and sundry...' Her words trailed away as she realised her colossal breach of etiquette.

His eyes narrowed and he towered over her, determined to give her the set-down she so richly deserved. He was drawing breath to speak when someone shouted a warning. Before he could react he was hit from behind by half a ton of angry stallion.

There was nothing he could do to prevent the accident. He was hurtled forward and cannoned into the unfortunate Miss DuPont, who fell backwards into the carriage wheel. The hideous sound of her head hitting the metal rim before she collapsed unconscious would remain with him forever.

He ended up on his knees but was on his feet in seconds and spun to face a horse with barred teeth and flattened ears. He didn't hesitate; he stepped in and punched the animal squarely between the eyes. This was enough to distract the horse whilst he grabbed the trailing reins. 'Enough, old fellow, you've caused sufficient damage for today.'

A terrified young groom appeared from behind the carriage, his face blood-streaked and one arm hanging uselessly by his side. Then one of the coachmen tumbled from the box and took the stallion from him.

Bennett turned to the prostate form of Miss DuPont to find that a lady of middle years was already there. He dropped to his knees and tore off his neckcloth. 'Here, madam, we need to stem the bleeding before we do anything else.'

'I daren't move her, sir. I fear she might have broken her neck.'

'Let me examine her. I spent years as a military man and have picked up a deal of medical knowledge on the way.'

The blood from the gash at the back of the girl's head had already soaked into her gown and showed no sign of stopping. He put his fingers at the juncture of her chin and neck and was relieved to feel a steady pulse. Then he carefully ran his hands from her neck to her hips and sighed with relief. 'I'm certain her neck and back are uninjured – however, she's taken a nasty blow to the back of her head and will require the immediate attentions of a physician, but first we must attempt to stop the bleeding.'

He didn't need to ask; she immediately tore off a strip from her petticoat and handed it to him. Deftly he folded his neckcloth into a pad and secured this across the wound. 'That will have to do for the moment.'

With her help he rolled the unconscious girl against his chest and regained his feet. There was no need to send word to the house; his brother and sisters were running towards them. Beau arrived first.

'I've sent for Dr Adams. This is a damnable thing, not a good way to start the summer party. Who is she, do you know?'

They were now halfway to the house. 'Miss DuPont – she's Lady Peabody's goddaughter and wasn't expected to arrive until tomorrow.'

Fortunately the entrance hall was empty of visitors and Bennett suspected that his sisters were responsible for this. The housekeeper was waiting to escort him to the designated chambers and he was dismayed to find this new arrival had been placed in a small room, which would better serve for a governess or companion.

'This won't do. Miss DuPont will go elsewhere.' Anderson didn't argue – nobody did when he used that tone.

The fact that some other young lady would now be banished to the small room didn't bother him at all. His concern was for the young lady he'd inadvertently injured so seriously.

* * *

Grace was heartily sick of being carried about like a parcel, but thought it prudent not to reveal she'd regained consciousness and was perfectly fine. Lord Sheldon was not a gentleman to toy with and she'd already caused more than enough excitement for one day. Her desire to remain in the shadows would no longer be possible. She kept her eyes closed until, to her relief, she was placed carefully on a bed.

'I'll leave you to take care of her; I'll wait next door for the physician.'

She remained still until the door closed and then risked a peep through her eyelashes. Good – he'd gone. There was a swish of material and Aunt Sarah and Annie were at her side.

'Thank the good Lord you're awake, my dear. You gave us quite a fright. Your head made a dreadful crack when it hit the carriage wheel.'

'Apart from a dull ache at the back of my head, and the fact that my gown is now covered in blood, I'm perfectly well, thank you and I've no wish to remain on this bed. Please help me to a chair.'

Her abigail carefully removed the ruined dress. 'We would have been here before you, miss, but Lord Sheldon didn't like the room you'd been given and brought you here instead. This is ever so smart, nearly as grand as the one you had at the manor.'

'I only have a vague recollection of how this accident occurred – tell me what happened.' When she'd heard how Rufus had attacked Lord Sheldon she was horrified. 'This is worse than anything I could have imagined. First my dogs knocked him from his feet and then my horse did the same. Thank goodness I was injured and he was forced to act as my saviour, otherwise I fear we would have been sent packing.'

They had been conversing in little more than whispers as they were aware this formidable gentleman was lurking in her sitting room. 'You will need stitches in that head wound, Grace, and we mustn't touch this makeshift bandage until the doctor's here. You lost a prodigious amount of blood and mustn't make matters worse.'

At this point Grace began to wonder why none of the Silchester staff were present. Surely there should at least be a chambermaid on hand to fetch what might be needed. The only explanation for this omission could be that her being moved to these rooms had offended the housekeeper.

'As soon as the doctor has put in the sutures I'll move from here to the room I was allocated. Annie, make sure my trunks are taken there and you can begin to unpack. Have you any idea where you'll be sleeping, Aunt Sarah?'

'None at all, but I'm not worried. They weren't expecting me to accompany you, so I'll be happy to sleep in the servants' quarters if necessary.'

'You'll do no such thing – I shall insist that you share with me if there's nothing else available.' She looked down at her petticoats. They were in little better case than her gown. 'Annie, would you find me some clean clothes? I've no intention of remaining here and can hardly parade around the place as I am.'

'I'll do that right away, miss. I'll be back in a jiffy; that's if I don't get lost.'

'Here, I think you should drink this lemonade unless you feel unwell?' Aunt Sarah suggested.

'I'm not going to cast up my accounts, if that's what you mean. I don't have a concussion. I think having fallen from a horse so many times my constitution is able to cope with these small mishaps.'

She watched the dressing room door anxiously, hoping that her maid would return with fresh garments before the doctor arrived to examine her. She wished to be respectably dressed and make it quite clear she was unharmed apart from the gash in her scalp.

'Aunt Sarah, could I ask you to do me an enormous favour? Would you go next door and inform Lord Sheldon that I'm quite well and there's no need for him to remain? I don't wish to draw any more attention to myself than I already have.'

'I should be happy to do so, my dear. Although the circumstances of your meeting was a trifle unfortunate, I couldn't help but notice he's an attractive gentleman, not at all what I'd expected.'

Grace couldn't hear their conversation through the closed door and hoped the message would be enough to send him away. The longer he spent attending on her the greater the risk that the other hopeful debutantes and their mamas would take a dislike to her, because she was monopolising the gentleman they'd come to ensnare for themselves.

Annie returned at the same time as Aunt Sarah and, despite her assurances to the contrary, Grace did feel a little unsteady and was grateful for their assistance as she stepped in and out of her garments.

Once she was safely clothed she asked what Lord Sheldon had said. 'He thanked me kindly for my message but has refused to move.'

'Are you saying that he's still ensconced in the sitting room? This won't do – this won't do at all. He's been up here for almost three-quarters of an hour and you can be very sure this will be noted by the guests who arrived ahead of us.' She stood up and took a few tentative steps around the room until she was sure her balance was restored. 'I shall go in and speak to him myself. He can hardly remain when he sees me freshly garbed and perfectly well.'

'I don't think that's a good idea. He's not the sort of gentleman who takes kindly to being told what to do.'

Undeterred, Grace paused to check in the overmantel mirror that she didn't look too much of a fright. 'Apart from the makeshift bandage I look quite respectable. Would you mind accompanying me, Aunt Sarah? I think it best if I don't speak to him unchaperoned.'

She took a few steadying breaths and then walked briskly into the sitting room. Who was the more astonished by her sudden appearance she couldn't say – but her jaw dropped as low as his. He had been slumped in an armchair, the picture of dejection, as if a member of his family was at their deathbed and not a complete stranger only slightly injured.

He was on his feet and moving towards her before she had recovered her wits. 'God's teeth! What the hell are you doing on your feet? You should be in bed waiting for the doctor to attend you.'

His less than obliging comment had the desired effect and her tongue was loosened. 'I'm sorry to inform you, my lord, that despite your best efforts I'm perfectly fine. When the doctor arrives please have him sent to my original chamber – not here – I've no wish to occupy rooms meant for someone else.'

He stopped a scant yard from her. For a moment the matter hung in the balance but then he smiled and something unexpected happened. Her anger vanished to be replaced by an emotion she didn't recognise.

'I apologise, Miss DuPont, I was under the erroneous impression you were at death's door. I'm delighted that I was wrong in my assessment of the situation. However, whether you like it or not this is now your accommodation. You will not remove yourself elsewhere.'

She was about to protest but something made her bite her tongue. She curtsied. 'In which case, my lord, I shall do as you bid and remain in these luxurious surroundings. I hope whoever has been ousted is not too disappointed with the inferior accommodation she must now occupy.'

His bow was suitably low. 'I can assure you, Miss DuPont, that you will hear no complaints from anyone on this score.'

No one would dare to quibble if he looked as fierce as he did right now. She was saved from making further inflammatory remarks by the arrival of the doctor. By the time he had put four stitches in her head she was heartily sick of the whole episode.

'There, Miss DuPont,' Dr Adams said as he stepped away. 'You need to wear a dressing on the gash for today, but if there is no infection then you can remove it tomorrow. I believe you will be able to arrange your hair in such a way your injury will not be visible.'

'Thank you, I shall remain in my rooms until I am fit to be seen. When will you return to remove the sutures?'

'I shall call in tomorrow as instructed by Lord Sheldon and make my decision then. I should think they can come out next week, or possibly sooner.' He dropped his instruments into his bag and collected the used swabs and these followed. He must have seen her surprise. 'I have nothing else of importance in my bag today and I like to take away everything I've used.'

She was about to stand up when he waved her back. 'Stay where you are. You might feel a little light-headed and it's far better that you rest. I've

asked the kitchen to send up a jug of watered wine – I find this very benefi-
cial after blood loss.' He pulled down his waistcoat and then turned to the
mirror in order to straighten his stock. He then pushed a few stray strands
of hair into place before nodding as if satisfied with his appearance.

He was remarkably vain for a man of his years, for he must be over
forty at the very least. Although his figure was reasonable, his complexion
clear and he had a decent head of mouse-brown hair, he certainly wasn't
an attractive gentleman.

However, he wasn't here for his charm and good looks but for his proficiency as a medical man, and she'd no complaints about his skills. He
picked up his bag, nodded politely, and departed promising to be back
before noon tomorrow.

'As I am to remain incommunicado for the next twenty-four hours I
might as well retire. I do feel rather lethargic and my head hurts
abominably.'

'An excellent notion, my dear girl – you look a trifle wan. I shall spend
the time settling myself into my own accommodation. It would appear that
I'm now to occupy the room originally intended for you. I'm more than
satisfied and if I use the backstairs I can be here within a few minutes.'

Grace told her maid she could continue to unpack the trunks, as with
the curtains drawn around the bed she wouldn't be disturbed by anything
going on in the adjacent dressing room where the wardrobes and closets
were.

She was drifting into a light doze when someone coming into the
bedchamber disturbed her, but she was too sleepy to open her eyes and
investigate.

5

Bennett sent the doctor on his way and was about to join the gentlemen who were playing a lively game of billiards, when an unaccountable urge to check for himself that this troublesome new guest was indeed suffering no ill effects from her accident overcame him.

He had no wish to announce himself, in fact had no wish for anyone to know he'd even been back to the apartment. He paused outside the sitting room until he was satisfied the room was empty then moved silently to the bedchamber door, which was fortunately ajar. Entering this room was a shocking breach of etiquette, but he couldn't help himself.

If he remained in the doorway, with one foot firmly in the sitting room, then hopefully this would be considered acceptable if anyone ever heard of it. Slowly he pushed the door wider until he could see across to the bed. The curtains had been partially drawn but not on the side that faced him.

She was lying on her side, her eyes were closed and he could hear the regular rhythm of her breathing. He stepped back and carefully pulled the door shut and then, satisfied he'd done no lasting harm by his actions, returned to join the guests.

The rise and fall of the conversation of the ladies coming from the grand drawing room gave him pause; he would leave them to their gossip and find more convivial company. Beau waylaid him before he reached the billiard room.

'How is Miss DuPont?'

'Amazingly, she appears to have suffered no serious harm apart from the gash on her head. Dr Adams advised she rest today so she won't be coming down again. I blame myself for the accident. The stallion was just trying to protect her; I was being unforgivably rude and the animal must have picked up on my anger.'

'I was just going out to inspect this horse myself – why don't you come with me? It's scarcely credible that an animal of this size and power is the property of that young lady.' Beau smiled. 'You might be interested to know that I checked the rules you drew up for your races and there's nothing there that would prevent her from entering if she so wished.'

'I know, and from the brief time I spent with her I can say with the utmost certainty she will definitely wish to enter. I suppose you heard about the damned dogs?'

'I'm afraid to tell you, brother, that every detail of both incidents is already the main topic of conversation inside.'

'It serves me right. I have an unfortunate tendency to forget I'm not still Colonel Sheldon and bark orders, expecting them to be instantly obeyed.'

As always word had travelled ahead and they were expected in the stable yard. When they enquired about the stallion it was to be told that he, and the carriage horses he'd arrived with, had been turned out as he'd objected strenuously to being put in a loose box.

Beau wandered off on an errand of his own and Bennett was on his way around the house to the terrace when Madeline called his name. At first he couldn't see where his sister was, but then saw she was beckoning to him from the shrubbery.

What the devil was she doing over there and behaving in such a secretive manner? He increased his pace, concerned that something else untoward had occurred.

'What's wrong, sweetheart? Why are you hiding out here?'

She grabbed his arms and drew him into the shadows where they couldn't be observed. 'You've caused the most frightful fuss by moving

Miss DuPont into the accommodation set aside for Lady Penelope, the Earl of Swindon's eldest daughter.'

He shook his head in bewilderment. 'There are plenty of other rooms available; surely Lady Penelope can have one of those? As she's not actually here, how can she object?'

'I know that; it's the fact that a commoner has been given precedence over a member of the *ton* that's causing all the discontent. Anderson and I spent hours going through the guest list and making sure everyone was in their proper place and given the chambers appropriate to their station. Miss DuPont might be a perfectly pleasant young lady, but she's a nobody as far as society is concerned. She cannot remain where she is.'

Bennett held on to his temper with difficulty. 'I don't give a damn what any of our guests think is appropriate. I allocated the rooms in order to recompense for the injury Miss DuPont sustained because of my behaviour. You may tell those who are complaining that the girl intended to remove herself to her original room, but I refused to allow it.' He stared at his sister and she got the message. 'Therefore, if they wish to complain they must do so to me, otherwise there will be no more said about it. If I hear Miss DuPont is being treated unfairly because of this then you will have me to answer to.'

His sister's surprise at his vehemence warned him too late that he'd served to make matters worse, rather than improve them. His interest would be misconstrued, the tabbies would already be linking his name to Miss DuPont and she was the last person he would consider offering for.

'No doubt there will be much said about this, but you can inform anyone who mentions it that I've no interest in making an alliance with a young lady who doesn't come from a similar background to ours.'

'I'm relieved to hear you say so and believe that will be sufficient to stem the rumours and allow Miss DuPont to enjoy her stay here. I've no wish for anyone to be ostracised through no fault of their own.'

'Now this has been settled satisfactorily, can you tell me why you're lurking in the shrubbery like an unwanted visitor?'

'I'm not exactly lurking; several guests have said they've seen a trio of strange animals here and I thought I'd better come and investigate.'

'It's those wretched dogs. I'd quite forgotten about them and I expect that those supposed to be looking after them have done so as well. Remind me, Madeline, did we extend our invitation to include pets and companions?'

She shook her head. 'Of course we didn't. I cannot think how Lady Peabody thought it would be acceptable for her goddaughter not only to arrive a day early, but to bring a menagerie with her.'

'Having met the young lady I would hazard a guess that Miss DuPont included them without asking for permission. I'll find the dogs and have them put in a barn where they can cause no further harm.'

His sister hurried off and he watched her go with a fond smile. She might be only nineteen years of age but she ran the household as well as his mother had ever done. Madeline would make some lucky gentleman an excellent wife, but hopefully not for another year or two. Her debut had been postponed because of the death of their father and until the coffers were refilled she refused to contemplate going to London for the Season.

It would help him find the animals if he knew their names, but he supposed he must make an effort anyway. He walked through the shrubbery into the edge of the wood and whistled loudly. Immediately there was crashing and snapping branches, and then he was surrounded by three tail-wagging animals.

'Sit. Stay.' To his astonishment they did as he bid, their eyes fixed on him, their long pink tongues lolling and their ears pricked. The gentle swish, swish in the leaves indicated their tails were still moving.

He moved away expecting them to follow but they remained put, waiting for his instruction to move. 'Come.' They were at his feet and sat down without being prompted.

He wanted to dislike them but they were in fact delightful creatures. They were obviously from the same litter, and identical in shape and size, but they were quite easy to distinguish as one was grey and black, the next a reddish colour and the third a mixture of the three.

'Well, if you promise to behave perhaps I won't banish you after all. However, I'll take it up with your mistress when she's recovered as to why she thought it permissible to bring her pets to visit.' He grinned and they smiled back. 'Come with me, boys; I'll show you your new home.'

They followed him, not barking or misbehaving, and he was

impressed. He met an anxious groom as he was about to enter the stable yard. The man bowed.

'I've been looking for them varmints this past half hour, my lord, and beg your pardon if they've been causing further trouble. They've never been away from home before and are a tad overexcited.'

This was certainly a day for surprises. Bennett was unused to being spoken to so informally and at such length by a minion. The dogs had sat in a row at his feet. 'What are their names?'

'That's Ginger, the grey and black's Buster and the other's Toby.' The man hesitated and then continued. 'Begging your pardon, my lord, but I'm Peterson and it's my job to take care of these three.' He scratched his head. 'I ain't ever seen them so quiet and well behaved. They must know they ain't popular.'

Bennett was warming to this garrulous groom. He reminded him of his sergeant who'd spoken to him in a similar fashion. 'I like them, but they must be kept away from the guests and certainly not come into the house. In case you haven't heard, your mistress is not seriously injured and will be up and about as usual tomorrow.'

The man's delighted expression said it all. 'Thank you, my lord, we've been that worried. The lad who was riding Rufus has broke his arm, but it weren't too bad and I've set it for him. I reckon Miss DuPont will want to know.' The man touched his cap, snapped his fingers and walked off; the three dogs trotted behind him.

* * *

When Grace eventually woke up the room was dark, but she was still in her petticoats. She was also ravenously hungry. She waited a few minutes for her eyes to become accustomed to the darkness and was then able to see enough to scramble out of bed and pull on her bedrobe.

She crept across to the shutters and pulled one back, letting in a shaft of moonlight. From this she found her way to the dressing room where the commode was situated.

When she was comfortable she searched for a tinderbox and located one on a shelf. She was adept at using this and soon had several candles lit and the room bathed in a flickering, golden glow. Now she saw that the time was just after midnight – small wonder she'd been abandoned.

Her head was sore but apart from that she was perfectly well. Having slept for the better part of a day already she was wide awake and had no wish to return to her bed. What she did want was something to eat and she could hardly go in search of food at this time of night.

She made her way into her sitting room and was delighted to discover a tray, the contents carefully covered with a damp cloth, waiting for her on a side table. She devoured the contents with relish and when she was done was ready to get dressed. She was perfectly capable of finding her own ensemble and so there was no need for her to wander about in her state of undress until her maid arrived in the morning.

There was an oil lamp in the dressing room and she quickly removed the glass, trimmed the wick and lit this. It gave a safer and better light in which she could go through her garments and find herself an outfit that would not require the services of Annie.

Before she dressed she washed and removed her bandage. The doctor was right, she could arrange her hair in such a way that the stitches were almost invisible. As she intended to exercise Rufus at first light she put on her riding habit. She wore men's breeches beneath the skirt as this meant she could ride astride or side-saddle without revealing an indecorous amount of ankle.

Obviously she never rode astride when she was likely to be seen. She hoped the dogs were being taken care of in her absence and that the three servants she had brought with her had been given decent accommodation outside.

Her ablutions and dressing had only taken an hour and it would be another four hours at least before she could venture downstairs. She'd no idea in which direction to go when she left this apartment as she'd had her eyes closed when she'd been carried here. Did this mean she must remain where she was until there were servants around to direct her?

She'd noticed an escritoire and if this held the necessary items for letter writing she would spend the time penning a missive to her best friend, Charlotte, and also to Collins to ask him to keep her informed about the progress of her brood mares and foals. She would send a short note to her parents informing them that she'd arrived safely.

When she'd finished her task she folded each letter and sealed the backs with blobs of melted wax. Then she wrote the address for each one on the front. At DuPont Manor there was a silver salver kept on a table by the front door for outgoing mail. She supposed there must be something similar here, but being a peer of the realm, the duke could frank her letters and they would go without extra cost.

She wondered, in retrospect, whether she had said rather too much about Lord Sheldon in her letter to Charlotte – would her friend misinterpret this and think she was really in the running for the position as his wife?

Although she had taken her time with her task, the hour was still too early to leave her chambers. Perhaps she could go at five o'clock – surely someone would be around by then to let her out of the house and direct her to the stable yard?

What should she do for the next two hours? Perhaps there was something of interest in one of the glass-fronted bookcases that stood either side of the door that led into the passageway. There were certainly plenty of books to choose from, so there must be something there that would keep her busy until she could leave.

Unfortunately most of the volumes were religious texts, or treatises on mathematics and on other boring subjects. There didn't seem to be a novel anywhere that would keep her occupied. The trunks were already unpacked so she couldn't busy herself with that. After pacing up and down the room for half an hour she decided she would try and find her way to a side door and let herself out, for surely she would go mad with *ennui* if she remained cooped up in here another minute.

After tossing the skirt of her habit over one arm, she picked up her gloves and riding whip and headed for the door. With a candlestick in the other hand, she was unable to close the door behind her and hoped it wouldn't bang shut and wake the other guests who were sleeping in this part of the house.

The shutters and curtains at the far end of the passageway hadn't been drawn and sufficient light came in from the oriel window to guide her towards it. Hopefully she would be able to see something through the glass that would give her her bearings and allow her to negotiate the way around this vast establishment without becoming completely lost.

The first glimmer of dawn on the horizon meant she could see she was facing east and acres of immaculately manicured parkland rolled away into the distance. There were stands of handsome cedar trees, yews and oaks and also what looked like a racetrack of some sort. She hadn't been aware that this family were interested in racing and her pulse quickened.

Did this mean there would be an opportunity to show off the prowess of her stallion? He was already in great demand for breeding and his progeny were much sought after in the locality. However, she'd yet to make any inroads with the gentlemen of the *ton*. If Rufus were to win a race or two whilst she was staying here, this might make all the difference to her stud.

Although ostensibly she was here to find herself an aristocratic husband, she now viewed this as an opportunity to further her business interests. The trust fund would not become available until she married or reached the anniversary of her twenty-fifth birthday. Her brow furrowed as she considered the implications.

The ideal arrangement would be for her to marry a compliant husband, someone who would make no demands on her whatsoever and allow her a free hand to run the stud. The exact opposite of Lord Sheldon. It was as if a great weight had lifted from her shoulders. Now she could be herself, not worry if she offended the prim and proper matrons and their simpering daughters – she had no wish to attract the sort of gentleman who was looking for a young lady of good breeding and impeccable manners.

From this point onwards she would search for either a very young gentleman who could be easily influenced or an older man who would be so besotted with his young bride he would allow her to do as she wished. The gentleman she was looking for must be an aristocrat of some sort, be kind and not lack for wit. She would prefer him to be personable, but the other criteria were far more important.

Surely there must be someone who would do amongst those spending the summer at Silchester Court? Someone her father would be happy with so he would give his permission and thus release her funds?

6

Grace tiptoed along the silent corridors until eventually she found the main staircase. She thought there might be maids on their knees scrubbing the floors but she was in advance of even those girls. There must be a side door that led directly to the stables and this would be easier to open than the front door.

After several false ventures she arrived at an exit that would do. This had no key, just two bolts that she pushed back easily enough. She pulled the door closed behind her and stood on the flagstone pathway that ran between two high hedges, listening. Yes – this led to the stables, for she could hear horses not far away.

The path ended at an archway and she stepped through into an immaculate yard – not a wisp of straw or forkful of manure to be seen anywhere. Even here no one was yet at work. The loose box doors were closed and she could hardly go from one to the other looking in until she found Rufus.

Then the familiar bark from one of her dogs led her to the rear of the stable block and she ran to unbolt the door that held them captive. She dropped to her knees and they jumped all over her. 'Good morning to you, boys. I see you have comfortable accommodation and have been well looked after. Now, show me where Rufus and the other horses are stabled.'

The dogs danced around her feet and then Toby shot off towards a paddock she could see in the distance and she gathered up her skirts and ran after him. The other two animals raced after their brother and by the time she reached the fence her stallion was galloping towards her.

He skidded to a halt, sending divots of grass flying up behind him, and lowered his massive head onto her shoulder. 'I'm glad they turned you out – you'll be much happier here.' She stared around the field and could see several empty fields stretching ahead, which would be ideal for an early morning gallop. As she had no notion where his tack was she would have to ride astride and bareback.

'Stand still, Rufus. I've no wish to further damage my head by falling on it again.' The horse calmed and remained stationary a few inches from the fence whilst she scrambled on his back. After arranging her skirts to her satisfaction she was ready to go.

'Remember, sweetheart, I've no saddle or bridle and you must be careful not to tip me off.'

She gently touched her heels to his sides and wound his long wiry mane around one hand. He needed no further encouragement and moved smoothly from trot to canter, increasing his stride when he saw the obstacle in front of them. She leaned forward, staring through his pricked ears, her blood pounding with excitement.

Rufus soared into the air and cleared the fence with a foot or two to spare and then they were galloping. The pins in her hair came out and it was streaming behind her. Forgetting she was at the home of the Duke of Silchester and that she was here for the sole purpose of finding herself a husband, and that her outrageous behaviour would offend, she laughed out loud.

* * *

Bennett had retired as early as he could do so without seeming uncivil. He wasn't a heavy drinker nor a gambler and found the twittering of society ladies unbearable after his years spent on the Continent as a soldier.

He rose at dawn as he always did, dressed quickly and took the backstairs so he could leave the house without disturbing anyone. He arrived at the side door and was startled to find it already unbolted. Surely no one else had come out so early?

As usual the stable yard was empty of grooms; he didn't expect one of them to get up just to saddle his horse as he was quite capable of doing so himself. He was walking to the tack room when he heard the uninvited dogs barking and was almost sure he also heard Miss DuPont.

He must have imagined this as she would hardly be out here at dawn when she had been so sorely injured less than a day ago. Although she'd looked well enough when he'd seen her sleeping, being out and about was another thing entirely.

The noise had come from the paddocks at the rear of the stable block where the chestnut stallion and the four grey carriage horses had been turned out. He couldn't believe his eyes and increased his pace until he was running flat out in a vain effort to reach the fence before the girl mounted her stallion.

Calling out would be disastrous. He would startle the animal and she would fall a second time and might not be so lucky. He arrived too late and watched helplessly as the horse took off. Then his horror turned to admiration as he realised the girl was in complete control and had a better seat than anyone he'd ever seen astride a horse.

He held his breath as the animal approached the fence and sighed as Miss DuPont – mounted astride and bareback – landed safely and continued her wild ride. Her three canine companions scampered after her. He turned and raced for the tack room and within five minutes he was on his own horse and galloping after her.

His initial admiration for her horsemanship had turned to fear that she was risking her life so casually. Lucifer cleared the fence with ease and thundered across the grass enjoying the unaccustomed race. The girl would have to slow her pace, if she was capable of doing so, when they reached the fourth fence as this bordered the woods that surrounded the property.

She might be an expert horsewoman but it defied credibility to think she could control such a powerful horse with no saddle or bridle. His worst fears were realised when he caught a glimpse of the chestnut without his rider on the far side of the hedge that bordered the final paddock.

'Steady, boy, we must not arrive at this speed.' He pulled on the reins and transferred his weight to the back of the saddle and the horse responded immediately, dropping from a gallop to a canter and then to a walk.

He was about to call out when three overexcited dogs shot through a hole at the bottom of the hedge and their sudden appearance caused Lucifer to rear at the precise moment he was dismounting.

* * *

After jumping the hedge Grace realised her small dog pack was several fields away. 'We will wait for them here, Rufus. I'll walk you until you're cool enough to graze.'

It took a while for the animals to catch up and by that time Rufus was happily munching at the lush grass that grew along the edge of the hedge in the clearing she'd jumped into. She greeted the dogs and then decided to explore before remounting. Although there was a track leading into the trees, she wasn't sure it would be suitable to ride along, as it looked more like one used by deer.

Suddenly the dogs turned tail and ran back the way they'd come and she could hear their excited barking in the distance. Something had attracted their attention so she followed them, hoping they didn't scare her horse as he could be somewhat temperamental. The hedge was too wide for her to see over when standing next to it, although Rufus was standing with his ears pricked looking in the direction of the noise.

There was a gap she could peer through. She was about to do so when the unmistakable sound of Lord Sheldon made her pause. Then something prompted her to peep through the shrubbery and her heart all but stopped.

His lordship was spreadeagled on the grass, there was no sign of his horse and her dogs were bouncing up and down around him. He was unhurt, which was fortunate, but so enraged she thought it better not to announce her presence. With luck he would think Toby and his brothers had arrived through their own volition and not associate her with his accident.

She clicked her fingers and the stallion trotted over to her. There was no way she could mount without something to stand on unless she removed her skirt. She hesitated for a moment, then decided it would be safer to remove herself from Lord Sheldon and risk being seen in men's attire than remain where she was.

She unhooked her skirt and draped it around her neck then grasped a handful of her stallion's mane and vaulted up. There was no need for her to urge Rufus into motion, he shot forward almost before she was settled and only her excellent balance kept her on his back.

Her horse had chosen to canter along the track adjacent to the hedge and Grace crouched over his neck, making sure she couldn't be seen from the field on the other side. With luck the dogs would be so interested in Lord Sheldon they wouldn't attempt to follow her and thus reveal that she'd been present and seen his humiliation.

The sun was slowly rising and there would soon be servants about and she'd no wish to be seen dressed as she was. The track eventually emerged at the rear of the stables and there was the clatter of buckets and the sound of voices. She dismounted and refastened her skirt. 'You must find your own way back to the field, Rufus. I daren't be seen.' She turned his head in the direction of the paddocks and slapped him on his hindquarters.

He whinnied loudly and his stablemates responded from the field. He needed no further encouragement and took off; she held her breath as he approached the fence but he jumped it with feet to spare. The horse was safely home; now all she had to do was get herself inside without being seen. She was certain there would be no guests down so early but there would be members of staff and they were bigger gossips than their masters and mistresses.

The house was rousing. There were maids and footmen already about their duties. She checked her skirt was correctly arranged, repinned her hair and then walked boldly through the side door. If she was going to be seen then she needed to look confident, not skulk about as if she had no right to be there.

She regained the sanctuary of her own apartment unobserved. She glanced at the overmantel clock and saw that the hour was still early – Annie would not be here until seven o'clock, which gave her almost an hour to recover her equilibrium and remove the evidence of her escapade.

There was little point in putting on her nightgown as she had no intention of going to bed. Therefore, she would wash and put on clean underpinnings and by then her abigail should have arrived to help her dress. Her head ached and she thought perhaps she'd overtaxed herself.

When she looked in the mirror she was horrified to see a trickle of blood running down the side of her face. She touched the wound and was unsurprised when her fingers came away red. The doctor had left no replacement dressings so she would have to improvise.

Tearing up a perfectly good petticoat was not an option, so she would have to find something else. Then she remembered the bandage she'd pulled off earlier – perhaps that would do. She was obliged to rummage through the laundry bin until she located it. The pad that had been pressed against the stitches was unusable but the bandage would do very well.

She wound it around her head and secured the end. She could hardly go down for breakfast as she was, so would have to send for something. If she was honest she was relieved she could postpone making her curtsy to the other toplofty guests for a few hours more.

'Good morning, miss, I've brought you a tray as I wasn't sure if you would be well enough to go down,' Annie called out cheerfully as she walked into the sitting room.

'I'm afraid I've overexerted myself this morning and have started the wound bleeding again. I think I might have loosened one of the sutures.'

Her maid dumped the tray on the sideboard with scant regard for the contents and was at her side in seconds. 'It's bleeding badly, miss. I'll send one of the girls down and ask for the doctor to be fetched back immediately.'

'He said he was returning this morning. There's no need to make a fuss; it can wait until he comes. We just need to apply a better dressing. I'm sure you can find something suitable that doesn't require destroying a chemise or petticoat.'

Annie looked unconvinced but didn't argue. Soon the bleeding was staunched by a second bandage being applied over the first. All traces of gore had been removed from Grace's face and she was dressed in one of her new gowns.

'There, that should hold until the doctor gets here. Now, miss, where do you want to eat your breakfast?'

'If you would place it on the hexagonal table that would be perfect. There's no need for you to remain, Annie. Go and have your own meal and then bring me any titbits of gossip you might glean.'

'I shall be back very shortly. If the physician arrives I'll come at once. Are you sure there's nothing else you want to eat or drink?'

Grace waved her away. 'Everything's perfect. One thing's for sure, I shan't go hungry here, for there's more than enough for a family on this tray.'

Although she'd thought herself hungry, she scarcely did justice to the delicious food. However, the jug of coffee was exactly what she fancied. She poured herself a second cup and carried it carefully to the upholstered window seat.

From here she could see the rose garden and, as soon as her wound had been tended to, she was determined to go there. She placed her cup and saucer on the windowsill and then positioned herself so her back was supported and she could stretch out her legs in front of her.

A short while later there was a sharp knock on the door. Good heavens! The doctor had arrived far earlier than she'd anticipated and her maid would still be eating her breakfast. She was reluctant to ask him to enter without a chaperone but decided as a medical man he would be exempt from the usual rules governing such things.

'Come in,' she called.

The door swung back and, to her horror, instead of the gentleman she was expecting, Lord Sheldon opened the door. Before she could protest he stepped in and she scarcely had time to swing her feet to the floor before he began his tirade.

'Have you no sense of decorum? No notion as to how a well-brought-up young lady should behave?' His question was rhetorical and she made no attempt to answer him. 'From the moment you arrived yesterday you've caused nothing but trouble and your wretched dogs are no better. As soon as you're recovered I wish you to leave Silchester Court. When Lady Peabody arrives I'll inform her of my decision. I suggest you remain in your apartment until you depart.'

He stepped back and closed the door behind him, leaving her aghast. Her head was spinning. There was only one reason he had evicted her – despite her precautions he had seen her lurking behind the hedge and knew she had broken all the rules this morning.

How could she have been so stupid? Her plans were in ruin and she would have to return to DuPont Manor as she had nowhere else to go.

Tears trickled unheeded down her cheeks and she collapsed onto the window seat and buried her head in her hands.

7

Bennett was on the stairs when he stopped. He'd barged into Miss DuPont's apartment and yelled at her as if she was a raw recruit, not allowing her to respond. What the hell was wrong with him? Then his stomach clenched when he realised that the girl had a blood-soaked bandage around her head and she'd been without it when he'd seen her earlier.

He bounded back up the stairs and ran to her sitting room. He didn't knock but threw open the door. She was huddled on the window seat sobbing quietly.

'Miss DuPont, please don't cry. I beg your pardon most humbly. I have the most appalling temper...'

She sniffed and slowly raised her tear-stained face. 'I'm well aware of that fact, sir – there's no need to state the obvious.' Her voice was scarcely above a whisper but he could hear every word.

He was somewhat taken aback by her comment but rallied and with a rueful smile handed her his handkerchief. 'Here, blow your nose and dry your eyes. Crying will only aggravate your injury.'

His brisk tone did the trick and her shoulders straightened. After a few minutes of mopping and blowing she was more composed. However, her wound was in urgent need of attention.

'You have reopened your gash by your exertions this morning...'

Again she interrupted him, but this time with a small smile. 'Yet again, my lord, you are telling me something I already know.'

'Miss DuPont, you are an impertinent young lady, but I'm sure that's something you already know as well.' Her gurgle of laughter was contagious and he couldn't prevent his chuckle. 'Dr Adams is not due to return until later this morning and this cannot be left until then. My valet has stitched me up a few times. I'll send for him; he can repair the damage.'

She didn't look overly impressed by this suggestion. 'If you don't mind, I prefer to wait for the doctor.'

He ignored her comment. She was looking decidedly pale and could be in trouble if the bleeding wasn't stopped immediately. Instead of pulling the bell strap he opened the door and yelled using his parade-ground voice.

As expected a footman hurtled around the corner and rushed off with the message. The fact that anyone within the vicinity would have heard him shouting bothered him not one jot. This was his home and he could do as he damned well pleased.

He left the sitting room door wide open – no need to give the tabbies anything else to gossip about. Miss DuPont had moved from the window seat and was sitting demurely in an upright chair. A streak of blood marred her face where she'd attempted to wipe it away with his handkerchief.

'I think that you're right, my lord – my injury is bleeding freely now and I'm beginning to feel a trifle light-headed.'

Without hesitation he ripped off his neckcloth. 'Let me have my handkerchief. I'll fold it into a pad and then secure it with this.' He grinned as he moved to stand behind her. 'This is becoming a habit, my dear, and it's fortunate I have a superfluity of such items.'

Deftly he pressed the folded handkerchief to the sodden bandage and then added his stock to secure it. She glanced up at him. 'If your manservant is coming to attend to me, then haven't you wasted a perfectly good neckcloth? I'm sure I wouldn't have suffered unduly if you'd waited until he arrived.'

He wasn't used to being contradicted and taken to task by anyone, and particularly not by a young lady who wasn't even a member of his family. 'No doubt that's correct, Miss DuPont, but I'd rather ruin my stock than risk your health.'

Her expression changed and her eyes brimmed again. 'I beg your pardon, my lord, I don't mean to be so contrary. I cannot think why I'm going out of my way to offend you.'

He squeezed her shoulder gently. 'There's no need to apologise – I've been damned rude to you as well.'

She rubbed her eyes dry before replying, 'I wasn't aware that I'd been "damned rude" – I merely thought I'd been slightly uncivil.'

This girl was an original. 'Miss DuPont, you're tying me in knots. Of course you haven't been as rude as I have and you certainly haven't been using such appalling language.'

There was no opportunity for her to reply as the bedchamber door burst open and Abbott, followed by two maids, rushed in. 'I've got everything we need, my lord, if the young lady's quite sure she wishes me to repair her stitches.'

'Thank you, Mr Abbott, I should be grateful if you would. It's entirely my own fault that the wound has reopened; I shouldn't have been gallivanting all over the countryside on my horse this morning.'

Her hands flew to her mouth as if she wished to push the words back in. This girl was outrageous, impossible, not at all the sort of young lady who should be visiting such a prestigious house as this, but the more he heard her speak and the more time he spent with her, the better he was coming to like her.

* * *

Grace wished the floor would open and swallow her up. To have admitted in front of two servants that she'd been out at dawn on her own was tantamount to tearing her reputation to shreds. Annie wouldn't dream of gossiping, and she was fairly sure that Lord Sheldon's man would be as discreet, but an unknown chambermaid couldn't be relied on.

She gripped the arms of the chair as Abbott began to unwind the bandage. Whilst his valet was completing this task his lordship picked up a matching chair and placed it beside her. Once he was seated he unpeeled her hands and held them firmly in his own. This was so unexpected it took her mind from what was about to happen.

'He will be done before you know it, little one, and then you must rest as you did yesterday.' He squeezed her hands and began to talk of something else entirely. 'I hope you're intending to enter Rufus in the races. However, you'll have to ride him side-saddle as I don't think my guests would survive the sight of a young lady astride, wearing men's breeches.'

Despite the horrible pain in her head she managed a weak smile and from somewhere summoned the words to reply. 'I ride him with a side-saddle as often as I do astride. Are you sure I'll be allowed to enter? Aren't these races meant for gentlemen only?'

His smile made her forget the pain. 'You're forgetting, Miss DuPont, that all the entertainment and events are at my instigation. Therefore it's up to me who participates or not. We're having several events on the water – do you have any interest in entering those as well?'

'I shall join in everything I'm allowed to, my lord, as there's nothing I like better than being outside. I'm an excellent swimmer, can row a boat but have never sailed a dinghy. Neither have I travelled in a punt – but I doubt it can be particularly difficult so am prepared to have a go at that as well.'

The excruciating agony stopped. 'There, all done, miss, and I reckon I've done a better job than the quack. These sutures won't come adrift. I've cleaned up the wound but it will be better left uncovered.'

'Whatever you think is best, Mr Abbott. Thank you for coming to my rescue.'

'I'm afraid I've had to cut away a deal of hair, miss, but once the injury begins to heal you've more than enough to cover it.'

She was about to put a hand up to explore just how much had been removed but Lord Sheldon wouldn't release her fingers.

'No, don't touch it. It would be better left alone. And I can assure you once you can brush your hair across the injury no one will know.'

'Very well, I'll take your word for it, sir. I meant to say that I'm grateful for the excellent care that's been given to my dogs and horses. Could I ask you to take my pets for a walk this afternoon as they seem, for some strange reason, to have taken to you.' Why had she said that? The remark could be misconstrued as a criticism. 'I don't mean...'

'I'm sure you don't; I understand exactly. Your dogs appear to have adopted me, which is certainly an odd thing to do on their part.' He was now on his feet and had moved a decent distance away from her. 'I'll explain to everybody that you will be unable to join us for a day or two. I'm sure that your godmother will wish to visit when she arrives later today.'

For a second Grace looked at him blankly. 'I'm sure that Lady Peabody will have better things to do than see me. I've never met her; she's merely doing my mother a favour by sponsoring me. They were bosom bows many years ago, I believe.'

'Whatever the reason, Miss DuPont, I'm glad she agreed to do so. I can honestly say that there's been more excitement in this house in the past twenty-four hours than in the past twenty-four years. I've not enjoyed myself so much since I returned from my soldiering.' He raised his hand in casual farewell and was gone, and the room seemed empty without him.

Annie began to fuss. 'I've never seen the like. You'd better come back to bed like his lordship said, miss; you look ever so peaky.'

It was useless to argue when her maid was in this mood, so Grace reluctantly agreed to return to her bedchamber, remove her garments and put her nightgown back on. By the time this was accomplished a jug of watered wine and another of lemonade arrived, as well as some sort of concoction prepared in the kitchen that would soothe her headache.

She drank half the watered wine and swallowed the tisane and she scarcely had time to settle into her pillows before her eyes became heavy and she drifted into slumber.

* * *

Bennett left Miss DuPont's sitting room, unable to stop himself from smiling. The girl might be headstrong, impertinent and unconventional but she was also a bruising rider, brave to a fault and undeniably attractive. Russet hair and green eyes were not a fashionable combination, neither was her unusual height and well-rounded figure, but there was something about her that appealed to him. Was it possible he'd found the girl he wanted to marry?

He descended the stairs two at a time and jumped the last four like a schoolboy. He would go through the motions of looking at the other candidates who'd been invited, but was sure none of them would come up to scratch. He'd told Beau he wanted an outdoor girl, someone with intelligence as well as money – Miss DuPont appeared to have all these attributes.

He met his older brother in the breakfast parlour, which was unoccupied apart from themselves. He doubted anyone else would be about before midday. 'You look inordinately pleased with yourself, Bennett. Tell me what's going on to give you such a spring in your step?'

Bennett regaled his brother with the events of the morning and at the end they were both laughing. 'I think we'd better make further enquiries about Miss DuPont. We're assuming she's an heiress because the Peabodys asked to have her included on the invitation list. However, we know nothing about her and if, as I suspect, she's likely to be my future sister-in-law, then we need to know more.'

'I'll leave that to your man of business, Beau, but I'll speak to Lord Peabody myself when they arrive.' He heaped his plate from the silver containers on the sideboard and took it to the table. There was no further opportunity for private conversation as, to his surprise, guests started to drift in and soon he was surrounded by hopeful girls and their doting mamas.

He did the pretty, was as charming as he could be, but was relieved when he could escape without causing offence. Fortunately there had been no mention of Miss DuPont and her occupation of a superior apartment, so he must suppose that his sister had done as he'd asked and stopped the gossip and speculation.

As he was strolling along the passageway he saw two travelling carriages bowling along the drive. He glanced at his pocket watch – a quarter to ten o'clock – whoever was arriving must have stayed overnight at a nearby hostelry. The baggage for all three families due to come today had arrived yesterday, so everything would be prepared for these guests.

He was about to enquire from Peebles as to the identity of these arrivals when he was approached by a matron of considerable size, dressed in the height of fashion and followed by not one but two hopeful debutantes. There was no escape – he would have to speak to them.

'Lord Sheldon, I am Lady Drusilla Forsyth, daughter to the Earl of Redbridge, and we've yet to be introduced. My daughters and I arrived later than expected last evening and were unable to join you for dinner.'

He bowed and she nodded. The two girls drifted forward and curtsied. Lady Drusilla pointed to the taller of the two, a pretty girl with blonde ringlets and sparkling blue eyes. 'Might I introduce you to my eldest daughter, Miss Amanda Forsyth?' The girl smiled shyly and curtsied a second time.

'I'm honoured to meet you, Miss Forsyth. I hope you enjoy your stay at Silchester Court.'

'This is my second daughter, Miss Rebecca Forsyth.' This young lady was equally attractive although her hair was not quite as golden nor her eyes as blue.

'Miss Rebecca, I'm pleased to make your acquaintance. If you require anything don't hesitate to ask any member of my staff. Breakfast is now being served in the main dining room at the rear of the house.' He bowed again and then with a smile moved away smartly.

It was decidedly unnerving being viewed with such speculation by all three ladies – even the youngest had been sizing him up. Was this how it was going to be all summer? Life would be unbearable if he was to be waylaid everywhere he went. The sooner he made his choice and announced it the better it would be for all concerned.

He would hide in the study for the remainder of the morning, and then spend the afternoon in the billiard room with the gentlemen after he'd taken the dogs for a walk. It would be time enough to meet all the suitable brides at dinner tonight. Madeline caught up with him as he opened the door to his retreat.

'Beau has just told me about the excitement this morning. The more I hear about Miss DuPont the better I like the sound of her. When do you think she will be able to join us downstairs?'

'Two days, I should think. I've just met Lady Drusilla and her daughters – I hope all the others are not so predatory, and that none of them are so desperate to catch me they try and get me to compromise them.'

His sister laughed at his comment. 'Don't be ridiculous – the idea of you allowing yourself to be gulled into such a position is nonsense. Make sure you don't pay particular attention to any one of them. When we have dancing don't dance more than once with any young lady, and check before you go into an empty room that you're not followed.'

His eyes widened in horror, but then she giggled. 'You're bamming me, Madeline. For a ghastly moment I believed you. You made it sound like something out of a Gothic novel – all we want is a ghost and a giant helmet to fall upon someone.'

'Now that's something I'd not thought of. It will add interest and excitement to the next few weeks if our guests believe the place is haunted. Excuse me, brother, I must find Giselle, Perry and Aubrey and see how we can set this up.'

His sister ran away, leaving him bemused. Surely there was more than enough going on without adding imaginary ghosts to the mix?

8

'My head hardly hurts at all, Annie, and from what you tell me it's healing well. I refuse to be held prisoner in my apartment for a moment longer and intend to get dressed and go down this morning.'

Grace had received no visitors apart from Aunt Sarah during the two days she'd been obliged to remain where she was – Lady Peabody and her daughter had not visited her as Lord Sheldon had suggested they would. She had an unpleasant feeling that her fictitious connection to Lady Peabody would already be under scrutiny because of this lady's apparent lack of concern for her goddaughter.

'Now I've washed the blood from your hair, miss, I can arrange it so your stitches won't show. It can't go up in your usual style; I'll have to do something else. It won't be as secure, so you'll have to be careful it doesn't come down.'

Aunt Sarah had been waiting patiently for more than a quarter of an hour. 'Mr Peabody has accompanied his mother and sister, and I found him a delightful gentleman – although I think you'll find Lady Peabody somewhat of a trial and Miss Peabody's so quiet I've not been able to discover anything about her. Have you had word from Peterson?'

'Yes, he sent word that the dogs and horses are managing perfectly well in my absence, so there's no necessity for me to gallivant around the countryside until my stitches have been removed. However, I wish to meet all the guests and be introduced to everyone. From what you've told me there seem to be at least four gentlemen who might do for me.'

'I do wish you would reconsider this foolish scheme of yours, my dear. I've no wish to see you married to anyone you don't have at least a strong affection for.'

'I've explained to you the reasons behind my decision, Aunt Sarah, and I'm confident my plan will be successful. All four of these gentlemen should be delighted to acquire an attractive young wife and a very substantial dowry.'

'If you're set on this, Grace, then might I suggest you concentrate on Mr Peabody? After all, he will already know your provenance so there will be no need to lie to him.'

'I do hope not, Aunt Sarah. Young gentlemen in their cups aren't famous for being discreet. Anyway, I shall find out for myself this morning.' She tilted her head to one side and then the other to make sure the loose arrangement resting at the nape of her neck didn't come adrift. Satisfied that unless she raced about her hair would stay in place, she stood up.

'Thank you, Annie, I'm ready to go down. Will you have my bonnet, gloves and parasol ready, as I'll need them when I take a stroll in the garden after breakfast.' She paused to read the neatly written itinerary that had been delivered to her apartment yesterday.

'The events don't begin until the weekend, which means I've not missed anything, and my stitches will be out before then so I'll be able to join in. However, it would appear there's to be dancing after dinner tonight, which fortunately I'll be able to avoid. I'll retire early saying that my head hurts.'

Aunt Sarah smiled affectionately. 'You'll have to dance in the end, my dear, and although you aren't overfond of this pastime, you're proficient in all the steps.'

'I am indeed – I certainly had enough lessons from that odious dance teacher Mama employed. Now, do I look acceptable?'

'That gown is perfect and brings out the colour of your eyes.'

'I expect all the others will be drifting around in clouds of pastel muslin and I'll be conspicuous wearing *eau-de-nil*.' She viewed her reflection in the long glass and nodded. 'I don't care what others think of me – I'm here to find myself a compliant husband so he might as well get to know the real me before he makes me an offer.'

She slipped her arm through that of her companion and together they left the apartment. She'd yet to meet the other guests who were residing in this part of the house, but she was quite sure they would be members of the *ton* and would have no wish to be associated with someone who was barely quality at all.

'I'm so glad you're here with me, Aunt Sarah. I shouldn't have the courage to go ahead with this if you weren't at my side.'

'Whatever you do in the future, I'll support you. Now, back straight, head up, and look confident, my love – you are the equal of anyone here and don't you forget it.'

Grace smiled. 'I don't think anyone here would agree with you, but I refuse to be cowed by those who think themselves better than me because of their position in society. I know that's a radical notion, but I have to believe this to be true if I'm going to succeed.'

'To think we could already have been on our way back to DuPont Manor if Lord Sheldon hadn't reconsidered.'

'Please don't remind me – he's quite terrifying when enraged. I don't think that spending ten years ordering soldiers about has improved his temperament. From what you've told me the duke and the other members of his family are perfectly pleasant.'

The vast entrance hall was empty and there was no sound of chatter coming from any of the reception rooms. Where was everyone? 'It's ten o'clock. Either the ladies are already taking breakfast or they have had trays sent to their rooms. I've no wish to go into breakfast if there are only gentlemen present.'

'Well, my dear, we can hardly investigate. If you wish to eat we must take that chance.'

'I find I'm no longer hungry. I can manage perfectly well until refreshments are served at midday.'

'If we're not to go into the dining room then, please excuse me. I shall return to my room and send for a tray. Perhaps you'd better do the same thing; it wouldn't do for you to become unwell because you haven't eaten.'

'Not eaten? That problem is easily solved. Good morning, Miss Newcomb, Miss DuPont. Might I say that I'm delighted to see you downstairs? Allow me to escort you to breakfast.' Lord Sheldon had overheard their conversation. For a large man he was remarkably light on his feet.

'Good morning, my lord, but...' She was unable to complete her sentence as he bustled them both along the passageway and into the dining room without allowing her to escape.

The room was already occupied by an assortment of gentlemen but a marked absence of ladies. If Lord Sheldon had not been behind her she would have turned tail, but she was inexorably moved forward until she and Aunt Sarah were inside.

Contrary to her expectations none of the gentlemen did more than rise in their chairs and nod and smile in her direction. They didn't require to be introduced; they were more interested in eating their meal.

'If you would care to be seated, Miss Newcomb, Miss DuPont, it will be my absolute pleasure to serve you.'

Reluctantly Grace took the seat as far away as possible from the others and her companion joined her. 'I require only a slice of toast and butter, and some conserve if there is any, thank you, my lord.' He nodded at her and waited for the second order.

'I should like a little of whatever is there, my lord – it's all so delicious.'

Aunt Sarah's reply pleased him and he beamed at her. He gestured towards the silver coffee and chocolate pots placed centrally on the large table. 'Help yourself to beverages. If you would prefer something else then it will be fetched from the kitchen.'

'Thank you, sir, we have everything we require.' One might have thought this conversation, although dull, would have attracted the attention of the other occupants of the table. After all she was unknown to them and although not a diamond of the first water, she was hardly bracket-faced.

However, they continued to eat and talk amongst themselves as if

Grace and Aunt Sarah were invisible. 'Should we not have been introduced? Isn't it rather uncivil of them to continue eating in that way?' The
words were quiet, spoken directly into her companion's ear.

The reply was equally soft. 'Believe me, my dear, you've been closely
inspected. Lord Sheldon could hardly introduce us to so many, so it's better
we all pretend we're in here alone.'

Grace raised her voice. 'Would you like coffee or chocolate?'

By the time she'd poured them both a coffee Lord Sheldon had
returned with their requests. When Grace saw what she'd missed she
regretted asking for so little. To her amusement his lordship filled his own
plate and then joined his cronies and she and Aunt Sarah were left to their
own devices.

The table was so long it was impossible to hear the conversation at the
far end so she must assume anything she said would also be audible only
to themselves. She swivelled in her seat so she had her back to the
gentlemen.

'I've been able to look at most of them and there are two that appear
promising. There's a fair-haired gentleman of middle years, wearing a
burgundy topcoat and a rather startling plum striped waistcoat. And a
little further along there's a younger man with light brown hair, a blue
topcoat and green waistcoat. Can you identify either of them?'

'The older gentleman's here with his wife and daughter, so you must
rule him out. However, the young man is Mr Peabody and he's certainly
interested as he's scarcely eaten another mouthful since we arrived.'

A flicker of excitement ran down her spine. 'Do you think he might be
curious rather than interested? Remember, I'm supposed to be his mama's
long-lost goddaughter. Unless, of course, he's already aware of my less
than illustrious family history.'

'I would say with absolute certainty, my dear, that that young
gentleman is halfway to becoming enamoured of you already. I'm sure you
will be introduced to him as soon as Lady Peabody is down.'

There was a second exit at the far end of the dining room and one by
one the gentlemen departed until only Lord Sheldon remained. Instead of
remaining where he was he picked up his half-eaten plate of food and
carried it down until he was sitting opposite them.

'You've been looking wistfully in the direction of the buffet, Miss DuPont. Are you sure I cannot tempt you to coddled eggs or a slice of crisply fried ham?'

'No, thank you, I'm quite content with what I've got.' A sudden rumble of thunder made her jump. 'Oh dear! I fear we're in for a storm and I was intending to visit the stables and check on my menagerie.'

'I've already taken your dogs for a constitutional. I cannot imagine why you chose to keep three such animals, but I must admit their charm is growing on me. I can also report that your stallion and your carriage horses are equally well cared for, although nobody has been brave enough to do more than pitch hay over the fence and check the water trough is full.'

A flash of lightning lit up the room and then the heavens opened and the noise of the rain drumming on the terrace outside the windows made it impossible to continue the conversation. Grace got to her feet and nodded to his lordship, then with a friendly wave she and her friend left him to finish his breakfast.

'Shall we go to the drawing room or do you wish to explore the library? I've not had a chance to investigate myself, but from what I hear it has thousands of books.'

'I'm going to return to my apartment and put on my cloak and outdoor boots. I cannot remain cooped up indoors a moment longer. If I get soaked, so be it – I can change before refreshments are served at noon.'

Just as Grace was walking across the grand entrance hall she was accosted by a very tall, thin lady dressed in the height of fashion and accompanied by a young lady who was obviously her daughter. 'Miss DuPont, I wish to speak to you immediately. Come with me.'

The lady didn't introduce herself, but Grace was certain this was Lady Peabody and the girl was Miss Amelia Peabody. She was tempted to ignore this uncivil command but decided it might be sensible to get this meeting over and done with. It was essential she knew exactly what Lady Peabody and her children knew of the situation and how much they had told the other guests.

The fact that Lord Peabody owed her father a massive debt would surely be a bargaining chip as this was also information that should be kept from the rest of the guests.

'In here, there's an anteroom we can use and not be disturbed.' Lady Peabody sailed in and her daughter followed, leaving Grace to enter last and close the door behind her.

She decided to speak first and not allow this obnoxious woman to dominate the conversation. 'You are Lady Peabody, I presume, as you've not had the courtesy to introduce yourself. If you wish the information about your husband's debts to remain a secret, I suggest you moderate your tone when speaking to me.'

'How dare you speak to me like that – I only agreed to this charade under duress. To be obliged to be associated with you in this way is decidedly unpleasant. I shall denounce you to the duke and you will be sent packing, for no one will wish someone like you to remain here.'

Grace swallowed a lump in her throat. 'Believe me, madam, if you do so I shall not be the only one sent packing. Do you really wish society to know your family's all but bankrupt? Miss Peabody will never find a suitable husband or Mr Peabody a wife.'

'Please, Mama, don't be too hasty. Miss DuPont might not be one of us, but she is incredibly wealthy and no one would know she wasn't acceptable from her conversation or her appearance.' Miss Peabody stared earnestly at her mother and Grace held her breath.

'Very well, I shall do as you ask, Amelia, but don't expect me to socialise with you, Miss DuPont. That would be the outside of enough. However, I'll confirm that you are indeed my goddaughter and the rest must be up to you.'

'In which case, my lady, I'll also hold my tongue. But be very sure if you are unwise enough to make disparaging comments about me then I'll not hesitate to reveal your secret. I think, on reflection, that you will understand that my not being a member of the *ton* is of far less importance than you being about to lose your home, estate and everything else.'

Her words appeared to resonate with Miss Peabody and she attempted a feeble smile, but her mother was not to be cowed by such threats. She drew herself up to her considerable height and stared down her long, aristocratic nose at Grace. 'Breeding, Miss DuPont, is far more important to the quality than money garnered from trade. You will be ostracised if your secret becomes known, whereas we will be offered sympathy and financial help if ours is revealed.'

There was little point in continuing this conversation. 'I bid you good day, madam. I have better things to do than waste my time with you.' Grace stalked past the two of them, not sure who had had the best of the encounter.

* * *

Bennett watched her go and wondered what had occurred between Lady Peabody and Miss DuPont to make the girl look so distressed. He strolled across to the anteroom, intending to greet his guests and perhaps elicit some useful information whilst doing so.

As he reached the door he could not help but hear the strident tones of Lady Peabody as she spoke to her daughter. 'I wish you to have nothing to do with that young lady and I shall speak to your brother and give him the same instruction. I cannot think that foisting her upon us like this is to anybody's benefit. I shall be writing to Lord Peabody this very afternoon to express my displeasure.'

He hurriedly stepped into the shadows as both women emerged and made their way towards the dining room. What had this remark meant? The girl was obviously Lord Peabody's goddaughter and not hers – Madeline must have been given incorrect information. This would explain why her ladyship had not bothered to visit Miss DuPont while she was forced to remain in her apartment.

However, it didn't explain why she'd taken the girl in such dislike. Then his lips curved and he smiled wryly. This young lady was an original and obviously her forthright manners and unconventional behaviour wasn't to Lady Peabody's taste. God knows what the wretched woman would say when she discovered Miss DuPont intended to enter her stallion in the races next week.

He would do his best to counteract any negative comments by asking his sisters to befriend the girl. Once the house guests were aware Miss DuPont was warmly regarded by the family she would be accepted by everyone else. In this way his conscience would be clear and he could get on with the business of finding himself a wife from the assortment his sisters had provided for him. Somehow he rather thought that he'd already made his choice and that however lovely, well-bred or impeccably mannered the other contenders might be, a red-headed, green-eyed girl had already captured his heart.

* * *

9

After getting thoroughly wet, Grace returned to her apartment with her good humour restored. There was nothing like a romp with one's dogs to restore one's equanimity. If the weather improved she would ride this afternoon and thus avoid the necessity of mingling with the other ladies.

Despite her firm stand with Lady Peabody, she was dreading having to pretend she was something she was not. It would be better to avoid going down for midday refreshments as well, however hungry she might be. If her first encounter with the others could take place when the gentlemen were present, there was less likelihood of being treated to an inquisition.

Her companion left Grace to her own devices, for which she was grateful. She was certain Aunt Sarah would be busily gathering useful information about the other house guests. The more they knew about everyone the easier it would be to find a man who would suit her.

Her ride was uneventful and Rufus behaved impeccably. She'd hoped that one or other of the gentlemen would decide to go out as well, but in this she was disappointed. She handed the reins to Peterson, the groom she'd brought with her, and made her way back to the side entrance.

The house was eerily quiet and for a moment she was taken aback. Then she checked the time on the longcase clock that ticked noisily in an alcove in the grand hall. Drinks would be served in the drawing room in less than half an hour and she still had to change – no wonder the house was deserted.

She picked up her skirts and ran up the stairs, ignoring the startled expressions of the footmen who waited to open and close doors. On bursting into her bedchamber she discovered not just Annie, but also Aunt Sarah and two other maids twittering and exclaiming.

'There you are at last, Grace. You've scarcely got time to dress. It will be an absolute catastrophe if you are late on your very first public appearance.'

'Don't wait for me, Aunt Sarah. I'll be down as soon as I can.'

Her riding habit was removed and she quickly pulled off her boots and breeches. She needed a strip wash as she could hardly appear reeking of the stables. Despite her hurry she was still horribly tardy and it was perfectly possible the guests would have gone into dinner without waiting for her.

She paused on the stairs to compose herself. There was no point rushing in red-faced and out of breath as this would only draw attention to her lateness. When she was sure she was calm she continued on her way, relieved to hear voices coming from the drawing room. The duke would consider her rag-mannered for keeping his guests waiting for almost twenty minutes and she would be unpopular with the chef as well.

'Ah! Miss DuPont, we are both fashionably late. Allow me to introduce myself.' The tall, dark man was a replica of Lord Sheldon so there was no need for him to tell her he was the Duke of Silchester.

She curtsied. 'Your grace, I apologise for keeping everyone waiting. I've no excuse at all.'

'And neither have I, so we will both be in disgrace together. Shall we brave the opprobrium of the assembled company or go straight to the dining room and pretend we've been there the whole time?' He offered his arm and she placed hers upon it.

She couldn't stop the bubble of laughter escaping and so they walked in together and instead of being received with frowns and disapproval everyone smiled and nodded.

The butler was hovering anxiously at the far end of the room and the duke signalled he should announce dinner. Grace expected to be led to the front of the queue and then lead the procession – after all, wasn't she on the arm of the duke?

Instead those nearest went through first and then everyone else made their way through the doors, across the passageway and into the biggest dining room she'd ever seen. 'Good heavens! You could dance a minuet on the table.'

'I hope you weren't thinking of doing so, Miss DuPont? My very expensive and highly sought-after French chef would pack his bags and leave immediately if we delayed dinner a moment longer.'

'In which case, your grace, I'll save my performance for later.'

She'd expected him to release her hand so she could find herself a seat, but he was guiding her to a row of empty chairs at the far end of the table. Only then did she notice that although guests were seating themselves in a higgledy-piggledy fashion anywhere they chose, these seats had been left vacant.

'I cannot possibly sit here. I've caused enough tongues to wag already.' She tried to pull her hand free but his grip was too strong.

'You will sit where you're told, young lady. And I choose to have you sitting with my family.' Although his tone was playful, there was no mistaking the steely glint in his eye.

'Beau, you've brought Miss DuPont with you. How splendid.' The young lady who'd spoken was obviously related to Lord Sheldon and the duke, for she had the same dark hair and remarkable blue eyes.

Grace's hand was finally released and she dropped into a deep curtsy. 'I am delighted to meet you, my lady. His grace insisted that I come, although I would far prefer to be somewhere less conspicuous.'

'I am Madeline. My sister Giselle is just about to sit down next to my brothers, Peregrine and Aubrey. You are to sit between me and Bennett tonight.'

This informality was decidedly unsettling and the thought that she would be sitting beside Lord Sheldon even more so. Was there still time to escape? Then her chair was pulled out for her by a waiting footman and she had no option but to take her place, knowing she was the very last person in this enormous chamber who deserved to have this position.

'I've never seen so many people sitting around so large a table in my life before. How many are there, Lady Madeline?'

'With family, there are sixty-three. I think the most there's ever been in here – and that wasn't in my lifetime – was eighty.'

The dinner was to be served *à la française* and the first course, which had more removes than she could count, was already positioned down the centre of the table. This meant that guests could help themselves to whatever they fancied.

Normally she had a robust appetite, but tonight she was overawed by her surroundings and uncomfortable being in such a prestigious position. Although the intention had been to smooth her passage into this grand gathering, she was aware she was being surreptitiously scrutinised.

'I shall give you a little of everything, Miss DuPont, as you seem reluctant to serve yourself.' Lord Sheldon picked up her empty plate and carefully placed a small amount of all that was within his reach.

When the food was placed in front of her, the appetising aroma made her mouth water and she forgot her nervousness. 'Thank you, my lord, I've not eaten since breakfast and then I only had toast.'

She risked a glance in his direction and he was smiling. 'In which case it's fortunate there are four courses, each with a dozen removes.'

She scarcely noticed what she ate but it was all quite delicious. Lady Madeline was charming and they discovered they shared the same anniversary.

'May Day is an auspicious time to be born, Miss DuPont, so I've been told.' She leaned across Grace and spoke directly to her brother. 'Miss DuPont and I are exactly the same age, Bennett. Isn't that amazing?'

Apart from their first brief exchange Grace had avoided any further conversation with him, believing that if she showed she was indifferent to him, and wasn't making a play to attract his attention, she would be less unpopular with the other guests.

'Quite extraordinary; but this information could have waited until we were able to converse without you being obliged to yell at me across Miss DuPont.'

Grace flattened herself against the back of her chair so they could talk more readily and her movement was seen by his lordship.

'There's no need to do that, Miss DuPont. I've no wish to converse with my sister at the moment. However, as I have your attention, I should like to speak to you instead.'

'Actually, my lord, I believe I've eaten something that disagrees with me.' Grace pushed her napkin against her mouth as if she was about to cast up her accounts. Her intention had been to slip away unnoticed and thus avoid the necessity of being seen talking to him. Unfortunately he believed her and his expression changed to one of concern.

'Come with me, sweetheart; there's a retiring room close by.' Her chair was pulled back with her still sitting on it. She had no option but to jump to her feet and hurry off as if she was indeed feeling unwell.

The fact that he had his arm resting lightly around her waist did nothing to improve her composure. He was such a kind man and she had ruined his dinner with her foolishness. She couldn't allow him to remain in ignorance of her deception.

They were now in the comparative privacy of the corridor, but the sound of conversation, cutlery and the clink of glasses was still audible. She stepped away from him and removed the napkin. 'I'm not feeling nauseous, my lord; there's no need for you to be concerned on my behalf.'

He stared down at her, his expression unreadable. 'In which case why did you wish to run away?'

'I didn't want to talk to you.' His eyes widened and his eyebrows rose. 'No, you don't understand. This is all such a dreadful muddle.'

'I'm waiting. Explain yourself.'

Her heart was hammering and her hands were clammy and she wished she could take to her heels and run away. There was no option but to tell him the truth – not who she was, but why she didn't wish to be seen as his favourite.

'I've already become a talking point with your other guests; by being singled out by you and your family I will be unpopular with those who have come here with the express purpose of ensnaring you.'

'And you are not here for the same reason?'

'No, I've come to find myself a husband, but not you. I thought perhaps that Mr Peabody might suit.' What had prompted her to tell him such an intimate detail?

'Look at me, if you please, my dear. I have no intention of conversing with the top of your head.' Reluctantly she met his eyes. There was something dangerous flickering behind his bland expression. 'That's better. Now, I thought myself the most eligible of fellows – that every young lady present was desperate to attract my interest. What is it you object to? Why am I not your choice?'

'You are a very attractive gentleman, with all the required attributes. However, I'm looking for a younger gentleman, one closer to me in interest and temperament.' This was a half-truth, but she could hardly tell him he was arrogant and dictatorial and she wanted a more malleable husband. Nor could she tell him that she was so far beneath his touch he wouldn't even give her a moment's notice if he knew her true circumstances.

He nodded. 'A reasonable explanation, Miss DuPont, and I thank you for being so honest. However, I fear you will be disappointed if you've truly set your sights on young Peabody. His mama has taken you in dislike and I believe he's unlikely to go against her wishes.' His smile was bland, but there was something unnerving about him. It was as if he was toying with her, playing a game she didn't know the rules to.

She tilted her head and gave him stare for stare. 'Thank you for your opinion, my lord, but please don't let me detain you. I'm returning to my apartment as I've no wish to spend the evening being grilled by the other guests.' Not allowing him the opportunity to reply, she spun and hurried towards the stairs that would lead her to safety.

* * *

Bennett watched her go through narrowed eyes. He had asked Beau to wait for her so she wouldn't be castigated for holding the company up. He had then included her in their family group in order to improve her standing with the other guests, and this is how she repaid him.

There could be no other young lady present who would have the temerity to reject him as a suitor in favour of a nonentity like young Peabody. Tarnation take it! If she wanted none of him then so be it – he would dismiss her from his mind and concentrate on finding himself a wife from the other candidates. He must also make sure Beau and his sisters no longer paid her any special attention. She could sink or swim amongst the society misses on her own.

His absence must have been remarked but he'd been gone for a few minutes only and hopefully the fact that he'd returned unaccompanied was explanation enough. His brother looked enquiringly in his direction.

'Miss DuPont was unwell. I directed her to the retiring room. She doesn't intend to return.' He turned to his sisters, wishing there wasn't a conspicuously empty place beside him. 'Although I've been introduced to everyone here, can you tell me which of the candidates you think is the most appropriate?'

It appeared there were four who not only had the necessary pedigree and fortune he needed, but also had the other necessary attributes.

'I'll make a point of speaking to those you've mentioned this evening. Is there to be dancing tonight, Madeline?'

'Yes, Giselle has offered to play the pianoforte and the carpet has already been removed from the far end of the drawing room. There will also be cards for those who don't participate and no doubt some of the gentlemen will escape to the billiard room.'

He glanced around the table, making sure he didn't seem to be looking at anyone in particular. 'There appear to be as many young gentlemen as ladies – how can that be?'

His sister frowned. 'Are you sure? Obviously the invitations included the head of the household, but only three accepted. As far as I can recall there were only a dozen male siblings accompanying their sisters and mamas.'

'Surely the housekeeper would have informed you of any additions to our guest list.' Under the pretence of wiping his lips on his napkin he did a quick headcount of those present at the table. 'There are approximately twenty-six girls, fifteen matrons, five older gentlemen and twenty unattached young men.'

Beau had overheard his comment. 'Small wonder Peebles wasn't ready to announce dinner at the usual time. He must have been frantically adding extra covers to accommodate these uninvited guests.'

'I cannot imagine why Anderson hasn't approached me with the prob-lem. I must speak to her after dinner and get an updated list of who is actually present. It must be quite unprecedented to host a prestigious house party like this and then discover we have acquired unknown guests.'

'Word must have got around that this is to be a marriage mart and the extra men will be those sons who initially refused our invitation,' Bennett told his sister.

No more was said on this subject and the dinner continued until Madeline stood up to lead the ladies away, leaving the gentlemen to their port. This was an ideal opportunity to discover who these interlopers were and whether they posed a threat to his intentions.

By the time the port had been passed three times he was certain only four of the men at the table were a danger to his marital plans. Five had come merely to participate in the horse races and he would have to examine their mounts before he could decide if they were a threat or not. He doubted anybody had a horse that could beat either Lucifer or Rufus. The rest were merely here to enjoy themselves and flirt with the females.

He'd had enough of socialising and, despite his intention to circulate this evening, he sloped off as soon as Beau stood up. He headed straight for the stables with the intention of talking to his head groom, if he was still available, about the contenders for the races next week.

A movement by the paddock which contained Miss DuPont's horses gave him pause. Was she outside too?

10

Grace returned to her apartment, carefully removed her evening gown and hung it on the rail. There was no point in creasing this as she would need to wear it again. She couldn't settle and it was far too early to retire.

She gazed longingly at the park and decided she would go for a ride. Hastily she donned her riding habit before slipping down the backstairs and out into the early evening sunshine. With luck there would be no one in the stables as the staff would expect their masters and mistresses to still be at dinner.

She'd been unable to pin on her military-style riding cap as the stitches got in the way. She would be relieved when the doctor returned to remove them and she could wash her hair properly and put it up the way she preferred.

There was a lone stable boy in the yard, sitting on an upturned bucket, and he jumped to his feet. 'I wish you to bring my saddle down to the paddock; I'll take the bridle. Has my stallion been groomed today?'

The lad shook his head vigorously. 'No, miss, he'll not let anyone near. I'll bring the brushes and such and then go back for his saddle, shall I?'

'Thank you – I expect his feet will need picking out as well.'

She wasn't surprised Rufus had been left to his own devices – he could be terrifying when he so wished. There was no sign of the horses when she reached the gate so they must be behind the stand of trees at the far end. She stood on the bars and called. Immediately he galloped into sight, closely followed by the four carriage horses.

Rufus had been rolling in the mud and it took both her and the willing stable boy over an hour to brush him clean. The sun was setting but she still had an hour or two before it got dark. After thanking the boy for his assistance, she mounted and set off to explore the grounds.

* * *

Fortunately there was sufficient moonlight to guide her back – she'd stayed out so long it was now full dark. She dismounted and quickly removed the heavy side-saddle and put it on the fence whilst she opened the gate and led Rufus into the field.

'Off you go, old fellow; go and find your companions. I'll see you tomorrow.' The stallion tossed his head and trotted into the darkness. Grace carefully closed the gate and fastened it and then was about to pick up the saddle when a shadowy figure stepped in beside her.

'Allow me, Miss DuPont, it's far too heavy for you.'

'Lord Sheldon, what are you doing out here? I thought everyone safe inside.' This was hardly a friendly response to his kind offer.

His teeth flashed white. 'Like you I prefer to be in the fresh air.' He reached across and removed the bridle from her unresisting hand. 'I'll put these away; you'd better get inside before you're seen.'

She was halfway along the path before it occurred to her that they had parted on bad terms earlier this evening, and she'd done nothing to improve the situation by her less than courteous reply. Tomorrow she would make a point of searching him out and apologising for her shrewish behaviour; she had no wish for him to think badly of her.

As she'd given Annie the evening free, her maid would not know about this night-time excursion. However, Aunt Sarah was waiting in her sitting room and didn't appear to be impressed by Grace's absence.

'Good gracious, what were you thinking of, my dear? Haven't you caused enough speculation this evening without wandering about outside in the dark on your own?'

'I don't care. In fact, I wish I'd never come here. I think it might be best if we leave as soon as my stitches are removed. We must find ourselves a small cottage to live in until I reach my majority and can access my inheritance.'

'Things aren't as bad as that, Grace. From my lowly position further down the table, I was privy to the gossip. The fact that you pointedly ignored Lord Sheldon and then left the table and didn't return has reassured the predatory matrons that you're not a contender for the position as his wife.'

'There's something about that man that brings out the very worst in me. I can't be in his company for more than a minute without us being at daggers drawn. He also told me that Mr Peabody's of no use to me as his mother would never allow an alliance between us.'

'Then shall we forget about your notion to marry? I think your suggestion that we find ourselves a small house and live there quietly for the next eighteen months is worth considering. I've managed to save sufficient to keep us for a few months – we just need another twenty guineas or so to put this plan into action.'

'I just remembered that there are monetary prizes for each race and a further generous amount for the overall winner. In fact I believe that every event carries some sort of financial reward.' She hugged her companion. 'We'll stay until I've garnered enough to keep us and then we shall leave. I think we'd better find somewhere to live before we go – I wonder if we could rent something in a village not too far away from the stud.'

'I shall start making enquiries, my dear, as I've got friends in the neighbourhood who can look for something suitable. Don't you think your father will search for you when you fail to return?'

'I doubt that he'll be too bothered. If he can't gain access to the drawing rooms of society by marrying me to an aristocrat, then I'm no use to him.'

'In which case, I'm happy to assist you in this endeavour. I can't tell you how relieved I am that you changed your mind about making a marriage of convenience. One day you will meet a gentleman you can love and will be glad you didn't throw away your chance of happiness.'

'That's a pleasant thought to retire with, Aunt Sarah. I need to look at the itinerary and see what's planned tomorrow – if there's something that's offering a monetary prize, then I shall enter.'

'Don't you remember, my love, nothing of any interest starts until the weekend, which is still two days away? The physician is coming the day after tomorrow to remove your stitches and then you'll be able to partici-pate in everything.'

They bid each other a fond goodnight and agreed to meet for breakfast at ten o'clock when the gentlemen should have eaten and gone about their business. Grace wished to make it clear to anyone who cared to listen that she wasn't in the running for the contest to secure Lord Sheldon's hand in marriage. Once she'd established this fact she hoped to be able to glean important information about the gentlemen's horses in order to know if there were any others, apart from Lucifer, that might prove a stumbling block to her plans.

As she settled down for the night she thought about the horse races. Presumably his lordship wouldn't accept the prize even if he won, but would give it to the contestant who came second, and this, God willing, would be her.

* * *

The next two days passed pleasantly enough and Grace found companionship with one or two of those present. She made certain she sat as far away as possible from the Silchester family. She avoided the neces-sity to dance as she retired immediately after dinner with the excuse that her head was still painful.

The sutures were removed and the doctor pronounced himself delighted. As soon as he'd gone Annie fetched several jugs of hot water and Grace was able to wash her hair. She sat in the window seat with it loose about her shoulders whilst the sun streamed in and dried it.

'Aunt Sarah, a dozen or more guests are going out for a hack in half an hour's time and I intend to be with them. However, I'm not riding Rufus but one of the duke's horses, as I don't want to reveal his prowess prema-turely and warn my adversaries what to expect.'

'I'm going to sit in the garden with two of the matrons and continue with my embroidery. It's fortunate indeed that not all of the ladies present are as unpleasant as Lady Peabody. She has endeared herself to no one and I feel sorry for her daughter who seems a perfectly pleasant young lady.'

They agreed to meet up before dinner in Grace's sitting room. The house had come alive in the past few days and was a positive hive of activity. Every chamber appeared to be occupied and there was a constant ebb and flow of guests from the reception rooms to the gardens and park.

She nodded and smiled at all she met and arrived at the stable yard confident she was no longer an outsider, but part of the group. Her dogs had also adapted to their new surroundings and were universally popular with those they came into contact with.

There were a dozen or more guests milling about in the yard, but there was only one other young lady present; all the rest were gentlemen.

A familiar voice hailed her. 'Miss DuPont, I gather you've requested one of my brother's mounts. Does that mean your stallion is unfit?'

She turned to speak to Lord Sheldon. 'I take him out at dawn, my lord, so he's been exercised already. However, I enjoy riding in company so have requested a horse from your stables. I hope that's not a problem?'

He shook his head. 'Not at all. And in case you're worried about being given a nag, you may rest assured that you'll like the animal I've had allocated to you. Not quite of the calibre of your stallion, but a fine beast.'

A groom approached with a tall bay gelding. He touched his cap and turned the horse so she could mount. Her bent leg was grasped by his lordship, and he tossed her into the saddle. Was it her imagination or had he gripped her booted ankle more tightly than was strictly necessary?

She gathered the reins and guided her horse through the archway and onto the expanse of grass that led to the home paddocks. There were already several other riders and her eyes were drawn immediately to a massive grey that was cavorting and prancing, making every effort to remove his rider.

The gentleman in question had an excellent seat and merely laughed each time the horse bucked. After a few minutes the animal settled and she raised her whip in an acknowledgement of his horsemanship.

He was not much older than herself, had corn-coloured hair cut short as was fashionable nowadays, and regular features. He was walking his horse towards her when Lord Sheldon appeared on his black stallion and came between them – whether deliberately or by happenstance, she'd no idea.

'There are so many of us I think it would be wise to move off and let the others fall in behind when they're ready. How do you like Bruno, Miss DuPont?'

'Very well indeed, thank you, sir.' She had no option but to follow his suggestion and was dismayed to be obliged to ride beside him after all her efforts to remain invisible these past two days.

Once they were a safe distance away from the milling horses she reined back. 'Excuse me, my lord, but I think it would be preferable for me to ride with the other lady, not with the gentlemen.'

'I doubt that Miss Forsyth will stay out very long – she's an indifferent horsewoman. No, you'd do far better staying with us if you want a decent hack across country.'

Grace kept her mount stationary and didn't reply. He was forced to continue, otherwise he would have created confusion when the other riders trotted up. The young lady was struggling to control her mount.

'Bring him alongside me, Miss Forsyth. He'll settle down then.'

The girl managed to do this with some difficulty but as soon as she was next to Bruno things became calmer. 'Thank you, Miss DuPont. Mama insisted that I come out this afternoon as everybody knows how much Lord Sheldon admires a good rider.' She smiled. 'Nothing I could say would convince her that I would do myself no good by demonstrating to him my shocking lack of proficiency.'

'Shall we let them go on ahead and find ourselves a more gentle route? There's a pleasant track that runs past the lake and requires no jumping of ditches or hedges.'

'In which case, Miss DuPont, I shall be delighted to accompany you. Mama has told me to stay away from you as you're a trifle wild. She'll be hopping mad when she discovers we've spent time together.'

Grace was unsure how to respond to this ingenuous remark. 'I've no wish to cause discord in your family – perhaps it would be better if you returned to the stables.'

'Absolutely not! Coming here was my mother's idea. For some reason she thinks I'll be able to attract Lord Sheldon. I cannot imagine what attributes she thinks I have that outshine everyone else here. I'm an indifferent rider, only passably pretty and not especially witty either. Fortunately I have the one thing that's essential – a staggeringly large dowry.'

They were now under a canopy of trees, but the path was too narrow to ride side by side and Bruno took the lead. This meant that their conversation must cease until they could be together again. However, her companion had other ideas and tried to push her horse closer by veering off the path.

Bruno, startled by the crashing of branches, snatched his bit between his teeth and bolted. Grace heard a despairing cry behind her but was too occupied in bringing her horse under control to turn back and help. Miss Forsyth had taken a tumble and her riderless mount was thundering along behind Bruno, adding to his terror.

* * *

Bennett intended to lead the group across country, taking in several massive hedges and fences in order to get a feel of the opposition. He watched Grace turn aside and take her companion into the trees then, just as he was about to push forward, he heard a scream coming from that direction.

He kicked Lucifer and his horse shot through the gathered riders, scattering them in all directions. He didn't think the scream had been from Grace, but something untoward had occurred and he needed to investigate.

It would be foolhardy to arrive at speed so he slowed his horse and entered the wood at a trot. There was no sign of Grace but Miss Forsyth lay weeping on the ground. He dismounted and quickly tethered his horse to a nearby branch.

'Miss Forsyth, are you hurt? What happened?'

The girl's sobs abated and she turned a piteous tear-stained face up to him. 'My lord, Miss DuPont insisted that we gallop although I'd told her I was unsafe. She has gone and she ignored my cry for help.'

He gently ran his hands along her legs and arms and was satisfied she was unhurt. 'Allow me to help you up, my dear, then I can carry you back to the house if you're unable to walk unaided.'

She held out her hands and he pulled her to her feet. Immediately she collapsed with a squeal of pain. 'I fear I've broken my ankle, my lord. I cannot bear to put my weight on it.'

'Then I'll carry you. I won't offer to put you up on Lucifer as he doesn't take kindly to other riders.' He scooped her up and set off for the house. He was met by the other gentlemen. He explained what had transpired, but when he saw the looks of disapproval and heard their mutterings he instantly regretted his frankness. He only had this young lady's account of what had happened and on reflection he rather thought the young lady had told a tale that suited her.

He approached his brother Perry. 'Here, take Miss Forsyth up with you. I need to find Miss DuPont.'

His burden successfully transferred, he strode back to his mount and vaulted into the saddle. The more he thought about it the less likely the given explanation seemed. Grace would never have put a less experienced rider at risk – something else had happened and he had a bad feeling about it.

He kicked his horse forward and, with his heart pounding, he pushed Lucifer into a gallop. As they thundered down the path he prayed he wouldn't find the girl, who already meant too much to him, lying broken on the ground.

11

Grace couldn't employ the standard method for halting a bolting horse of circling them as the path was too narrow, so all she could do was sit tight and hope he slowed down of his own accord. The branches whipped past her face, her hat became dislodged and her hair was in no better state.

There was a clearing ahead if she remembered rightly and this would be perfect for her purposes. She threw her weight back and transferred both hands to the inside rein. As the frantic animal emerged into the sunlight she applied all her strength to the single rein and wrenched his head round, managing to dislodge the bit from between his teeth.

Being an expert horsewoman she regained both reins and circled him a few times until he calmed. She was leaning forward, patting the horse's lathered neck, when Miss Forsyth's mount erupted into the clearing. Its sudden appearance caused Bruno to shy and she was pitched headlong into the bushes.

As she'd had the good sense to hang on to the reins her horse didn't take off again. She was unhurt, merely snagged in the brambles, and matters weren't improved by Bruno pushing his big head in to investigate.

'Get out of the way, you idiot. Haven't you caused enough trouble already?'

To her astonishment the animal laughed at her. Then Lord Sheldon's face appeared above her. 'I'm glad to see you're unhurt, Miss DuPont, but mystified as to why you think the debacle was my fault or that I'm an idiot.'

She was too cross to bandy words with him and surged to her feet, ignoring his friendly comment. 'I take it that my erstwhile companion is not injured. She attempted to barge past and my horse bolted. I heard her fall but could do nothing about it.'

Ignoring his outstretched hand she fought her way out of the brambles, glad she'd had the sense to wear gloves. 'If you would be kind enough to assist me to remount, my lord, I shall return to the stables. I've had more than enough excitement for today.'

She turned her back on him and presented her bent leg and was thrown up with more vigour than was strictly necessary. 'Thank you for your assistance, my lord. Do you wish me to lead the loose horse back or will you do it yourself?'

'You take him; I've wasted enough time already and must catch up with the other gentlemen.' He handed her the reins of the second animal, remounted and vanished without another word.

Although she'd offered to lead the horse back she now realised it was going to be impossible as there wasn't room on the path for the horses to be side by side. She wished now she'd not been so curmudgeonly, had thanked him for arriving so promptly – but now she was left with an insurmountable problem of her own making.

She leaned across and tied the horse's reins around his neck so he couldn't tread on them. 'Right, let's hope you have the sense to follow me and don't wander off.'

Eventually she arrived at her destination but was somewhat surprised to find no anxious crowd, no grooms, awaiting her arrival. Now there was room she reached over and pulled the spare horse's reins over his head so she could lead him into the yard.

Peterson, her own groom, strolled round from the rear of the yard and stopped in surprise when he saw her – then hurried across the cobbles. 'Did you take a tumble? Are you hurt? We thought you'd gone on with the gentlemen, miss. I didn't expect you back for an hour or more. Why have you got an extra horse in tow?'

Grace dismounted, puzzled that word of the mishap hadn't reached the grooms. She quickly explained what had happened, but omitted to repeat what had taken place between her and Lord Sheldon, and her groom was shocked.

'Didn't hear a word about it, miss, otherwise I'd have been out to look for you. You want me to send the boy to find your hat?'

'Yes, if he has time. I'd better try and repair some of the damage before I venture into public view.' She pulled off her leather gloves and quickly twisted her hair into some sort of shape, and then rammed the few remaining pins into it, praying it would remain in place until she could get back to her chamber.

As usual the passageway was quiet when she stepped through the side door. However, she could hear the murmur of voices coming from the main reception areas so decided to take the backstairs and hope she didn't meet any servants coming down with full slop pails, or worse.

Annie was pottering around in the dressing room when Grace arrived and was suitably dismayed at her mistress's dishevelled appearance.

'My word, miss, you've quite ruined your new habit and I doubt that I can repair it. It's a good thing you've got a spare one with you.'

'Has Miss Newcomb called in this morning?'

'Yes, miss, she said to tell you she'll see you when luncheon's served at noon.'

Freshly gowned in a delightful green sprigged muslin, her hair freshly arranged, Grace made her way to yet another dining room in which a cold collation had been laid out for the ladies.

When she walked into the room she'd expected to be greeted with friendly smiles, nods and the occasional good wishes, but instead she was stared at with opprobrium. There were more than a dozen ladies present and all of them gave her the cut direct.

She was tempted to run out, but something prompted her to stiffen her shoulders and ignore the disapproval. There could only be one reason for this – Lady Drusilla and her daughter had spread their falsehoods and blackened her name.

'Grace, come away; you'll do no good remaining here,' Aunt Sarah whispered from beside her.

'No, I'll not be driven out. I've done nothing wrong and I'm as entitled to eat as anyone else. Are you going to join me?' She half-expected her companion to refuse.

'Of course I am, my dear. We can take our plates somewhere more convivial. There are tables set out on the terrace for anyone who wishes to eat *al fresco*.'

The assembled ladies moved away as if they were in danger of contamination and muttered – in small, disapproving groups – in the far corners of the room. Whilst they piled their plates with an assortment of delicacies, Grace explained what had actually transpired. Then they headed for the French doors at the far end of the room.

'That was most unpleasant, my dear. I just hope Lord Sheldon puts matters straight before this evening. I hope not to experience something of that nature again.'

'They're like sheep. They follow the leader and don't think for themselves. I'm heartily sick of all this nonsense and cannot wait to leave. I don't fit in with the *ton* – I'm not one of them and never will be.'

Grace was enjoying her lunch when she saw the gentlemen returning from their ride. The three Sheldon brothers led the pack and the rest struggled along behind. 'I think the duke's horses are going to be excellent competition for Rufus. I don't think there are any other animals in the same class.'

'I doubt that the younger brothers will be so gentlemanly as to hand the prize over to you, so let's hope you beat them in the races. Look – there seems to be some activity over at the maze. Shall we go down and investigate when we've finished our repast?'

'I seem to recall there's to be a treasure hunt this afternoon and we must enter together. I expect that the young ladies will hope to entice a gentleman to accompany them, but we are made of sterner stuff than that and can accomplish so simple a task without the assistance of a man.'

* * *

Bennett dismounted and slapped his mount on the neck. 'I hope you two intend to enter the treasure hunt, which begins at two o'clock. It's obligatory to ask a female to join one's team – do you have anyone in particular in mind, Aubrey, Perry?'

'I thought I'd ask your Miss DuPont, old chap. She is a damn sight more interesting than any of the others our sister invited,' Aubrey said.

'That reminds me, I'd better make sure the true story of the fall is circulated or things might be rather unpleasant for Miss DuPont.' He saw his brothers exchange a knowing look and glared at them. 'I've told you, I've no interest in that young lady and she has even less in me. She certainly didn't come here in the hope of becoming my wife. I think she's got some other scheme in mind.'

He had their full attention and had no alternative but to expound his theory. 'It seems there's a DuPont Stud. A couple of the gentlemen here have heard good things of it. It's an unusual name so that has to be the same family. Miss DuPont has come to attract new customers for their business venture.'

They looked at him as if he was speaking in tongues. 'That's fustian, brother. Where did you come up with a half-baked notion like that?' Perry said.

'Running a stud is a man's business – I hardly think a gently born young lady would be involved. No, Bennett, she's here for the same reason as all the rest – she's hoping to snag herself an aristocratic husband. Possibly not yourself, but there are several other suitable candidates she might have her eye on.' Aubrey wandered off with his twin and Bennett could hear them laughing at his expense.

He'd sent his brother's man of business away to make more extensive enquiries about the DuPont family. Her faults, and they were too numerous to catalogue, should outweigh her advantages but, for some obscure reason, none of the rest appealed to him as much as Grace did.

His lips twitched. Already he thought of her by her given name and he didn't even *know* the names of most of those present. He was almost certain he'd seen her eating her lunch with her companion on the terrace. If he hurried he could change and be back in time to ask her to be his partner in the treasure hunt.

He didn't, of course, want to escort her for a romantic reason, but merely to discover on what pretext she was here. On his way back from his apartment, he bumped into Beau.

'What is it about that young lady of yours, Bennett, that puts the cat among the pigeons so readily? The house is humming with her latest exploit and she doesn't come out of it well.'

Once he'd explained the facts, his brother patted him on the shoulder. 'We know nothing about this girl. Don't do anything that would put you under an obligation to offer for her until Carstairs returns.'

'Devil take it, Beau, I don't even like the chit and she certainly doesn't like me. I can assure you that even if I was stupid enough to make an offer, she wouldn't accept.'

'As head of the family it behoves me to remind you to be vigilant. I think you're correct in your opinion about Miss DuPont, but there are several other scheming minxes here who wouldn't hesitate to compromise you in order to get an offer. I'd prefer you to remain unmarried and our coffers unfilled rather than have you make an unwise choice.'

'I intend to invite Miss DuPont and Miss Newcomb to join me in the treasure hunt. That way I'll be safe from the machinations of the others.'

'True enough, Bennett, but singling her out in this way might give the wrong impression to your guests.'

'I assume that you won't be joining in? Remember, I'm not the only eligible bachelor living under this roof. It's possible that the majority here are secretly hoping to become a duchess rather than a lady.'

His brother laughed. 'I've no intention of becoming leg-shackled. There's not a young lady in the country who wouldn't bore me to death within a month of being wed. No, I'll leave that tomfoolery to the rest of you. I thank the good Lord every day our parents had the good sense to produce a plethora of heirs and thus leave me free to remain a bachelor.' He grinned. 'My ladybird in Town provides me with all the entertainment I need.'

'In which case, as your heir, I'd better get on with the task of finding myself a wife. I'll bear your comments in mind, Beau, and make sure I'm not alone with any of our unmarried guests. However, as Miss DuPont is chaperoned I shall be safe with her.'

As he rounded the corner the two ladies jumped to their feet and dashed away towards the maze. Unless he cared to shout, or run after them, they would have entered the treasure hunt without him. He had no intention of taking part with anyone else, so he ducked back the way he'd come and made his way to the billiard room where he would be safe from predatory mamas and their daughters.

Aubrey turned from his position at the window. 'What have you done to offend those two ladies? When the companion spotted you and told Miss DuPont, she was on her feet and off like a rabbit from a fox.'

'The young lady in question has no more desire to further her acquaintance with me than I do with her.' He unclenched his fists and forced his mouth into a resemblance of a smile. 'I've no intention of joining in the treasure hunt so have come to play billiards.'

He moved away from his brothers and pretended to be occupied in selecting a suitable cue. How dare the girl run away from him and make him a figure of fun? He glanced around the assembled company and several of the gentlemen present smirked in his direction. This wouldn't do – this wouldn't do at all.

The slender cue snapped in two and he hurled the broken pieces against the wall and strode off, ignoring the laughter behind him, and headed for the maze.

* * *

'I must warn you, my dear, that Lord Sheldon is coming this way with a determined look on his face.'

Grace was on her feet and heading for the maze before Aunt Sarah had finished her sentence. She wished to participate in all the events with just the two of them – and if she did change her mind it wouldn't be to team up with this particular gentleman.

'Wait for me, Grace, it's most unseemly to go everywhere in such a rush.'

'I apologise. I'm behaving like a schoolroom miss.' She slowed her pace and linked her arm with her companion's. 'I'm sure that his lordship had no intention of inviting me to partner him in the treasure hunt. I cannot think what possessed me to dash off like this.'

Aunt Sarah patted her hand. 'He's gone now, so you can relax. I think we might be the first to arrive. I wonder how this will be organised as we might well have solved the puzzles before anyone else has even started.'

'I would think that we probably just collect the clues and take them with us when we've completed the hunt and the time we've taken will be noted.'

They both signed in the book and were handed the first clue. This merely required them to reach the centre of the maze where they would find the next one.

'This is a magnificent maze, Aunt Sarah. The hedges must be over two yards tall.' She led the way towards the dark interior, hoping that the time she'd taken to study the maze from an upstairs window would be sufficient to lead her to the centre without difficulty.

'I think we should have taken the flag with us, Grace. I don't like the thought of being lost in here.'

'Yes, that's quite true but it would also mean we were eliminated from the contest before we've even started. There's a prize of a guinea for the winner and I'm determined to have it.'

She was about to move forward when her companion grasped her hand. 'My dear, I apologise, but I cannot go in here. It's making me feel quite ill. You must continue on your own and I'll rejoin you when you've emerged. I can make my way surreptitiously around the outside and no one will know I'm not with you.'

'The footmen with the book have their backs to us. If you go now you won't be seen.' She must complete this task on her own and hope she didn't lose her way.

She closed her eyes and visualised the centre of the maze and the way the hedges had been laid out to confuse those within its walls. If she remembered rightly she must take the first path, and then turn right and right again and then straight ahead before turning left. This should lead her directly to the centre in no time at all.

12

Bennett had no intention of playing fairly. Members of the family knew about a secret route to the centre of the maze. This didn't require going past the footmen as the entry was at the far side, and invisible to anyone who didn't know it was there.

There was plenty of time as it would take the girl at least half an hour to find her way to the centre where he would be waiting. He wasn't sure exactly what he was going to do when he confronted her, but he was damn sure she wasn't going to make a fool of him again.

He ignored the basket of clues placed neatly on the stone obelisk upon which the directions for escaping were carved. He sat on the moss-covered marble bench, crossed his legs at the ankles, then threw his arms over the back of the seat in order to give the impression that he was relaxed – when the very opposite was true.

The sun was warm on his face and he closed his eyes, letting his mind drift. Despite his anger, the warmth and peace of the maze worked its magic and the tension left his limbs. What was it about this girl that ruffled his normal calm persona? He couldn't remember the last time he'd lost his temper and was rarely even mildly irritated since he returned from his soldiering. And yet in the space of a few days he'd been snapping and snarling at the slightest thing.

The only explanation he could think of was that his decision to marry for expediency was unsettling him. Perhaps his altruistic offer to save the family through sacrificing himself in parson's mousetrap had been a grave error of judgement.

'Excuse me, Lord Sheldon, are you quite well? Do you wish me to send for assistance?'

This concerned enquiry jerked him from his reverie and he almost catapulted from the bench. How the devil had she arrived so quickly?

'You startled me, Miss DuPont.' He gathered his wits and scrambled to his feet.

Her smile defused his irritation. 'Obviously, my lord, and I beg your pardon for doing so. However, I'm mystified as to how you're here before me. Is there a secret entrance somewhere?'

'There is indeed, and I intended to surprise you – not the other way round.' He reached out and removed one of the clues from the basket and handed it over to her. 'This is what you've come for; I'd better leave you to continue your hunt.'

She read the clue and waved the paper in excitement. 'We must go to the clock tower. I've not seen one, so must rely on you to take me. I'm quite determined to win this challenge and now you're here you might as well assist me.'

He flipped the paper from her fingers and perused it. 'Two hands aloft – well deduced, it took me a moment to work it out.'

She was already halfway down the path that led to the exit. 'Come along, sir, there's not a minute to waste.'

He ran to catch up with her – he seemed to be doing a lot of that lately. 'Miss DuPont, where's your companion? I can't possibly accompany you unchaperoned.'

'Fiddlesticks to that! I gave you my word I'm not here to seek a husband – even one as toplofty as yourself. Miss Newcomb is waiting for me at the exit so, unless you intend to inform your cronies that we were alone in here, no one will be any the wiser.' She pursed her lips and stared at him. 'And anyway, it's rather too late for you to be complaining about decorum, my lord, as it was you who accosted me and not the other way round. What exactly were your intentions?'

His neckcloth became unaccountably tight and he ran his finger around it. He was hoist by his own petard and could think of no way to wriggle out of this awkward situation without looking ridiculous. He shrugged and smiled. 'I'd better own up to my misdeeds. You were seen running away from me and this caused considerable hilarity in the billiard room at my expense. I decided I would wait for you and... and I've no idea what I intended to do.'

Her delighted burst of laughter was totally unexpected. 'If you hadn't fallen asleep and had hidden behind the bench you could have jumped out at me – that would have sent me into hysterics. However, I apologise for causing you embarrassment and promise to do better in future.'

They emerged from the exit together and the look of astonishment on Miss Newcomb's face when she saw them made up for the earlier missed opportunity.

'My lord, I didn't expect to see you with Miss DuPont.'

'I'm sure you didn't, madam, but here we are. We're determined to claim victory in this event and are on our way to the clock tower, which is on the far side of the stable block.'

One by one they deciphered the clues, sometimes Miss Newcomb providing the answer, sometimes himself, but far more often it was Grace who deciphered the riddle first. By the time they collected the final piece of paper an hour and a half had passed.

During this time more than the puzzles of the treasure hunt had been solved – he now understood why this particular young lady was making him behave so out of character. For some inexplicable reason his heart had decided she was the one for him when his head was telling him the opposite.

* * *

Grace handed in their clues, delighted they'd managed to accomplish the task in so short a time. 'That was a thoroughly enjoyable experience. Thank you both for helping me.'

Lord Sheldon had been quiet for some time and she rather thought he'd lost interest in the whole proceedings. However, he smiled. 'It was my pleasure, Miss DuPont. Now, if you would excuse me I must spend time with my other guests.'

She watched him stroll away, unsure exactly how she felt about this gentleman.

Aunt Sarah took her arm. 'I doubt that any other team will complete the hunt so quickly, my dear, so I think you stand a good chance of being the winner.'

'I hope so. We need all the gold we can accumulate before we leave here. By the way, did you send your letters to your friends yesterday?'

'I did indeed. There's a silver plate by the front door for any guests to place their correspondence and the duke franks them. I expect I'll get replies sometime next week.'

Grace was still thinking about Lord Sheldon's strange behaviour. 'I'm at a loss to understand why his lordship decided to join us and then left so hurriedly. Did I do something to offend him?'

'Not whilst we were solving the clues. I thought we all got on splen-didly considering who he is. But you must remember, my dear, that he can't be seen to be giving you more attention.'

'Good heavens! Anyone who thinks so must be touched in the attic, for I'm the least eligible young lady present.'

'You are one of the prettiest girls, one of the liveliest and almost certainly one of the richest – all you lack is pedigree. I know of several impecunious aristocrats who have married beneath them in order to fill their coffers. Why should Lord Sheldon not do the same?'

Grace snorted inelegantly. 'Aunt Sarah, this is one of the foremost fami-lies in the country. Only a girl with an impeccable background would be acceptable.' She didn't want to discuss this further as she had better things to think about than a tall, blue-eyed gentleman. 'I'm wondering if I should join the card tables each evening as I'm sure there's money to be won playing Loo.'

'There's also a risk that you would lose. I should avoid gaming, my dear, and stick to the things that you know you excel at.'

They found a secluded arbour in the rose garden and as soon as they were settled Grace removed the itinerary from her reticule. 'Tonight there's to be a musical evening and it says here one must enter one's name on a list in the drawing room if one wishes to perform.'

'I hope you're going to play. You are more than proficient on the pianoforte.'

'This would just draw more attention to myself. It wouldn't do to appear to excel at the ladylike pursuits as well as the outdoor ones. I shall attend and appear suitably appreciative of the performances of others.' She ran her finger down the paper. 'See, there's to be a cricket tournament tomorrow and there's to be a prize for the winning team.'

'I'm considered an excellent bowler, my dear. Would you like to practise as I can't recall you playing this game before.'

'I can throw a ball, but I've never tried to hit one with a bat. I wonder if we can find the equipment without having to ask.'

They headed for a quiet part of the grounds and Aunt Sarah began her lesson. After a highly enjoyable hour or so, Grace believed she had the requisite rules in her head and the skills to be able to join in.

'We must go at once and sign the list and make sure that we're included in one of the teams. Gentlemen have an unfair advantage in this game as we shall be sadly hampered by our skirts. I'd no idea cricket could be so aggressive.'

'It's part of the fun, my dear. I can't tell you how much I've enjoyed today – whatever the outcome of this visit, I shall look back on these few weeks with pleasure. I doubt that either of us will ever have such entertainment again.'

'Oh, please don't say that. How dreary you make our future sound. Once I have access to my trust fund, we'll be able to do whatever we want. God willing the war with France will be over by then and we can travel on the Continent.'

'We shall have to hurry, Grace, if we don't want to be tardy. I doubt that his grace will cover for your absence a second time.'

'I shall be ready in good time. Come to my sitting room in one hour and we'll go down together.'

Annie had hot water waiting and within the allotted time Grace was ready. 'I'm not sure about the amount of bosom on display. Do you think I should put in a *fichu*?'

'No, miss, it's not nearly as low as some I've seen here. I think that colour is perfect on you.'

'I know that debutantes should dress only in white, but that makes me look like a ghost. Jonquil is an unusual shade for an evening gown, but not too bright, so I don't think it will offend the matrons.'

Her maid fastened the stunning amber and diamond necklace in place. 'There, that finishes the ensemble perfectly. I think Miss Newcomb has just come in, so you're ready in perfect time.'

Grace decided the evening was too warm to require her to take her matching gossamer wrap. She stared down at her silk gloves and frowned. 'I don't care what the rule is; I'm not going to wear these tonight. It's far too hot for gloves.'

She quickly peeled them off, shook out her skirts and whisked into the sitting room where her companion was waiting. 'That's a delightful gown, Aunt Sarah – russet silk is perfect on you. However, I'm not as fond of your matching turban with the egret feather.'

'I intend to blend in with the other matrons, Grace my dear, and I noticed that many of them are similarly dressed. They tend to forget to whom I'm affiliated and I can pick up a lot of interesting gossip.'

Grace did a quick twirl, sending her skirts out in a cloud around her ankles. 'Do you like this ensemble? It's slightly more daring than last night's gown, but I'm feeling more confident and believe I can carry it off.'

'Jonquil is ideal with your colouring – as long as a young lady doesn't wear bright colours, I don't think anyone can object. I noticed that several girls were wearing pale blues and pinks last night. You look quite delightful and I'm sure you're by far the prettiest girl here.'

* * *

Bennett had spent an excruciatingly tedious afternoon talking to some of the hopeful debutantes. None of them had anything pertinent to say and all they did was simper and giggle and flutter their eyelashes at him.

Madeline, looking enchanting in a pale green confection, was waiting for him in the drawing room.

'Beau is to announce the winners of the treasure hunt before we go into dinner. I'm sure you already have a good idea who that will be.'

'The speed with which Miss DuPont and her companion solved the clues was remarkable. I doubt that anyone else would have matched their time.'

'They were a full half an hour ahead of every other competitor. Your Miss DuPont has entered her name in all the competitions. She was seen practising for the cricket tournament and if what I've heard is true, she and Miss Newcomb will be an asset to any team.'

'Is she to perform tonight?'

'Her name isn't on the list – I doubt that anyone so skilled in outdoor pursuits is likely to be as good at the more ladylike activities.' His sister paused and her eyes widened, and he turned to see what had caught her attention.

It was as if a fist had punched him in the chest. For a second he found it difficult to breathe. Gliding across the grand hall was the most beautiful young woman he'd ever set eyes on. Grace looked like a princess – put every other hopeful young miss in the shade.

He no longer cared who she was or why she was here – his mind was made up. He would have no other for his wife and would spend every available moment from now on courting her until she fell in love with him.

As he stepped forward intending to waylay her, a hand dropped on his arm. 'No, brother, she will not do. I must speak to you in private.'

Beau's expression was grim and Bennett's stomach roiled. He was about to refuse to accompany his brother but decided against it. 'Very well, but I'm telling you now, there's nothing you can say that will deter me from making her an offer.'

He strode beside the duke into the nearest small chamber where they wouldn't be disturbed. Beau closed the door and gestured to a seat. Bennett remained where he was.

'I have just received word by express from London. It seems Lord Peabody is in hock to DuPont and was forced to bring the girl here. The family's fortune comes from trade. Her great-grandfather was a black-smith, for God's sake. She will not do. You must forget her and find your-self a wife from an acceptable family.'

'Have you finished?' His brother nodded. 'I shall marry Grace DuPont whatever you have to say on the matter. If you're worried that our progeny will taint the line, then you know what to do about it. Find yourself a suitable duchess and provide your own heirs.'

He walked out, his anger barely contained. He loved the duke, knew he was passionate about the family, but had not thought him so proud that he'd stand in the way of his own brother's happiness. He would speak to Grace tonight, call a halt to this house party farce, and then return with her to her family home and ask her father for her hand in marriage.

He strode outside, needing to calm down and clear his head before he mingled with the crowd. His evening pumps would become mired, but he cared not for that. How could the man he looked up to, loved and admired, behave so callously? He was being forced to choose and it would break his heart to cut himself off from his family – but do it he would.

He doubted he would return to Silchester Court. Once Beau made up his mind, he never changed it. If his beloved Grace wasn't to be welcomed here, then neither was he. His siblings could visit him at his estate, or ignore him; that would be their choice.

He would keep his word and transfer his wife's dowry to the family, but that would be an end to his contact with the duke. He decided he'd better return to the drawing room – the prize for the treasure hunt would have been given and dinner would have already been announced. He'd been outside too long.

The drawing room was full, and there was a strange atmosphere in the room. Why hadn't everyone gone into dinner? If his brother was anything less than courteous to Grace when he presented the prize, he would floor him. He looked over the heads of the crowd to find Grace.

Strange that he could see neither her, nor her companion, as they were both distinctively dressed. He spotted Giselle standing by the window and she beckoned to him. Her eyes were red. What was going on here?

'What's wrong, little one? Has someone upset you?'

She turned a tear-stained face to him. 'I can't believe he would do something like that. Beau asked Miss DuPont to leave immediately. He says that she's an imposter. I'm so sorry, Bennett, I know that you were becoming fond of her.'

13

Grace and her companion mingled with the assembled guests and although not exactly friendly, no one turned their back as they had done at lunchtime.

'They are serving champagne. Do you want a glass, Aunt Sarah?'

'I think not, my dear; alcohol doesn't agree with my digestion. Shall we wait on the terrace – it's rather crowded and hot in here.'

'As long as we remain where we can hear the announcement about the treasure hunt; we mustn't miss that. I'm certain we'll be the winners.'

There were one or two other people enjoying the fresh air but they remained apart. 'I didn't see the duke or Lord Sheldon in the drawing room, did you?'

'No, Grace, I didn't. I expect they'll be here soon.'

'The duke's coming this way.' She had a sinking feeling inside that his purpose wasn't to give her any good news. His expression was distant; he looked every inch a haughty aristocrat.

He stopped in front of them and didn't bow – in fact he didn't acknowledge them at all. Grace knew that she should curtsy, but refrained.

'Miss Newcomb, today I received information that Miss DuPont is not who she purports to be. I wish you both to leave Silchester Court immediately. Instructions have already been sent to your servants to pack your trunks and your grooms are harnessing your carriage.'

How dare he ignore her and speak to her companion instead? He might be a duke, but he was no gentleman. Instead of being humiliated or upset by his rudeness she was incensed.

'Unless you intend to physically remove us from your house, sir, I've no intention of being evicted tonight. If you expect my staff, my companion and I to spend the night without a roof over our heads, then you can think again. I shall be delighted to depart before breakfast tomorrow morning.' She let her gaze travel slowly from his crown to his toes. 'Anyone who marries into this family has my sympathy. You are arrogant and unpleasant, and being the Duke of Silchester is no excuse for your behaviour.'

She didn't wait to see his reaction but stalked back through the drawing room, head held high, looking to neither left nor right. She kept her composure until she reached her apartment but then she began to shake and collapsed into the nearest chair.

Aunt Sarah followed her in. 'My word, that was absolutely splendid, my dear. You were magnificent and put that man to shame. However, perhaps we'd better lock the door just in case he does send men to carry us out.'

The idea was so nonsensical that Grace recovered her composure and laughed. 'Can you imagine the scandal if we were to be dragged kicking and screaming through the house in front of the cream of society? I almost wish he'd try.'

'So you don't wish me to lock the doors?'

'Absolutely not. That man is despicable – I'm not surprised he's still a bachelor – even his title isn't enough to persuade anyone to marry him.'

Annie rushed in from the bedchamber. 'We've been told to pack your belongings, miss. Is it true that we're to leave?'

'Yes, but not tonight, so there's no urgency. However, if you've already begun the task I should complete it, as I intend to leave at first light.'

'Are you going to change out of your evening gown?'

'We might as well, my dear, for there is no point in spoiling them,' Aunt Sarah said. 'I'll return here when I'm ready. I wonder if the duke has sent word to the kitchen not to give us anything to eat.'

'I was thinking that myself. Annie, can you send down and order supper to be brought to us? If it doesn't arrive, then we'll know we must remain hungry until we leave here and find refreshments elsewhere.'

She had no intention of discussing the debacle with her maid and Annie had the good sense not to ask why they were to leave so unexpectedly. For all her calm exterior, Grace was at a loss to know how to proceed. They had nowhere to go, only ten guineas between them, and she now had five horses and five adults to house and feed.

She paced the floor, trying to see a way out of this disaster. Returning to DuPont Manor was not an option – but perhaps the farmhouse in which Collins had set up the stud could accommodate them all. Aunt Sarah would be able to support them for a while with her savings, but these wouldn't last forever – and certainly not for the year and a half until her trust fund was available.

When her companion returned she was ready to put forward her plan. The request for supper trays had been ignored so obviously word had been sent to the kitchen. 'I cannot believe that anybody would behave in such a monstrous way. To leave us without food or drink is quite abominable.'

'It is indeed. The duke was so kind to you last night – it's hardly credible he's now behaving like this. Have you sent word to Peterson that we're not leaving until first thing tomorrow?'

'Botheration! Annie must take the message. Hopefully my grooms will not be starved as well.'

She hated to be trapped in her apartment, but she could hardly wander about the place as before as she was now *persona non grata*. Her companion, once they were sure that no sustenance was to arrive, left to pack her trunk, promising to be ready at dawn.

As she had Annie to do this task for her, Grace now had the prospect of being trapped in her chambers until she could retire with nothing to do apart from think about what had happened. She wouldn't be sorry to leave. She didn't like most of the guests, didn't fit in with their rules and regulations, but she was disappointed she couldn't show off the prowess of her stallion.

Although she tried not to think about him, the image of Lord Sheldon kept drifting into her mind. Similar in appearance to his obnoxious older brother, but there the resemblance ended. His lordship although somewhat irascible, would never have behaved so badly; of that she was quite certain.

*   *   *

Bennett was speechless. Had he heard aright? 'Let me get this straight. My brother has told Miss DuPont she must leave here immediately? Has he gone quite mad?'

He turned but was held back by his sister's hand gripping his elbow. 'No, you mustn't confront him. It will make matters so much worse.'

Gently he removed her fingers. 'I'm sorry, sweetheart, but I cannot let this go. He might be the duke, but he can't treat my guests like this. They were to leave straightaway?'

She nodded. 'Yes, but I don't think she's gone yet.'

Bennett frowned as he considered the problem. Should he find his brother and draw his cork or make sure that Grace was still on the premises? There was no way on this earth that the woman he loved was going to be turfed from his familial home. They would leave together in the morning and he would make damn sure everybody here was aware of that fact.

As he reached the French doors Perry stepped in front of him. Although his younger brother was almost as tall as he, he had half his bulk. 'No, Bennett, I'll not let you pass. Not until you've heard what I've got to say.'

'Go ahead – but make it brief.'

'Our imbecilic older brother told Miss DuPont to leave but she refused to go and gave him a dressing-down that's the talk of the drawing room.'

This was the last thing he expected to be told. 'How the hell do you know this?'

Perry grinned. 'Although they were out here, a couple of tabbies were lurking by the door and overheard it all. I'm not sure which bit of information is being relished more – the fact that Miss DuPont is not who she says she is and that Beau wishes to evict her, or that she refused to go and told him he was arrogant and objectionable and that she wasn't surprised he remained unmarried.'

Some of his fury abated at this news. 'Where is our brother now? Why haven't we been called into dinner?'

'He's gone off in high dudgeon and the butler doesn't want to send us in without him.'

'Tell him to announce dinner. There's no point in the meal being spoiled because our brother has behaved like a nincompoop. I'd better tell you, this is my fault. I'm sure he didn't intend to send her packing, just to warn me off making her an offer. I told him I intended to marry her, whatever his opinion, and that must have been the trigger. It doesn't excuse what he did, but perhaps it explains it.'

'This is going to be interesting, Bennett. I can't remember when I've had such an entertaining time.'

'Collect Giselle; she's sniffing on the terrace. You know how she hates unpleasantness of any kind. I'll not be coming into dinner so you must take the lead tonight.'

He decided to make his way to Grace's apartment by a circuitous route and thus avoid the speculation and sniggers he'd encounter in the drawing room.

He knocked on her sitting room door and was pleased to hear a firm command to come in. Somehow he expected her to be in floods of tears, needing his comfort and reassurance. What he found was something else entirely. She viewed him with something bordering on dislike and his optimism began to fade.

'Lord Sheldon, what an unexpected surprise. No doubt you've heard what happened. I do hope you've been sent to physically eject us. I'm quite looking forward to creating a disturbance that will never be forgotten.'

'Don't be ridiculous, Grace. Of course I haven't. I've come to apologise...'

She looked even more disapproving. 'I don't recall giving you permission to use my given name, my lord. I am Miss DuPont to you.'

This was not going well. 'I apologise...'

'So you've already said. If there's nothing more, I suggest you go and eat your dinner and leave me in peace.'

'Devil take it, will you let me get a word in?' He hadn't meant to sound so terse, but his temper was fraying badly. She raised an eyebrow and half-smiled in a most irritating way. This was too much for his fragile control. 'I'm not surprised that you've angered my brother, for you must be the most aggravating young lady I've ever had the misfortune to meet.'

Instead of recoiling from his anger she stepped closer, her eyes flashing dangerously. 'I didn't want to come here; I was given no choice by my father. I despise your kind – you think yourselves above the common people, that you can behave despicably, treat people not of your class as of no account and never feel a moment of remorse for doing so.' She moved nearer, forcing him to be the one to step backwards.

'I'm certain the duke would not have even considered sending a member of society from his house in the middle of the night. I doubt that anyone else would be denied food as we have been. I cannot wait to leave here. I dislike you and your kind and regret every moment I've spent under this roof.'

She raised her hand and pushed him violently in the chest. He lost his balance and tumbled backwards through the open door. He heard her laugh as she slammed it behind him.

He surged to his feet with the intention of barging back in and putting her straight on a few matters, but then something she'd said prevented him. Surely he'd misheard – his brother couldn't have ordered the kitchen not to send supper trays.

He stood with his hand against the door frame breathing heavily, controlling his anger. This was no longer directed at Grace, but at his brother. Before he acted precipitously he would check the facts.

'Miss DuPont, did you say that the kitchen has refused to send you food?' He spoke loudly, knowing she could hear him quite clearly through the door.

To his surprise the door opened. 'I did say that. Are you saying that you didn't know?'

'Of course I didn't, you pea-goose. I shall attend to the matter directly; you will have your supper very shortly.'

'Thank you. I'm sorry for pushing you – I don't know what came over me. Ever since I met you I've been behaving out of character and I cannot understand why this should be so.'

He bowed. 'I accept your apology. Pray excuse me, my love, but I have a matter of the utmost urgency to attend to. I'll return and join you for supper.'

* * *

With a casual wave he strode off and Grace watched him go with a deep sense of foreboding. He'd called her 'my love'. That could only mean one thing. For some inexplicable reason he'd developed feelings for her, and she feared she might actually reciprocate these.

This was not something to celebrate, because whatever her feelings for Lord Sheldon she could never marry him and become part of this family. She was a commoner, well, perhaps not quite that, she was gently born, but definitely not of their aristocratic class.

However, she'd no wish to be the cause of a permanent rift between the brothers and she had a horrible suspicion that her would-be suitor had gone in search of his grace and intended to wreak physical punishment on the duke, and this she couldn't allow.

Without a moment's hesitation she picked up her skirts and ran pell-mell along the corridor, down the stairs and into the grand hall. The drawing room was now empty – she sighed with relief. Lord Sheldon would hardly accost his brother at the dinner table.

She saw a footman emerge from a narrow passageway and called him over. 'Has his grace gone into dinner?'

'No, miss, neither he nor Lord Sheldon are there.'

Where could they be? She would try outside in the stables – no, the duke would have gone somewhere more private. She thought for a moment and then decided to go to the boathouse. Which would be the quickest route? Fortunately she was no longer dressed in an evening gown, but something more practical – a muslin day dress – and had sturdy slippers on.

The sun was just sinking below the horizon, bathing the water of the ornamental lake in rippling gold. The reflection made it difficult to see, but she was certain she'd spotted Lord Sheldon striding in that direction. She picked up her skirts and raced after him. Should she call out? It would be most unladylike – but she no longer had a reputation to protect so she might as well.

'Lord Sheldon, stop. I must speak to you immediately.' Her voice echoed and she was certain that anyone within five miles would have heard her shout.

Her quarry certainly did as he shot round as if poked by a large hatpin. He didn't walk towards her, but he didn't continue on his journey either.

She arrived at his side breathless and scarcely able to speak coherently. He waited with narrowed eyes until she recovered but offered no comment.

'My lord, why have you called me "my love"?' This was a nonsensical thing to say, but she could think of nothing else and she could hardly ask him if he had come out here intending to fight with his brother over her.

'You have run after me, screamed like a fishwife, and this is the reason? I scarcely know how to reply. I thought some further catastrophe had occurred.'

She was still floundering, unable to think of anything sensible to say, when a third party joined them. The duke had overheard them. 'I believe, Bennett, that Miss DuPont is here in order to stop you from assaulting me.' His eyes glimmered with amusement as he looked at her. 'Am I not right?'

'You are, your grace. Although why I should wish to do so, I've no idea, after the way you've behaved towards me this evening.'

Before she could reply, or warn the duke, Lord Sheldon drew back his arm and punched his brother square on the nose. The duke staggered backwards, clutching his face, and for an awful moment Grace thought more punishment was to come.

'You deserve to be horsewhipped, Beau, but a bloody nose will suffice. It's too late to turn your charm on us; the damage is done. My future wife and I will leave here tomorrow and will not come back. What you did was unforgivable.'

The duke was holding a handkerchief to his injured nose and it was rapidly turning red. He offered no reply but his eyes were sad and she regretted with all her heart that she'd been the cause of this catastrophic rift between Lord Sheldon and his brother.

She was given no opportunity to offer her assistance to the injured man as her elbow was gripped firmly and she was marched away. She wasn't a recalcitrant child to be dragged across the grass. 'Let go of me, sir. I dislike being manhandled.' She threw her weight back on her heels and he was forced to stop unless he wished to pull her over.

Once they were stationary she was ready with her question. 'I wasn't aware, my lord, that I was betrothed to you. I don't remember you having asked for my hand in marriage – I can assure you that's not something I would easily forget.'

His cheeks flushed and he looked uncomfortable. She allowed him no opportunity to respond but continued. 'Indeed, sir, I'm as likely to accept an offer from a member of this family as I am to sprout wings and fly. I'm sorry that you've fallen out with your brother, but that's not my concern. I intend to leave here tomorrow and I shall do so without your company.'

14

Grace opened the door to her sitting room and stopped in shock as Aunt Sarah rushed forward to greet her.

'See, we have our supper, and what a magnificent one it is too. The only reason we didn't get our food earlier was because dinner was delayed and the kitchen was too busy.'

'I didn't think matters could get any worse – Lord Sheldon has just punched the duke and he did it because I told him we had been denied food as well as being evicted.'

'How dreadful! Well, I for one am starving and have no intention of letting this delicious repast go to waste. If his lordship wishes to fight with his brother then it's no concern of ours.'

The food did smell appetising and Grace overcame her qualms. Eventually she was replete and pushed away her empty plate with a sigh of satisfaction. 'That was absolutely delicious. I was half-expecting our supper to be interrupted by Lord Sheldon but am relieved that he listened to what I said to him and didn't come.'

Her companion wiped her lips on a napkin and waited expectantly for the rest of the story. 'You've yet to explain to me exactly what took place in the garden.'

When Grace had finished her friend was astounded. 'Received an offer from Lord Sheldon and rejected it out of hand? Surely it was worth giving it a moment's consideration...'

'I couldn't marry into a grand family such as this as it would mean spending the remainder of my life being treated as an inferior. For people like this birth is everything – what's inside a person is of no account. Until I arrived a few days ago this was a close and happy family and I've ruined that.'

'I shall retire. I wouldn't have returned if Annie had not sent word that food had arrived. Goodnight, my dear, I shall see you at first light tomorrow.'

The door closed quietly leaving Grace to her thoughts. Then she noticed that her companion had forgotten her reticule. A few minutes later there was a soft tap on the door – Aunt Sarah must have come back for her bag. 'Come in, I've been expecting you.'

'Have you indeed? I'm relieved that you're prepared to speak to me after what you said outside.'

She was on her feet and staring at her visitor in horror. 'What are you doing here? I thought it was my companion returning – if I'd known it was you, I wouldn't have invited you in.'

* * *

Bennett kicked the door closed behind him, hoping that being closeted with his beloved girl would compromise them both and force her to accept his offer. She was wise to his move and dodged around him and threw the door open again.

'Go away, my lord. I've no wish to speak to you.'

'I've come to tell you that the duke has reconsidered his demand that you leave and you are now free to stay. My sisters and brothers are circulating through the guests, making sure that everyone is aware the whole episode was a dreadful misunderstanding.'

She didn't appear particularly pleased to hear this. 'The fact that your brother has a broken nose could not have gone unremarked. How have you explained that away?'

'He was drunk as a wheelbarrow and walked into the boathouse. The first is true – the second appears to have been accepted. And his nose isn't broken, merely a little bent.' What could he say to convince her? There was little point in pursuing his courtship as she'd made it perfectly plain she wanted none of him. However, he wasn't going to let her go without a fight. If he could somehow persuade her to remain here, he was sure he could change her mind.

'My brother heard you reject my offer and, now he knows you're not here in the hope of becoming my wife, his objections to your remaining have been removed.'

'How typical of someone like him – he cares little for anyone's feelings and will only be happy if you marry a young lady with an impeccable pedigree.' She stopped and he was almost sure her eyes filled. He wasn't mistaken – for all her protestations she did have feelings for him. All he had to do was wait and she would be his.

'I'm sorry that I misled you about the food – that was an unfortunate misunderstanding.' She gestured towards the half-empty trays and his stomach rumbled loudly. He hadn't been fortunate enough to find himself anything to eat and was sharp-set.

'Forgive me, but if you've finished with that meal I've not eaten since first light.' He didn't wait for her to refuse but moved swiftly to the table and filled up a plate.

'Do help yourself, my lord. I'd hate to think that you were going hungry on my account.' She pointed to the jug of lemonade. 'I'm sure you would prefer wine with your meal, but you'll have to make do with that instead.' She turned to go towards her bedchamber. 'I'll leave you to eat. Forgive me, I have to be up very early tomorrow and it's already past ten o'clock.'

'Please, don't go. If you retire I'll have to take this to my apartment to eat and then I'll get no second helpings.'

'Very well, I'll remain until you've finished.' She picked up a book and took it to a chair on the far side of the chamber. She couldn't have made it clearer – she wished to have nothing else to do with him and he didn't blame her.

This was an unmitigated disaster. How could he have found the young lady he wished to spend the remainder of his days with only to have her slip from his grasp? He came to a decision. There was one slim chance of getting her to stay. If he could convince her that he'd accepted her rejection and was looking elsewhere for a wife, then maybe she'd remain.

'It's a great shame that you are leaving tomorrow as I was looking forward to beating your stallion in the races that start on Saturday. In fact, one of the younger gentlemen is running a book on the result.'

He had her full attention now. 'I didn't know such a thing would take place. If I did decide to stay, would it be possible for me to place a wager?'

He continued to eat, trying not to show his excitement. After a suitable pause to swallow his mouthful he replied. 'You couldn't, but one of your men could. As far as I recall, Rufus is considered an outsider – Lucifer is favourite.'

'Then I'll stay and put my guineas down as a wager for my stallion to win all the races that he's entered in. Which reminds me, my lord, I believe that I've yet to be awarded my prize from the treasure hunt.'

He dipped into his waistcoat pocket and tossed her a golden coin. 'Here you are. I collected it for you as I was, please correct me if I'm wrong, part of the team.'

She gave him the first genuine smile of the evening. 'I'm sure that as a member of the family you don't want the prize divided. I'm assuming that, in the unlikely event that I come second to you, you'd be happy with the applause and donate the prize money to myself.'

He refilled his plate and tucked in with relish. She could hardly send him packing whilst he was eating. She returned to her place at the far side of the chamber and left him to his meal. He couldn't help thinking that for a young lady with a massive fortune she was remarkably interested in acquiring money. He would make some subtle enquiries with her outside men and discover why this was. 'I shall convey the fact that you no longer intend to leave to everyone downstairs. Why don't you give me your purse and I'll hand it on to your groom so he can put his name down in the book?'

She hesitated and then nodded. 'Just a moment, I'll fetch it from my bedchamber.' She vanished and he heard her rummaging around. He could hardly contain his excitement that his ploy to keep her here had worked.

'Here you are, my lord, there are five guineas in there and I wish all of it to be wagered on my winning every race I enter. No doubt Rufus remains an outsider because the gentlemen believe he's too strong for me and I won't be able to control him in a race. They are in for a disappointment.'

Her eyes flashed and it took all his strength of will not to close the gap between them and take her in his arms. He caught the purse one-handed. 'I'll take care of this matter immediately, Miss DuPont. And I can only apologise again for my brother's behaviour and give you my word that you will be treated with the utmost respect for the remainder of your stay.'

'I would be more impressed, sir, if the duke had come himself to apologise. However, I care not for the opinion of anyone here. I intend to remain in my apartment in future and shall only mingle with your guests when I participate in one of the events.'

He shrugged as if unperturbed by her news. 'You must do whatever you wish, but I can assure you that...'

Her friendly smile had been replaced by a look of disdain. 'Thank you for your offer, Lord Sheldon, but we both know that I'm unwelcome here. Whatever your assurances to the contrary, I'm not one of you and have no intention of being treated like a poor relation.' She barely inclined her head. 'Goodnight, my lord. Don't let me detain you any longer.'

He bit back his sharp retort and deliberately bowed low. 'Goodnight, Miss DuPont, I look forward to seeing you at the cricket matches tomorrow afternoon.'

How was it that he could love a young woman to distraction and yet still want to put her over his knee? Being married to her would certainly not be boring. His momentary anger at her incivility dissipated and he was smiling by the time he reached the side door that led to the stable yard.

He sent a lad to find Peterson, telling the man to meet him by the paddock in which his horses were being kept. Five minutes later the man arrived. He touched his cap and waited politely to be told why he'd been summoned.

'I'm not sure if word has reached yet, Peterson, but your mistress is now remaining here. Matters have been smoothed over and his grace has made it clear he regrets his actions.'

'I'm right glad to hear that, my lord. The longer we stay here the better as we've nowhere else to go.' The man scowled, realising he'd revealed too much.

'Tell me, I want to know why Miss DuPont has sent me to give you this purse to wager on her winning all the races. Why should someone as rich as she is be so eager to gain more money? And why have you nowhere to go?'

'It's like this, my lord, Miss DuPont don't get on with her parents – they want her to marry a toff and gain them entry into the grand houses. That's why she was sent here. She ain't interested in folk who think her not good enough for them. She doesn't intend to return to her family home but find herself somewhere she can live quietly with Miss Newcomb until she comes into her inheritance.'

The man looked relieved that he'd been able to tell this secret to somebody.

'Thank you for being so frank. Take this purse and get the wager entered – no doubt you know who's running the book. This information shall remain confidential.' Bennett could see the ghostly shapes of the horses at the far side of the field and called softly to them.

'They won't come to you, sir, right choosy they are.'

The stallion was looking towards them and Bennett called again. This time Rufus broke into a canter and halted a few feet from him. 'Come along, old fellow, time you got to know me.' The animal snorted, tossed his head and vanished back into the darkness. 'He's a magnificent beast. Winning here will improve his status as a sire. I've heard good things about the DuPont Stud.'

He looked round but found himself alone – the groom had obviously regretted revealing so much and made himself scarce before he could be asked anything else. Bennett was well satisfied with this conversation as it explained a lot about Grace.

Persuading her to change her mind while she was at Silchester Court was highly unlikely, so he would allow her to depart and then renew his courtship once she was settled in her cottage. After being brought up in the lap of luxury, he was certain she would find living in straitened circum-stances extremely unpleasant.

* * *

After an exhilarating ride at dawn, Grace returned to her apartment and had barely completed her ablutions when Aunt Sarah arrived.

'I was up early because I thought we were leaving. I've only just discovered that you changed your mind.'

'I beg your pardon, I quite forgot to send a message to your room last night. My maid will come and unpack for you later. I must tell you why we're staying.'

Instead of being shocked by the news that all their money had been put in a wager on the races, her companion was thrilled. 'How exciting! I'm so glad you decided to remain until the races and other competitions are completed. This will allow time for my friends to respond and with luck we won't be obliged to live in that derelict farmhouse with your horses.'

'I should like to have one more practice at my batting and bowling before the tournament this afternoon. I doubt that anyone else will be there at this time in the morning. If the racket outside in the passageway in the small hours is any indication, most of them will still be abed.'

The house was quiet, but everywhere sparkled and there was no evidence of there having been any sort of party last night. They left through the side door and made their way round to a secluded part of the lawn.

'The grass is still wet, Grace – it's fortunate we had the foresight to put on our boots. Now, my dear, do you wish to bowl or bat?'

Aunt Sarah hit a cracking shot and Grace prepared to run after it but was forestalled by one of three young gentlemen who had obviously come out to join in the fun.

Two of them were Lord Sheldon's twin brothers – but she hadn't been introduced to the third.

One of the twins caught the ball and threw it back to her and she was obliged to jump in order to catch it. 'Miss DuPont, forgive us for interrupting you at your practice but we have a proposition for you both.' He grinned and tapped his chest. 'I'm Peregrine and that's my younger brother, Aubrey. This other fellow is Edward Buchanan. We'll have Fletcher playing with us too.'

She curtsied and they all bowed. 'I'm intrigued to know what you are going to propose, my lord. Have you come to join in our practice?'

'If you've no objection, we'd love to. But first, we're putting together a team for this afternoon's tournament and each team must have at least three young ladies in it. My sister Giselle is already down and we'd like you to join us too.'

'We'd be delighted, wouldn't we, Aunt Sarah? As each team has to have only eight members and not the usual eleven – who is to be the other one in our team?'

Lord Perry answered. 'We haven't decided, but you can be sure he will be an excellent player.'

The gentlemen removed their topcoats and waistcoats and rolled up their shirtsleeves and Grace soon discovered she wasn't quite as skilful as she'd thought. After a further hour dashing about, she was hot and dishevelled but couldn't remember having had such a good time before.

'I think that's enough, my dear. I'm quite exhausted.'

'I'm calling a team meeting at one o'clock in the library,' Lord Perry said as he recovered his garments. 'It's a great shame ladies can't play in breeches – it would make it so much easier.'

'Actually, I believe I have the perfect solution, my lord. I have a garment that will fulfil the proprieties and yet allow me to run more freely.'

'Good show – we'd better be getting in – don't want to let the opposition know we've acquired the best two lady players available.'

The three gentlemen bowed and wandered off, slapping each other on the back and laughing gaily.

'I'm looking forward to this afternoon, but I believe I'll need a rest before the tournament. I'm quite exhausted – I'm not as young as I used to be.'

'Nonsense, you're in your prime, Aunt Sarah. We must hurry. I've no wish to be seen in such disarray.'

'I assume you were referring to your divided skirt, the one you had made up for riding astride. Do you have a second one that I could borrow for this afternoon?'

'I do. However, as I'm considerably taller than you it will need to be turned up. It will be a simple task to ensure the skirt will fit you. Do you have a suitable top to wear with it?'

'I can find something – don't worry, my dear. I'm going to wash and change before I join you for breakfast. I hope they send up a full tray as I find myself sharp-set. All this exercise has given me an unladylike desire to eat.'

* * *

At one o'clock precisely, Grace and her companion made their way to the library, each wearing a divided skirt, a smart white top and a serviceable spencer. Their footwear was sensible boots. The doors were open and the sound of voices drifted out.

'I hope we're not tardy, Aunt Sarah. We should have left longer to get here – I'd forgotten just how vast this place is.'

'You're not last, Miss DuPont – I have that distinction,' Lord Sheldon spoke from behind her.

Her heart flipped. She should have realised he would be the eighth member of the team.

15

Grace could hardly refuse to be on the team at this juncture – she would just have to do her best to ignore Lord Sheldon. Although this was going to be difficult as he was a rather large gentleman and quite the most attractive man she'd ever seen.

'Then we shall be tardy together, my lord, and Lord Perry will hardly scold his older brother.'

'He'd be unwise to try, Miss DuPont. My brother didn't tell me you and Miss Newcomb were to be on his team. I take it that playing cricket is another one of your skills.'

'My companion is the expert, but I believe I won't let the side down.'

Lord Perry greeted them enthusiastically. 'At last, we feared you three were not coming. Now, I must tell you in what order you will be batting and whereabouts I shall position you in the field.' He nodded approvingly at Grace's attire. 'An excellent solution, ladies. I doubt that any others will have such an ingenious skirt.'

Aunt Sarah appeared to understand the technical terms and joined in the discussion and Grace was pleased to notice all the gentlemen listened to her contributions with respect. Grace was to bat last and would be fielding somewhere in between the two sets of wickets. That was all she required to know – the rest would surely be better seen than talked about.

She moved away from the group to gaze through the window. There were already teams making their way to the designated playing area and she was pleased to see that their team would have the advantage, because the other ladies would be hampered by their skirts.

The meeting came to a conclusion and she was called over. Lord Perry addressed them all once more. 'There are four teams participating in the tournament and we have been drawn to play first against Lord Peabody's eight. Whoever wins will play the winner of the other match tomorrow – unless, of course, there's time today.'

The gentlemen led the way from the library and Lord Sheldon walked with his brothers, having paid her no more attention than he did Aunt Sarah. Lady Giselle joined Grace at the rear of the group.

'I've adjusted my ensemble too.' She raised the hem of her plain blue gown. 'Look, I'm wearing a pair of my brother's old breeches so if I take a tumble I'll not reveal anything I shouldn't.' She pointed to the gathering crowd. 'I think the entire party is out here to watch. The duke's playing in one of the other teams, so we won't be against him unless we win our first match.'

'You sound relieved, my lady; is he a skilled player?'

'Miss DuPont, he's fiendish and can hit a ball for six every time. I can't tell you how competitive my family is. My sister's in his team. I'm rather surprised that Bennett is with us. I heard that he was to join Beau, but I'm glad he hasn't.'

The grass had been close-cropped by the small flock of sheep kept for that purpose and Grace was unsurprised that the surface had been swept clear of droppings. It wouldn't do for any of the players to step in something unsavoury.

Lord Perry and Lord Peabody were doing something in the centre of the field and then beckoned them over. 'I've won the toss and decided we should bat first. Bennett is to be one of the umpires and a crony of Peabody's is to be the other. You three ladies are batting last so must sit with the rest of the team and wait until it's your turn to go in.'

There had been chairs brought out from the house and the spectators and other teams were arranging themselves. 'I can't believe the ladies in Lord Peabody's team intend to play with their bonnets on,' Grace said.

'Quite ridiculous! By the way, Aunt Sarah, I asked Peterson to put my last guinea on us – we stand to gain six more if we win. He told me he'd got excellent odds for the horse races and if fortune favours us we shall leave next week with over a hundred guineas.'

'Splendid, my dear, with what I have saved we shall have more than enough to survive in comfort until you reach your majority next year.'

She watched the match progressing with growing interest. Lord Sheldon had opened the batting and although five wickets had fallen he was still there striking the ball well and scoring an abundance of runs.

The other gentlemen in her team continued to be dismissed and although they had a satisfactory score of more than a hundred she was dreading her turn. Aunt Sarah scored a satisfactory six runs before she returned to her seat and Lady Giselle took her place. So far none of the bowlers had managed to dislodge Lord Sheldon so she would be obliged to bat alongside him very soon.

His sister was out first ball to great cheering from the spectators and derisive shouts from the opposition. She collected her bat and began the long walk to the centre. She was met by Lord Sheldon before she reached her position.

'We have a decent score, so don't worry if you're out without making any runs.'

'I'll try and hit it towards one of the girls who are spending more time chatting to each other than concentrating on the game.'

He grinned, making him look less austere and much younger. 'I've been doing exactly that, which is why we have such a good total.'

Grace took her position and watched the bowler draw back his arm and throw the ball. She swung her bat and brought it round with such force the ball flew into the air and vanished over the heads of the spectators. She was so surprised she forgot to run, but fortunately there was no need as she'd scored a six.

Shouts of 'bravo' echoed around the field. This game was easier than she'd thought. She hit the second ball with equal force and this time aimed it in the direction suggested. As she began to run she watched with horror as the ball struck one of the girls in the chest.

The young lady toppled backwards and her companions screamed.

Pandemonium followed as an elegant lady in an extraordinary hat, which looked as if it had a fruit bowl attached to it, joined in the racket. Grace dropped the bat and was preparing to run over and offer her assistance when Lord Sheldon arrived at her side.

'No, you must remain where you are. The game will continue once the girl has been helped from the field. Don't look so worried, little one, it wasn't your fault. They should have been paying attention and it was Lord Peabody's job as captain to see that they did. I'll go and see as I'm one of the umpires.'

He strode off and as soon as he arrived at the scene the racket ceased and the unfortunate girl was carried from the field. She watched with amusement as the other two went with her, refusing to return and finish the game.

Grace noticed that despite her agitation the girl's mother had not come out to investigate but remained fussing and flapping until her daughter was returned to her side. She was relieved to see no serious harm had been caused by the blow but was at a loss to know how the game could continue when the opposition had only five members remaining in the team.

Lord Perry had now joined his brother in the huddle where the accident had taken place. He jogged over with a broad smile on his face. 'Excellent news, Miss DuPont, Peabody's team has conceded defeat and we're through to the final without having to field and all due to your excellent batting.'

This was doing it too brown. 'My lord, I hardly think I'm to be congratulated for almost killing one of the other team.'

He shrugged. 'Serves her right for not paying attention. Anyway, she was merely winded and made more of a fuss than was necessary. I've a feeling there might be difficulties for the duke's opponents as it looks as if the three young ladies in that team have also withdrawn.'

Lord Sheldon strolled across to join them as they made their way from the field of play. 'It would appear that my brother's team doesn't have to play, so the final will take place in fifteen minutes. I hope you're not thinking of withdrawing from our team?'

'I was considering it, but I've decided to play on. However, can I make a suggestion, Lord Perry?'

'Go ahead, I'll be happy to accommodate you if I can.'

'Might I suggest that if you win the toss, our side could field first this time? Then it's quite possible I won't have to bat again if Lord Sheldon performs as well a second time.'

He nodded. 'Excellent notion, I should have thought of that myself. Are you to be one of the umpires again, Bennett?'

'I believe my brother and I are to share the privilege. Don't place our ladies together as Peabody did with his. I'm sure Beau will target them if we do.'

Grace was positioned at a safe distance from the batsmen and had ample opportunity to look around. The cricket field had been made from an area of the park that was edged at one end by shrubbery and trees (where the spectators were sitting); the opposite boundary was the lake. The other two sides had a border of long grass and she noticed the ground sloped away in this direction so that only the top half of the fielder standing there was visible.

She hoped she didn't have to run after the ball down there. Fortunately the lake was on the opposite side to her so she didn't have to worry about falling in. The match started and the first blow from the duke went in the opposite direction and was safely fielded before he'd scored any runs. The second sailed over her head and she turned to see if the gentleman guarding the boundary was going to collect it. He was nowhere in sight.

Without hesitation she turned and raced after it. There was no sign of the wretched ball – it must have gone into the long grass and she'd have to go in after it. She hadn't intended to run quite so fast, but the slope turned out to be more of a hill and by the time she reached the long grass she was out of control.

Desperately she tried to stop but to no avail and when her left foot came in contact with a tussock, she somersaulted into the air and vanished face first into the grass.

* * *

Bennett took off after Grace. His brother hadn't bothered to run as he knew his hit would score him the maximum runs without him having to move from the stumps. When Bennett reached the edge of the incline he'd expected to see her returning with the ball in her hand. She was nowhere in sight – the area was empty – no sign of her anywhere.

He stopped and rubbed his eyes. Then he was joined by his brothers. 'Where the hell is she? In fact – where the hell's Fletcher? He should be patrolling the boundary and should have caught the ball.' Perry sounded as perplexed as he was.

'I'm going to investigate. We can't continue until we've recovered the ball and God knows where that is.' He broke into a run and just as he reached the edge of the playing area, Grace emerged rear end first from the long grass a few feet away. 'Are you all right? Have you found the ball?'

She sprung to her feet and turned to face him. 'No, sir, I don't have your stupid ball. I suggest you find another one as this will never be discovered in this jungle.' There was grass stuck to her clothes, and her face was liberally covered with mud. He couldn't prevent his smile, and this did nothing to endear him to her.

'Do you require my assistance, Miss DuPont?'

'I do not – you may remain where you are and continue to smirk at my misfortune.' Then her eyes widened and she turned a delightful shade of pink. He glanced over his shoulder and saw the entire team had gathered to enjoy the spectacle.

He bounded into the grass and stood directly in front of her, blocking her from view. He handed her a clean handkerchief. 'You have smuts on your face; I suggest you remove them before you rejoin the game.'

For an interesting moment he thought she would strike him and then she thought better of it. 'Good God! I can see Fletcher asleep over there; at least I think he's asleep – he could very well be dead. Very dangerous business playing cricket.'

She turned and looked where he was pointing. Her gurgle of laughter made him want to snatch her from her feet and kiss her breathless. 'You're quite ridiculous, my lord, and I suggest you go and investigate whilst I search for this missing cricket ball. I assume that those watching with interest are not intending to assist with this matter?'

'I shouldn't bother; I have another one in my pocket. An umpire always carries a spare.'

They picked their way through the grass to the prostrate body of the missing fielder. As they got nearer his snores were quite audible.

'I do believe he's inebriated, sir. I must say I thought he looked a trifle unsteady earlier. I'm at a loss to know where he found sufficient alcohol to get into this state whilst playing cricket.'

Bennett prodded the comatose form with his boot but the man didn't stir. 'No doubt he has a flask in his pocket. I suggest we leave him here to sleep it off. Let's hope Perry can find a substitute or we're going to lose this match.'

'I sincerely hope that we don't as I have placed a wager on the result.'

They hurried back to the centre of the field and amidst much jollity the match resumed. As expected Beau was impossible to get out, but no one else survived for very long and the entire team was dismissed for ninety-eight runs. He noticed that only a handful of spectators remained.

Perry spoke urgently to him as they left the field. 'Fletcher was a decent batsman; it's a damn shame we won't have him playing.' He gestured towards a bank of black clouds that were rolling in. 'I doubt this match will be completed today. It's going to rain in the next half an hour.'

'I'll score as quickly as I can, but I can't do it all on my own like last time. Will Miss DuPont be prepared to bat again?'

'Absolutely not – I'm going to suggest the ladies abandon the match and leave it to us. There's no point in all of us getting drenched.'

Grace was talking to Giselle and her companion. 'Excuse me, ladies, there's no need for you to remain out here...' He was interrupted by a crash of thunder followed by a flash of lightning and the heavens opened.

There was no need to finish his sentence. The remaining spectators and the players were too far away from the house to get there without being soaked to the skin, so everyone dashed for the shelter of the trees. By the time they were under the thick canopy most of them were rather damp. His own shirt was sticking to his chest and the thin muslin gowns left nothing to the imagination.

However, his attention was fixed on Grace. Her serviceable garments remained opaque not revealing any more than they should; her face was still somewhat grubby and there were grass stalks in her hair. To him she was the most beautiful woman there.

Someone had had the foresight to rescue the blankets and chairs abandoned by the spectators and these were soon set out. The young ladies were sitting chatting companionably together in a group some distance from the gentlemen.

The light touch on his arm reminded him he was paying this group too much attention. 'What are you going to do about Miss DuPont?' Perry asked him.

'Do? Nothing, of course. She made it very clear she's no interest in my offer and I've no intention of making a jackass of myself. There are plenty of more suitable candidates and I'll select my wife from one of those.'

His brother looked relieved. 'Marrying her would have been a disaster for the family. Beau will never accept someone from her background and you would have been forced to choose between her and us.'

Bennett's fists clenched and he pretended to be rubbing his face dry in order to regain his composure. 'I'm well aware of that. He made it abundantly clear what he thought of her and it's something that neither of us is likely to forget.'

'It's a great shame she isn't one of us, as I like her – but you've made the right decision.' His brother sighed and stared sadly at the torrential rain. 'I'm going to suggest we call this match a draw, Bennett. The wicket will be waterlogged and I doubt we'll be able to resume the match tomorrow anyway. What do you think?'

'You're the captain; it's nothing to do with me. However, if we can't play tomorrow then the match would have to be abandoned anyway as the races start the next day.'

Somehow Grace sensed he was talking about her and looked his way. Her radiant smile rocked him to the core. He couldn't stop himself from reciprocating and prayed his brother hadn't seen his face.

16

The rain continued to pour down and, even with the protection of a blanket and the trees, Grace and the other ladies were becoming chilled to the marrow.

'I refuse to remain here a moment longer,' she said. 'I'd rather get soaked and then be able to change into dry clothes than sit here for an hour or more whilst we wait for the rain to pass.'

A chorus of approval greeted her decision and with the blankets held over their heads they made a dash for shelter. They ran up the flight of stairs that led to the terrace and then in through the French doors, receiving a spontaneous round of applause from the occupants as they burst in.

Lady Madeline removed the blanket from her head and shook herself like a dog. 'I'm considerably warmer now, but I still need to change.'

Grace did likewise. 'Thank you for an enjoyable afternoon, my lady, but I don't think I'll be taking part in another cricket match. We're dripping on the fine carpet so had better take ourselves off and get dry.'

'Please don't remain in your room tonight, Miss DuPont – there's to be charades after dinner and I should love you to be in my team.'

'Thank you, Lady Madeline, but I'm *persona non grata* with the duke and think it better I keep myself separate. I've no wish to cause embarrassment to your family.'

'Fiddlesticks to that! My brother can be decidedly stuffy at times – but we do our best to ignore this unfortunate trait. I can assure you the rest of us are not like him. It comes of him being brought up with the expectation of becoming one of the most powerful men in the land and owning vast estates. He has always been feted and fawned over and it has rather gone to his head.'

'In which case, my lady, I'll come down for dinner and will be delighted to join your charades team. I've not played this game since I was away at my seminary – but I've always enjoyed any form of play-acting.'

She glanced nervously towards the terrace where she could see the gentlemen were bounding up the steps and would be inside at any moment. She didn't want to talk to any of them – and especially not to Lord Sheldon. The other girls felt the same way and as one they turned and scurried from the room.

She hoped her pink cheeks would be put down to exertion and not to the embarrassment she felt at having inadvertently revealed her feelings to his lordship. When she'd looked up and seen him staring in her direction she hadn't been able to stop herself smiling, and he'd been delighted by her response.

Aunt Sarah was close behind her. 'There's little point in changing twice, my dear, so I shall remain in my room until it's time for dinner. I'm glad you've decided to come down. We might as well enjoy being part of such a prestigious house party as it's unlikely we'll ever be in this position again.'

Impulsively Grace hugged her friend. 'I could hardly refuse such a kind invitation. As long as I stay away from the Sheldon gentlemen, I'm sure I'll not receive the opprobrium of either the duke or the other aristocratic members of this company.'

She spent the remainder of the afternoon curled up on the window seat, reading and watching the rain. She hoped Peterson had brought in her horses as they weren't accustomed to being out in such inclement weather. She wished Rufus to be in peak condition for the first of the races.

Fortunately the final of the gentlemen's race wouldn't be until the Tuesday, which would give her stallion two days to recuperate.

When her maid called her in to begin preparations for the evening, Grace was a trifle apprehensive. Although the girls she'd been mixing with this afternoon had been friendly, she doubted that she would be received as well by the others. Having hit one of their friends in the chest with a cricket ball would not have endeared her to them.

Annie shook out the skirt of the evening gown Grace had decided to wear that night. 'You look pretty as a picture in that, miss. Although the underskirt is emerald green the silver gauze overskirt makes it almost impossible to see.'

'Are you trying to tell me you don't approve of my having selected such a vibrant colour?'

'It's not for me to say, miss, but I doubt that anyone else of my age will be wearing anything so bright.'

'However, you must admit that this ensemble suits me to perfection. The matching green ribbons you have threaded through my hair are the perfect complement. I hope I'm not obliged to sit with the family tonight.'

Her maid sniffed and handed over the fingerless gloves and reticule that completed the outfit – these too were made from emerald green silk.

Her dear companion was just about to knock on the sitting room door when Grace stepped out into the corridor. 'My, you do look splendid, my dear. An inspired choice, if I might say so.'

The corridor was busy with other guests making their way downstairs and private conversation was impossible. Grace was expecting to be ostracised. However, all but a couple of those they mingled with greeted her politely.

* * *

When Bennett heard that Grace was to come down that evening he had mixed feelings. Having the woman he loved within arm's reach and not being able to show his feelings would be hell. He'd given his word he wouldn't repeat his offer, but he had no intention of allowing any other gentleman to make advances to her.

He circulated the grand drawing room, nodding and smiling and offering the odd remark, but his attention was on the double doors through which she would come. He was talking to one of Beau's friends when the man faltered in his conversation and his mouth dropped open.

Bennett swung round and his breath caught in his throat. Standing framed in the doorway, completely unaware of the sensation she was causing, was his darling girl. Her gown was astonishing – he'd never seen anything like it. Every man in the room was staring slack-jawed at this vision of loveliness.

He didn't know a lot about women's gowns but even he could see this was something quite exceptional. The shimmery material of the skirt revealed tantalising glimpses of a shocking emerald green. He glanced around the crowd and wasn't surprised to see that the ladies were equally spellbound.

In that moment he decided he didn't give a damn for his family's reservations – if he didn't stake *his* claim tonight then somebody else would do so. When a girl was as lovely as this it really didn't matter where she came from – she might not be part of high society, but she was gently born and far wealthier than many of the eager debutantes who'd come hoping to entice him into offering for them.

He moved smoothly through the gawping crowd and arrived at her side before anyone else had a chance to move. He bowed deeply and she reciprocated with a curtsy.

'Good evening, Miss DuPont, you look *ravissante* tonight. That gown is a triumph. You will be besieged by the other ladies for the name of your modiste.'

'Thank you, my lord. I'm relieved to hear you say so, for I feared the amount of attention being paid to me was for another reason entirely.' Her friendly smile slipped a little. 'Could I ask you to step aside please. I must find somewhere less conspicuous to stand.'

Instead of doing what she asked he moved to her side and offered his arm. For a heart-stopping moment he thought she was going to refuse, but then her gloved hand was resting where it belonged. 'Will you come with me to the library?'

She shook her head. 'That wouldn't be appropriate, my lord. However,

I would be prepared to promenade around the music room where we will be in full view at all times.'

'Very well, that will have to do. Don't look so prune-faced, Miss DuPont. I don't intend to make you an offer. That's not why I wish to speak to you.'

The fingers on his arm relaxed. He'd said the right thing even though it was untrue, as he'd had every intention of asking her to marry him if she'd agreed to go to the library. Her companion had drifted away to join the older ladies, leaving them to talk freely.

The music room was relatively quiet, just two other couples wandering about, and the chamber was sufficiently large to mean they could all converse without being overheard and yet were breaching no rules of etiquette.

As they walked past the piano she paused. 'This is a beautiful instrument, far better than the one I had at home. Would you object to me playing? I doubt I'll get an opportunity to do so again as I'm intending to leave directly the races are finished.'

Before he could object she pulled out the piano stool, threw back the lid and sat down. It was obvious she had no wish to have a private conversation with him and this was her way of preventing it.

Then she began to play and he forgot his annoyance as the beautiful sound filled the space. He was transfixed and let the liquid notes pour over him, scarcely able to credit the girl he'd fallen in love with was a virtuoso on the pianoforte.

* * *

Grace hadn't intended to play for more than a few minutes but as always she was immediately lost in the sonata and forgot where she was or who she was with. It had been too long since she'd had the opportunity to play, and music had always been a solace when her life had become difficult and her parents too demanding.

She played the last chords and sat with her eyes closed, satisfied she'd done the piece justice. Then she was jerked back to the present by Lord

Sheldon dropping his hands to her shoulders. This intimate contact sent unexpected heatwaves racing around her body.

'My love, I've never heard anyone play so exquisitely. You must play again after dinner and before the dancing starts.'

'My lord, please let me get up. It must be time to go in and I mustn't be tardy yet again.'

He removed his hands, allowing her to regain her feet. She was dismayed to find him standing a hand's width from her, his heat pulsing towards her. The piano stool pressed against the back of her legs, making it impossible for her to move that way. She was trapped and didn't dare to raise her head and see his face.

'Look at me, Grace – please don't hide your feelings from me.'

Reluctantly she tilted her chin and as she did so his arms closed around her waist, drawing her close. The light was blotted out as his mouth claimed hers in a searing kiss. The moment his lips touched hers she knew the decision had been taken out of her hands. She could no longer deny that she loved him.

It was he who raised his head and brought the kiss to an end. Her heart was hammering as if it wished to escape from the confines of her bodice and without his firm support she feared she might have collapsed into a heap on the floor.

'My darling, do you wish me to go down on one knee and ask you formally to be my wife?' His eyes were damp and his voice gruff – he was as moved as she.

She couldn't find her voice and shook her head and smiled, hoping this would be enough to tell him he didn't need to make a cake of himself.

'In which case, sweetheart, will you make me the happiest of men and agree to be my wife? I love you and cannot live without you at my side.'

'I will – I love you too.'

To her astonishment she was lifted into the air and spun around like a child until she was quite giddy. 'Put me down, my lord. I'm sure I'm showing an unseemly amount of ankle.'

He laughed and stopped his mad gyrations. He didn't place her immediately on the boards but allowed her to slide down his chest and the contact made her dizzy all over again.

'My name is Bennett; in future I wish you to address me by this. We must hurry – everyone is going into the dining room.'

He took her hand and raised it to his lips and then kissed each knuckle in turn. 'I shall announce our betrothal tonight. I take it I don't need to apply formally for your hand to your father?'

She found it difficult to concentrate on his words whilst he was caressing her so delightfully. She pulled her hand away so she could think more clearly.

'I don't wish you to announce anything, Bennett. Please can we keep this information to ourselves?'

'If that's what you want, then so be it. However, I think it's perfectly possible the news will already be out. Don't forget there were two other couples in here when we came and they might well have remained to hear you play and seen me kiss you.'

They joined the milling crowd of people making their way to the dining room and she saw at once Aunt Sarah was making her way towards them and from her expression she was deeply upset about something. Grace moved to one side so she could speak privately to her companion.

'My dear girl, what were you thinking of? How could you have been so indiscreet?'

'Aunt Sarah, what are people saying?'

'Your reputation is gone. You were already considered a trifle fast, but now I've heard two of the tabbies saying you'd accepted a *carte blanche* from Lord Sheldon.'

He had joined them and overheard this last remark. 'Madam, I hope you will be the first to congratulate us. Grace has agreed to be my wife.'

'No, Bennett, we must leave things as they are. I don't care what anyone thinks about me, but I'm causing friction in your family. Please, let people think I'm going to be your mistress. It will make things easier for you.'

'Good heavens! What a preposterous suggestion, Grace. A lady's reputation is the most precious thing she owns. Do you wish his lordship and any progeny you might have in the future to be ostracised by society? This must be put right immediately.'

'Miss Newcomb is right, my love. I thank you for your concern, but I made my choice a week ago. I shall be married to the woman I love and my family can accept it or not. I'll not be swayed by their disapproval.' He reached out and brushed a finger across her cheek, sending tingles to the tips of her toes.

'I think you're making a catastrophic error, Bennett. The duke's a formidable man and he'll do everything in his power to prevent us being wed. Also you're forgetting that all those debutantes and their mamas will be equally enraged that a cit has stolen the prize from beneath their aristocratic noses.'

He took her hand and placed it possessively on his arm. 'We'll go in together and I'll make the announcement as soon as everybody is seated. I'll send to Doctors' Commons in Town and obtain a special licence so we can be married immediately.'

The smile he gave her banished her reservations. His brother might be the head of the family, but Bennett was equally determined and would protect her from any unpleasantness. She'd never been so happy in her life – she wouldn't have to hide away until she reached her majority but would be married to this wonderful man and they could live anywhere they chose.

As soon as the knot was tied he would receive her massive trust fund and would be able to replenish the Silchester family coffers. There should be ample left over to supplement whatever income he derived from his own estates to allow them to live in luxury for the rest of their lives.

Aunt Sarah slipped away to take a seat at the far end of the chamber but Bennett led her to the top table. She was uncomfortably aware of the accusatory stares burning into her back as they walked the length of the vast room.

By the time they reached the duke and his siblings, she could scarcely move one foot in front of the other. Bennett smiled down at her, his eyes filled with love, and this gave her the courage to take her seat despite the icy disapproval from his older brother.

When the footmen had retreated her beloved stood. He ignored the duke and raised his hand. 'My lords, ladies and gentlemen, I'm delighted to announce that Miss Grace DuPont and I are engaged to be married.'

This announcement was greeted in stunned silence. The duke got to his feet and Grace waited in terror for him to shatter her dreams.

17

The duke smiled at Bennett and Grace but his eyes remained unfriendly. 'Might I be the first to offer my congratulations to you both? Please raise your glasses. I give you Lord Sheldon and Miss Grace DuPont.'

There was a hurried shuffle as the guests snatched up their glasses and rose to repeat the toast. Her smile was fixed, her hands were shaking – she knew this wouldn't be the end of it. The duke wouldn't give in so easily.

The fact that half the glasses raised were empty only served to add to her unease. This had to be a bad omen. Everybody sat down and conversation began again and she was certain the only topic would be this unexpected and unwanted betrothal of one of them to someone like her.

She scarcely noticed what was placed in front of her and was able to eat no more than a few morsels. Her future husband gave the appearance of being relaxed and happy but she was certain he wasn't – how could he be when his entire family was against him?

The interminable meal eventually drew to a close and Lady Madeline rose gracefully to her feet, indicating that the ladies should leave the gentlemen to their port. She was tempted to flee, to hide in her rooms and avoid the inevitable unpleasantness that was about to come her way.

Then her dear friend was at her side and slipped a comforting arm through hers. 'The worst is all but over, my dear. You must just get through this evening and the matter will be settled. The announcement has been made, the duke congratulated you and Lord Sheldon cannot retract. However disgruntled these ladies might be, there's nothing they can do about it.'

'If I didn't love him so much, Aunt Sarah, I'd never have agreed to this. I didn't come here to ensnare him, certainly had no expectation of falling in love – but now I cannot envisage a life without him.'

As they entered the grand drawing room the other ladies hurried away. Despite the announcement, her scandalous behaviour in the music room had made her even more socially unacceptable. Well-brought-up young ladies didn't kiss their future husbands – but if they did, it took place in private.

Grace saw Lady Madeline and her sister look her way and tentatively smiled. Her gesture wasn't reciprocated. Both girls turned away as if Grace had become invisible. She blinked away tears, not wishing to show her distress. She hadn't expected Bennett's sisters to side with the tabbies, and their desertion meant he would lose his entire family if he continued his engagement to her.

'I can't remain in here and be ignored, Aunt Sarah. We must go into the music room and I'll play you something.' She didn't give her friend the opportunity to refuse, but turned and marched, shoulders back and head up, down the length of the room and out through the doors that led directly to the chamber she sought.

The music room was empty. 'Kindly close the doors. I've no wish for an audience.' Once this was done her anxiety lessened and her breathing slowly returned to normal.

'That was most distressing, my dear. We cannot remain here and be ostracised in this way. As you are now going to become the wife of Lord Sheldon, surely there's no further need for you to participate in the races, and we can leave here tomorrow morning? Mr DuPont will be delighted that you've achieved his aim and will welcome you home – however unorthodox your departure was last week.'

'I was thinking the same. Could I prevail upon you to set matters in motion? I must remain here until Lord Sheldon joins me, so I can tell him my decision. I'll return to my apartment as soon as I've spoken to him.'

They embraced fondly and then Aunt Sarah hurried away to send messages to the stables and make sure that the trunks were repacked. She settled herself at the piano but was unable to lose herself entirely in the music and therefore heard Bennett come in to join her.

She finished the passage she was playing and prepared to close the instrument and stand up. 'No, continue to play, sweetheart. I'll sit quietly on the end of the stool and listen.'

Once he was settled, his thigh deliciously pressed against hers, she resumed. She played another sonata, this one a recent composition by the composer Beethoven.

'That was superb. Come, my love, we must return to the others. There's to be dancing and I'm determined to waltz with you.'

'I'm not going back in there to be ignored and humiliated. I'm beginning to have second thoughts about our betrothal, Bennett. You'll be ostracised by your peers and I'll never be accepted.'

He lifted her from her feet and then sat down again, placing her on his lap. 'I don't give a damn what anyone else says, I'm not marrying them, but marrying the woman I love. My brother has accepted our engagement, albeit reluctantly, and that's all that matters to me.'

'I expect the majority of your guests will leave now that you've made your decision.'

'I doubt that very much. There are few people who don't enjoy being entertained in the lap of luxury and rubbing shoulders with the highest in the land. They will be disappointed, but none of them will go.'

His arms tightened and one hand cupped her face, turning it so he could kiss her. The feel of his mouth against hers, the touch of his tongue on her lips, was making her forget her reservations. Her back arched and she buried her fingers in the hair at the nape of his neck.

Then she was rudely ejected from his embrace and he was standing with his back to her breathing heavily. 'What's wrong? Are you unwell, my love?'

'No – give me a moment to recover. Play something else; it will calm me.'

This was all very strange. She'd no idea why he'd become so agitated but was happy to do as he asked. This time she attempted to play a prelude

by Bach but her fingers fumbled a few times and she couldn't concentrate
on the music. Frustrated by her ineptitude, she slammed down the piano
lid and marched across to stand behind him.

'I refuse to be ignored by you as well, sir. What have I done to offend
you?'

Slowly he turned and his eyes were dark and there was a hectic flush
along his cheekbones. 'Do you have any idea what happens in the
marriage bed, sweetheart?'

Scalding colour flooded her cheeks at his question. She turned away,
too embarrassed to meet his amused gaze. 'It's not a subject I've had any
interest in until now – so the answer to your question is no.'

His smile was tender and he reached out and took her hand and led
her back to the piano stool. He pressed her shoulders and she sat once
more. Then he fetched one of the small chairs, spun it round and strad-
dled it a yard from her.

'This is something that your mother should have explained. I'm at a
loss to know how to begin, but until you understand things are going to be
– how can I put it – difficult for us.'

'I know that I feel a strange heat all over when you kiss me. That I
yearn for something else, to be even closer...'

He smiled lazily. 'Well, darling, that's a start. What you're experiencing
is passion, desire – it's part of being in love.' He stopped and closed his
eyes as if lost in thought. Then he continued. 'I don't know how to explain
this delicately. Presumably you've seen what happens between your stallion and a mare in order to produce a foal?'

Her eyes widened and her mouth went dry. Surely he didn't mean? He
nodded. 'I see you understand. The same process occurs between a man
and woman when they make love.'

She couldn't stop her eyes from travelling to his nether regions and his
shout of laughter at her indelicacy was enough to make her smile.

'How extraordinary! I cannot imagine how such a thing is possible
when men and women are so disparate in size.'

'I can assure you, my love, that when a couple are as in love as we are
the intimacy of the marriage bed is something to be enjoyed not feared. I

was obliged to move away from you before I anticipated our wedding night.'

She shot to her feet as if stabbed by a needle. 'Good heavens! I think the less time we spend alone the better, Lord Sheldon. We've already scandalised your guests by kissing – I can't believe you've just suggested you intended to do something even more shocking – and in the middle of the music room too.'

'Don't fly into the boughs – I was teasing you. I've no intention of making love to you until you are my wife, however much I should like to.'

The sound of the musicians tuning up interrupted their conversation. 'The dancing is about to begin. I believe I can now return with you by my side.'

They were halfway to the door when she recalled she'd sent her companion to arrange for their departure the next morning. When she explained he was unsurprised.

'Don't worry, my love, I'll send word to the stables that you're not leaving after all. I'm glad you decided to return to your familial home as you cannot move to my estate until we're married, for the scandal would follow us for the rest of our lives. I know I rail against the restrictions of my upbringing, but I was born into one of the most powerful families in the kingdom and I want my wife and any progeny we have to enjoy the same status that I have.'

'I thought you were prepared to throw it all away in order to be at my side.' She stopped and clutched her bosom in a theatrical way. 'Are you not to be my gallant protector after all?'

'You're an impertinent baggage and I see I shall be run ragged once we're wed.' He gathered her close and his kiss was hard and demanding. She melted into his arms and forgot where she was or the fact that they could be seen by anyone who cared to step into the music room.

A delightful and breathless few minutes later he released her. 'You know I would die for you, give up my heritage and family without a second thought. However, I shall be much happier remaining part of the Silchester dynasty and you will come to love all this too. Being privileged is not just about wealth, sweetheart, it's also about responsibility. Those privileged enough to be born into power have an obligation to take care of those less fortunate.'

'In which case, Bennett, I'm relieved you have neither to give up your life nor your heritage for my sake.' She slipped her arm back through his and squeezed it. 'I shan't dance with anyone else and certainly have no intention of spending a moment with anyone apart from you. So when we've danced I shall retire as I intended to before.'

'You'll do no such thing. As we're already so far beyond the pale as to be almost invisible, I intend to dance every dance with you and be damned to the rules of etiquette.'

She wasn't sure this was a sensible suggestion but his enthusiasm was infectious and she didn't demur. They walked arm in arm to the far end of the grand drawing room where the carpets had been removed for the evening. The ballroom was only used for formal occasions and Grace wasn't sure if she was glad or disappointed she would never experience the grandeur of this chamber.

There was no sign of the duke, for which she was profoundly grateful, but his other siblings were there and appeared as eager to dance as the other guests who were milling about waiting for the quartet to begin playing.

'As Beau has made himself scarce, I believe I'm the most senior member of the family here. Therefore, my love, we shall lead the proceedings. Come with me whilst I talk to the musicians.'

He made it quite clear that he wished for only country dances and waltzes to be played tonight – both of which involved her remaining with him and not being obliged to dance with any other gentleman.

He led her to the centre of the space and they stepped apart so they were at the head of each line of dancers. Immediately the next four places in the set were taken by his two sisters and two brothers, which meant that the remaining couples had to join the end of the lines.

Although she had been well taught and danced with other girls when she was at the seminary, Grace had never danced with a gentleman before. She curtsied to him and he bowed and then they joined hands in the centre of the set and began their promenade. She needn't have worried as Bennett was an expert dancer and soon she began to enjoy every moment.

There was scarcely time to draw breath before the second country dance began and after two more she was ready to sit down for a while in order to catch her breath. She'd had no time to observe closely what others were saying about their scandalous behaviour but as far as she could tell from the smiling, friendly faces around her none of the younger members of the party held her in dislike.

'Are you enjoying yourself, sweetheart?'

'Indeed I am. I'd no idea dancing could be such fun. Have you noticed anyone giving us disapproving stares for dancing so often together?'

'They wouldn't dare. The rules are different at a private party, and I believe that several have already danced more than once with my brothers.' He stared thoughtfully at the gaggle of excited debutantes. 'I rather think they've transferred their attentions to Aubrey and Perry – a younger Sheldon is better than none at all.'

'That's a disgraceful thing to say, Bennett.' She tapped him playfully on the arm and his smile made her toes curl in her slippers. Now she knew what to expect in the marriage bed, his every look made her heart race.

A few minutes later the opening bars of a waltz were played. 'At last – this is what I've been waiting for. Come along, darling, we shall take to the floor.' He grinned and nodded towards the other dancers. 'I don't suppose any of them would consider taking the floor for such a *risqué* dance if they were anywhere else. In fact,' he whispered to her as he led her to a very prominent place in the centre of the empty floor, 'I fear we may be the only ones dancing.'

'As you said before, my love, we have already broken all the rules so a waltz or two is not going to make matters worse.'

He swept her away in time to the music and she forgot everything but the joy of dancing in the arms of the man she loved. After they had twirled around the floor a couple of times the other couples decided to ignore conventions too and they were no longer alone.

When the music finished she was quite dizzy and not sure if it was the dance or the excitement. 'I've had a truly memorable evening, Bennett, but I'm quite exhausted and intend to retire. I have to be up at dawn to exercise Rufus and my dogs, and will be unable to do so if I stay here any longer.'

'In which case, sweetheart, I too shall go to my rooms. We'll ride together in future. I want to see how your horse compares to mine before the races on Saturday.'

He didn't take her through the lower end of the huge chamber where everyone else was gathered, but led her out through the side doors and into the spacious passageway.

'I'd no idea a military man could dance as well as you do – I thought you spent your time on more physical pursuits.'

'Wellesley insists that all his officers are proficient so we can acquit ourselves with charm and dignity at any functions we're obliged to attend. It isn't all battles and glory, my love.'

'To my mind war can never be considered glorious and I'd much prefer it if these political differences could be solved in a more peaceful way.'

They continued to chat about this and that as they made their way up the wide staircase. He escorted her into the guest wing and up to her sitting room door.

'I won't come in, sweetheart, as that would test my resolve to breaking point.'

'Then you must kiss me here, for I refuse to go in until you've done so.' She moved closer and threaded her hands around his neck, giving him no opportunity to refuse her request.

He needed no more prompting. After a delightful and intoxicating few minutes he stepped away. 'Go in, darling, or I swear I'll accompany you.'

She opened the door and dashed in, closing it behind her. She leaned against the wood, letting the cold surface cool her overheated body. 'Goodnight, Bennett, I love you.'

There was a slight bump on the other side. 'Goodnight, my darling, I love you too. I'll see you in the stables at first light.'

She remained where she was until his footsteps faded into the distance and then pushed herself away from the support of the door. Small wonder that there was so much written about love and passion if it made everyone feel the way she did at this moment.

18

Last night's storm had cleared and Grace arrived at the stables pleased she wouldn't get soaked for a second time. Her horse was saddled and waiting but there was no sign of Lucifer or Bennett.

'Peterson, Lord Sheldon is supposed to be riding out with me this morning. Do you know why he's not here?'

'He's waiting for you in the lane, miss – he's only just gone. That stallion of his was doing his best to toss him off so he thought it wise to take him out of the yard before the animal injured himself or one of the grooms.'

'Let's hope Rufus is in a better frame of mind.' She scarcely had time to put her foot in the single stirrup iron and adjust her skirts before her horse surged forward. They left the yard at speed and she was greeted by her beloved as she calmed her mount.

'Good morning, sweetheart, it seems that our horses are a trifle overexcited this morning. Shall we gallop out their fidgets?'

'I'll follow your lead, Bennett. The going is soft so if we take a tumble we shouldn't be too badly injured.'

'I've no intention of losing my seat – and I sincerely hope that you don't do so either.' Expertly he turned his plunging horse and sent him into a canter. Rufus needed no urging and fell in behind him. The speed increased until they were galloping at full stretch.

The path was wide enough to overtake and she encouraged her horse to increase his pace. Gradually he drew level until they were racing side by side and then he was past and Lucifer was unable to match his speed.

After a mile or two she sat back in the saddle and hauled gently on the reins. Immediately Rufus responded, shortening his stride and dropping into a collected canter, and then into an easy walk.

Bennett arrived a few seconds later. 'I can't believe your horse has beaten mine. I didn't think there was another animal in the land as fast as Lucifer.'

'I told you my stallion's invincible. I intend to win both the lady's and the gentleman's cup.' She bent forward and slapped her mount's neck. 'Well done, my boy, I knew you could do it.'

'I don't think the rules will allow you to enter the same horse in both categories, my love.'

'Then I shall ride Silver Lady, one of the carriage horses. She goes like the wind under saddle.'

They continued their ride, stopping every now and again to allow the three dogs to catch up. The stable yard was bustling when they returned and there were several other gentlemen about to take their own mounts out for morning exercise.

One of them called out cheerfully. 'I think I might as well withdraw from the races, Sheldon. My Sam here hasn't a hope in hell of beating either of your stallions.'

A chorus of agreement ran around the yard, but it was humorous and she was certain that none of the gentlemen present had any intention of withdrawing.

Peterson was waiting to take her horse and he nodded at Lucifer. 'The honours were ours. Keep him inside today as I don't wish him to overexert himself. I'll be riding Silver Lady as well, so will you bring her in too?'

Bennett had already dismounted and was at her side ready to lift her from the saddle before her groom would offer to do this task. 'None of the ladies will be up yet. Shall we breakfast together before we change?'

Grace viewed her dusty habit with disfavour. 'I think not, my dear. I'll have a tray in my room as usual. However, when you're ready I should be delighted to have you join us.'

'I'll be there in a quarter of an hour – can you be changed by then?'

'Of course. I'm famous for my punctuality.'

He chuckled and his gloved hand stretched out to brush her cheek before he bounded off to his own apartment in the main part of the house.

Annie had the hot water waiting and Grace was ready in the allotted time. Aunt Sarah arrived before he did. 'I'm glad Lord Sheldon is joining us. I have something of interest to tell you both.'

Three maids appeared with trays, crisp white tablecloths and the other paraphernalia necessary to eat their breakfast. The girls had just departed when Bennett knocked on the door and strolled in without waiting for her response.

He nodded to her friend and turned to admire the substantial feast set out for them on the sideboard. 'Excellent, my instructions have been followed to the letter. We have everything here that they have in the breakfast room.'

Once they were seated in front of plates heaped with delicious food, Aunt Sarah explained what she'd learned. 'It would seem that none of your guests intend to leave even though you're now spoken for, my lord. Indeed, I gather that there are several extra gentlemen arriving today with the sole intention of taking part in the horse races tomorrow.'

'How extraordinary – surely nobody arrives here without an invitation?' Grace was puzzled by this news.

'No, my dear, they don't intend to stay here – they have taken lodgings at a local hostelry. Word of the races has spread and I believe, though of course you probably already know, my lord, that there are a dozen or more entrants from your neighbours as well.'

'How many do you think there'll be, Bennett? Can you accommodate all the extra horses?'

He appeared remarkably relaxed about this new development. 'I'm not surprised, my love – there's little to do in the summer months once the Season's over. The track I've had prepared can accommodate ten horses safely at one time so the entrants will be divided. All the names of the participants are to be put in a hat and withdrawn tonight to see which heat they'll run in.'

'Although that's the fairest way to arrange things, it could mean that all the best horses are in the same heat.'

'I thought of that, Grace. The first five will go through to the final – this should ensure we have the best horses racing together at the end.'

When the meal was finished he left to attend to the details of the races and they agreed to meet in the library at three o'clock.

'What do you wish to do this morning, my dear? I'm expecting to get a reply from my friends about vacant accommodation near your horses. I must write to them and tell them we no longer require their assistance as we'll be returning to DuPont Manor until your nuptials.'

'I intend to write to my parents and give them the good news. Lord Sheldon is writing as well, and I will put my note in with his. I'll give it to him this afternoon. I've also to write to Collins and update him on the situation. I'm hoping my mares and foals can be transferred to Lord Sheldon's estate and that he will allow me to continue with my endeavours.'

'I'm sure he will, my dear. He seems a most accommodating gentleman where you're concerned. I must own I was pleasantly surprised by the reaction of the duke to your shock announcement last night. I thought him adamantly opposed to such a match.'

'As did I, but he could hardly do anything else as he was presented with a *fait accompli*. None of his siblings has actually spoken directly to me or offered their congratulations and I think that is significant, don't you?'

'You refine on this too much, my love. They will be delighted to have you in the family. You might not be of the same class as they are, but you are far wealthier and equally well educated. They cannot fail to be aware you are the most beautiful young lady present and will make Lord Sheldon an excellent wife.'

'I do hope you're correct. I'm sure this won't be the first marriage that could be labelled a misalliance.'

* * *

Bennett discovered he now had more than thirty horses entered for his race, which meant there would now have to be four heats in order to accommodate them all safely. By the time he'd spoken to his grooms, and written the necessary letter to Grace's father, the time had moved on to almost two o'clock.

He had no inclination join the guests in any of the activities his sisters had organised so remained in the library. After a few minutes of quiet consideration he came to a decision. He quickly wrote a letter to Doctors' Commons requesting a special licence for himself and Grace; he would send his man of affairs to London to fetch it for him. There was no necessity to travel post, which was exorbitantly expensive. This task could be accomplished comfortably within four days.

Once he had this document he would marry her, and the house guests would become the guests at their wedding. The garden party that was planned for the following week would be the ideal occasion for the tenants and villagers to celebrate their wedding. There was also to be a grand ball the same evening to which all the families in the neighbourhood had been invited and this event would make it a double celebration.

This would mean that Grace wouldn't need to return to her family home. They could leave the day after the ball and go at once to his estate, which was no more than two hours' drive from Silchester Court. He wrote the letter and his man of affairs departed on his errand.

The door opened and he looked up with a smile expecting to see his beloved enter; however, it was his sister.

'Madeline, just the person I was looking for.'

'I've been looking for you everywhere, Bennett, did you know there are now thirty-six horses entered in your race?'

'I did indeed and I've already taken care of the arrangements necessary to accommodate them all.' He then told her of his plans for the wedding and she looked at him as if he was speaking in tongues.

'Good heavens, Bennett, you cannot expect the poor girl to marry you in such a rush. She will want her parents here and also needs to prepare her bride clothes. Getting married with such indecent haste will not do either of your reputations any good.'

'I've sent word to her parents asking them to join us here immediately.

I'm sure they'll be more than delighted to be part of this house party. There's no point in scowling at me; Grace and I will be married next week and there's nothing any of you can say to prevent it.' She was unconvinced. 'I love her, Madeline. I've never been so happy in my life. If I was to discover she didn't have a dowry that would save the family, was as impecunious as I, I should still marry her. I cannot live without her and do not intend to do so.'

'In which case, brother, you have my full support. I hope that one day I might feel as passionately as you do about a gentleman. I warn you, though, Beau isn't happy about your engagement and has sent to London in the hope of discovering something detrimental that will prevent your marriage.'

'Then can I ask you not to tell him I'll have a special licence? My man left an hour ago and should be back within four days – once he's here we can be married and there will be nothing he can do about it.'

* * *

The afternoon passed speedily and Grace was, for once, ready to go down at the appointed time. However, Aunt Sarah had yet to appear and her friend was never late. Annie had already been dismissed for the evening so she would have to go herself and see what was causing the delay.

The chamber was on the next floor. The early evening sunshine streaming in through the windows made this upper floor unpleasantly hot. She hurried to her companion's sitting room door, but receiving no response she walked in. This was very strange – where was she?

The bedchamber door was closed but she thought she heard a sound behind it. Her heart jumped into her mouth – was the reason for this tardiness that Aunt Sarah was unwell?

She knocked and pushed open the door to find the room in darkness. 'Don't come any further, my dear. I'm feeling very unwell. I have a high fever and have cast up my accounts several times. I've no wish for you to catch whatever ailment I've got.'

'Fiddlesticks to that! I'll run back and change into something more suitable and then return to take care of you.'

She returned to her room in a rush and was glad the evening gown she'd selected didn't require the assistance of her maid to remove it. She draped it over the end of the bed, removed the matching underskirt and then found herself a plain morning gown. There was nothing she could do about the elaborate arrangement of her hair, which looked rather strange now she was dressed so drably.

She had pulled the bell strap when she'd arrived and only had to wait a few moments before Annie burst in. 'Is something wrong, miss? I didn't think you needed me this evening.'

'Miss Newcomb is unwell. I wish you to help me take care of her.'

This time she was accompanied by her abigail and took the more direct route that the servants used through the narrow passages and staircases that ran throughout this enormous edifice.

'Miss Newcomb has a fever and has been nauseous. The room's oppressive and I think the first thing we must do is open all the windows, even if we keep the curtains closed.'

By midnight the fever had broken and her dearest friend was sleeping. Only then did she remember she had not sent word to Bennett and he would have been wondering where she was.

'You go on to bed, miss; I'll stay with her until the morning. I reckon she's over the worst and will be well enough tomorrow.'

Grace was certain she would become lost if she took the back route to her apartment so this time she went out into the corridor. She could hear the sound of laughter and loud conversation drifting up from the main reception rooms and paused for a moment by an open window, breathing in the cool air gratefully. After being closeted in the small bedchamber with Aunt Sarah for several hours she decided she needed to go outside and clear her head before she retired.

She glanced down at her crumpled gown and thought it might be sensible to change, but she didn't have the energy. If she remained in the shadows and slipped out through the side door that led to the stables she doubted she would be seen by anyone.

She'd not been outside many minutes before her dogs joined her. 'How did you know I was here? Clever boys – I'm going to go for a little walk. Are you coming with me?'

'I should be delighted, sweetheart. I've been wandering about here like a lost sheep for the past few hours in the hope that you might come out before you went to bed. How is Miss Newcomb?'

'She's much better, thank you. I'm so sorry I didn't send word to you...' She was unable to complete her sentence as he enfolded her in his arms, pulling her close so her back was resting against his chest.

For a few moments they were quiet, enjoying the contact. Then her stomach gurgled loudly and quite spoilt the moment. 'I beg your pardon, how indelicate of me.'

'I had supper trays sent up to your sitting room, my love. I think it time we both went and ate.'

'Did you not go into dinner either? Or are you just hungry again?' She turned in his arms so she could see his face in the moonlight.

'I didn't go in – I was too worried about you both. But I can assure you I'm as hungry as you are.'

Hand in hand they walked companionably to her apartment and sure enough there was a veritable feast awaiting them. Eventually they were replete.

'I'd better go, sweetheart, before I'm discovered leaving your rooms so late.'

'I don't care if anyone knows. After all we're going to be married at the end of the week, are we not?'

His eyes darkened and she knew what he was thinking. Would it really matter if they anticipated their wedding night by a few days?

He got up so abruptly that his chair tipped over, startling them both. 'No, darling, you mustn't look at me like that. I'm going before I do something we'll both regret.'

He didn't even pause to kiss her goodnight but left the room at a run. The hour was approaching two o'clock and if she didn't retire immediately she would be too tired to perform at her best in the lady's race, which took place at midday.

19

Grace slept fitfully and was up again after a few hours. She pulled on her second-best riding habit and left for the stable yard. She'd told Annie to remain with Aunt Sarah for today so would have to manage without her maid's assistance.

This morning she intended to take Silver Lady out for a gentle hack so they could both become accustomed to this new arrangement. She had ridden the mare a few times, but not for several months. Indeed, she didn't think the mare had had a saddle on since she last rode her.

The dogs were scampering about as if they belonged there and all the grooms appeared to enjoy the company of her lively pets.

'Good morning, miss, I'm just about to saddle Silver Lady. Are you going to take Rufus out afterwards?'

'I am, Peterson. I need to make sure they are both sound before we enter the races.' She looked around surprised to find there were no other gentlemen, especially the new arrivals, doing the same thing with their mounts.

'Is Lord Sheldon down?'

'No, miss, you're the first. I heard as it was a late night for the gentlemen, a lot of wagering and such took place in the billiard room until the small hours. I doubt we'll have any of them here before noon.'

This suited her – the fewer of the competitors who saw her expertise in the saddle the better. 'What are the odds on me winning either of the races?'

'They shortened. Word got round that you beat his lordship in that race yesterday. I'm right glad I put the money on before that. We have ten to one – you're odds-on favourite now.'

She wasn't sure if this was a good thing or not. She'd forgotten to ask Bennett in which heat they were to run this afternoon and hoped they weren't together. The other contestants would know she was a danger to them – was it possible they could join forces to prevent her from winning?

'Have you heard in which heat Rufus is running, Peterson?'

'You're in the second one, and you're racing against the duke and Lord Peregrine – I don't know much about the other entrants as they're all horses from elsewhere and not stabled here.'

The mare looked in fine fettle, her dapple-grey coat shining and her eyes bright. When she was tossed onto the side-saddle the horse looked round, but made no further objection.

'I'm going to have a quiet ride through the woods. If Lord Sheldon enquires, will you tell him where I am?'

The groom touched his cap and returned to his work. The dogs scampered around the mare's hooves but even this didn't disturb Silver Lady. The hour was still unfashionably early and she didn't really expect Bennett to be up in time to join her on this hack.

Then Toby and Buster began to bark – she'd not seen Ginger for a while, but he was usually the one sniffing down a rabbit hole so she wasn't unduly perturbed about his absence. She swivelled in the saddle and saw her beloved on his magnificent stallion cantering towards her.

'Good morning, sweetheart, I can't believe you're out so early. That mare of yours is looking very smart. However, Madeline is riding a powerful gelding and thinks he might be a match for your horse.'

He drew alongside and the presence of a different stallion made her mare misbehave. After a series of bucks Grace managed to settle her and they were able to resume their ride.

'Having seen the way you handled that disgraceful exhibition, my love,

I withdraw my previous remark. My sister is a competent horsewoman, but she's no match for you.'

'I expect you've seen the lists for the races this afternoon. Would it be unsporting of you to tell me a little about your brothers' mounts?'

'Beau's horse will not be a rival; the animal's built for stamina and endurance not speed. If the races were for more than three miles then you might have a problem. Perry's mount is part Arab and goes like the wind – he might well be faster than Lucifer or Rufus, but he only runs well from the front. If he can't get that position he'll not do well.'

'Actually, I've been thinking I might run the first heat tactically. I will allow your brothers to beat me and come in third. There's no point in pushing Rufus until the final.'

'I wish to ride with you to the races, my love. I want everybody to know we're a couple. Meet me in the entrance hall at half past eleven.'

She returned to the stable satisfied her mount for the lady's race wouldn't let her down. Bennett had continued without her as he wished to let Lucifer stretch his legs and neither of them wanted a repeat of the race they'd had yesterday.

By the time she'd exercised Rufus and returned him to his loose box, the yard was busy. Grooms were busy tacking up and she was surprised that none of the saddles were for a lady. Obviously she was the only one who was taking this event seriously enough to make sure her mount was ready for the event at midday.

* * *

Annie was back in the apartment when Grace returned and greeted her with a happy smile. 'Miss Newcomb is able to keep down food now and her fever has completely gone. She will be up and about in time to see you race your big stallion, miss, but won't be there for the first event.'

'I'm so glad she's feeling better, as I was very worried about her.' She tossed her gloves, hat and whip on a side table. 'I see you've put out my new riding habit – I want to look my best this afternoon.'

'Green is perfect on you, miss, and brings out the colour of your eyes.

I'm glad you decided not to have all the gold braid and buttons that the modiste suggested – the military style is all very well but you don't want to scare the horses.'

Although she hadn't eaten since the small hours, Grace wasn't hungry. It was never a good idea to do anything strenuous on a full stomach. Once she'd completed her ablutions and changed she went to sit on the window seat from where she could view the racecourse.

There were now two wooden structures positioned on either side of the track at the place where the start and finish would be. She assumed they had been built for the race officials to stand on so they could see there was no cheating.

An area of grass had been roped off, presumably as a collecting ring. The racetrack itself had already been marked out with white-painted posts and there were men busy nailing rope to them to prevent the spectators from wandering into the path of the horses when they were racing. Hopefully they would remain on the seats provided either side of the finishing line.

Each race would be two circuits of the track and would be a test of horsemanship as well as of the ability of the horses themselves. There were two sharp bends to negotiate and a shallow stream to jump. The track also narrowed at both the bends, which meant that the participants would have to be vigilant if they didn't want to be unseated.

As she watched she saw several carriages approaching along the drive and at the head of those were half a dozen horsemen. She glanced at the mantel clock – there was no need for her to go down for another half an hour.

The clumping of feet and excited chatter from the ladies outside in the passageway indicated the time had come for her to make her way downstairs.

* * *

Bennett decided to remain in his apartment until it was time to meet his darling girl in the grand entrance hall. From his sitting room window he could watch the goings-on in the park. His reverie was disturbed by the arrival of his sister who wasted no time in getting to the point.

'I suppose you won't be supporting me this afternoon, Bennett.'

He lifted her from her feet and placed an affectionate kiss on top of her head. 'Of course I will – it's perfectly possible to support both you and Grace. I warn you, she's determined to win.'

'And so am I – I think all the races should be won by members of this family...' He frowned and she stuttered to a halt. 'I'm sorry, I shouldn't have said that. Miss DuPont will also be a member of this family very soon.'

'She will indeed, sweetheart, and I hope you'll welcome her without reservation. If I'm forced to choose, then you know what will happen.'

There was no need for him to finish his sentence. The colour left her cheeks and her eyes filled. Immediately he felt ashamed that he'd upset her. He loved his sisters and would do everything in his power to keep them safe – but one thing he would never do was give up the woman he loved.

She hurried off and he didn't call her back. There was something going on that he wasn't privy to and he had an unpleasant sinking feeling in the pit of his stomach. He pushed his worries aside. Today was about the races – about Grace. He refused to consider the remotest possibility that something would happen to force him to make that impossible choice.

There was a steady stream of spectators heading for the racetrack and already there were several mounted ladies in the collecting ring. The time had arrived to collect Grace and escort her to the start line. He wanted it made clear to everyone present that they were now inextricably linked.

The rules and etiquette of high society meant that once an engagement was official only the lady could break the arrangement, not the gentleman. As he had no intention of releasing Grace, whatever scurrilous gossip was unearthed about her family, his marriage could go ahead as planned and he had nothing to worry about.

She was there before him and he looked down on her from the gallery and was almost unmanned. He was a military gentleman, had thought romantic love was for other fellows, but now he knew different.

Somehow she sensed he was there and looked up. Her face lit with such love he wanted to vault over the banisters in order to be with her. He took the stairs three at a time and she laughed at his unorthodox arrival. 'I've not seen anyone do that before. You're lucky you didn't break your neck.'

'I was tempted to slide down the banister, but refrained. We must hurry, sweetheart, or you're going to be late. By the by, that's a spectacular ensemble you have on. I'll have no difficulty picking you out from the other entrants.'

'If my dressmaker had had her way I would be even more visible.' She ran her fingers over the gold braid and large brass buttons on the front of the jacket. 'I've not worn this before – I do hope I'm not going to be too conspicuous.'

He pulled her hand through his arm when what he really wanted to do was crush her to him and kiss her breathless. 'I can assure you there are at least two with more ornamentation on their habits than you have. I also saw a girl in scarlet – now that's certainly making a statement.'

Why in God's name were they discussing something so trivial? This was a momentous occasion for both of them and yet here they were talking about costume.

'I'm glad Rufus is not to run until the second heat as this will give me time to return Silver Lady to the stables. I've asked Peterson to shut my dogs up this afternoon as I don't want them getting in the way of the horses or the spectators. I sincerely hope they remain incarcerated.'

'I've become inordinately fond of your pets. They've proved excellent ratters, far better than the cats. Our barns are now free of rodents because of your dogs.'

Her mare whickered eagerly when she saw her mistress approaching. He tossed Grace into the saddle and checked the girth was tight and her stirrup leather the correct length. He was more nervous about this than she. He wasn't happy at the thought of her thundering around the race-track on a horse that was more used to pulling a carriage than being ridden under side-saddle.

He mounted Lucifer and together they left the stables. 'As you know my heat's immediately after yours, so I'll watch your race from horseback.

Please be careful, sweetheart. Don't take any unnecessary risks. Remember, you no longer need to win the purse.'

She tapped him playfully with her whip. 'It's a matter of pride, my love; I intend to show everybody my horses are second to none.'

The groom in charge of ensuring the correct horses were ready to race came forward and handed her a number painted on a piece of card through which string had been threaded.

'Give it to me, Grace. I'll tie it around your arm.'

She held this out so he could do so and both horses remained commendably still during the process. 'Thank you, my lord, I must go as the other contestants are gathering at the starting line.'

* * *

Bennett was right; her riding habit was comparatively subdued compared to one or two of the others. She nodded and smiled when spoken to but her attention was mostly on the other horses, seeing which would be the ones to beat.

Lady Madeline came alongside her with a friendly smile. 'I don't think there are any others to touch us, Miss DuPont. We will leave the rest of the field behind and conduct the race between ourselves.' She patted her massive gelding's neck and grinned. 'I warn you I intend to win. It's a family failing – none of the Sheldon clan like to lose.'

'And neither do I, my lady. However, I'm in agreement that our mounts are the only two with a chance of winning.' Grace didn't say that she knew the gelding only ran well from the front. She intended to take the lead and hold it all the way round.

A smartly dressed gentleman that she didn't recognise had climbed one of the structures and was holding a brightly coloured flag aloft. All the horses turned to face the start. The spectators fell silent and her heart hammered loudly.

Silver Lady shifted beneath her, as eager as the others to be off. The flag came down and she threw herself forward. The mare sprung from stationary to a flat gallop and they were several lengths ahead. She concentrated on her own race, ignored the yelling and shouting going on from the sidelines, and urged her horse faster.

They thundered around the course, increasing their lead with every stride the mare took. The two sharp bends were negotiated with ease and the stream cleared with feet to spare. When Grace galloped past the spectators for the first time the roar from the crowd was deafening.

There was no time to think about that – she must stay ahead and win the race. There was so great a distance between her and the other horses she could no longer hear them behind her, but then something made her look over her shoulder and to her surprise she saw Lady Madeline was no more than a length behind her.

The second circuit was as successful as the first and Silver Lady came into the finishing straight still ahead of the gelding. She glanced back and saw that her future sister-in-law wanted to win this race more than she did.

She eased back on the reins a touch and her mare responded immediately. She held Silver Lady in check until the gelding was parallel and then she turned and yelled. 'This is going to be a dead heat, my lady. That should give the gentlemen something to think about.'

The girl's face lit up and she nodded. They steadied their mounts until they were galloping stride for stride and then crossed the finishing line together.

The cheering from their audience told Grace she'd made the correct decision. She guided her exhausted mare back into the collecting ring where Bennett was waiting for her.

He greeted her with enthusiasm. 'That was well done of you, sweetheart. The race was yours to win. I cannot accompany you back to the stables as mine starts as soon as the final competitor has finished.'

'Were there any fallers, Bennett?'

'No, unless someone has come to grief in the last few hundred yards. You must go; you need to refresh yourself before you return for your second race on Rufus.'

He raised a hand in salute and trotted across to join the other gentlemen gathering at the far side of the collecting ring. The race had taken more out of her than she'd anticipated and she wasn't sure she would be able to do the whole thing again in half an hour.

This wasn't an option – she'd come here to show members of the *ton* that any progeny Rufus sired would be worth having. Her stallion would take care of her. All she had to do was remain in the saddle and he would do the rest. He'd never been beaten and she believed that there wasn't a horse here that could do so.

However, there was one thing she could do that would vastly improve her chances of winning. If she rode astride she would scandalise everyone present, but she would win the race.

20
_____

Grace explained her intentions to her groom and they agreed to have her stallion waiting by the paddock so she could at least be mounted before she was seen by the other contestants to be riding in so disgraceful a fashion.

She flew up the stairs and was obliged to rummage about for her divided skirt without the assistance of her maid as she'd given Annie the afternoon off to watch the races. She left the jacket from her habit on which made things a bit speedier.

With scarcely ten minutes before the race began she arrived at the paddock. 'Are you sure about this, miss? I don't reckon Lord Sheldon will take too kindly to seeing his future wife riding like this.'

'It's too late to repine, Peterson, the decision's made.' She should really have reprimanded him for his impertinence, but he was right to remind her she was taking a big risk.

Rufus was plunging and rearing at the noise coming from the race-track. She would never have been able to control him riding side-saddle.

She was justifying her decision, rehearsing her excuses, as Bennett would have plenty to say on the matter. Perhaps it would be better to withdraw – after all she no longer needed the money and once she was married the stud would be his concern, not hers.

Then it was too late and she was being swept towards the start line surrounded by the gentlemen, who appeared too busy trying to find a position at the front to take any notice of her. Rufus was as eager as the others to barge his way to the front and even riding astride she was in danger of being unseated.

'Miss DuPont, let us protect you from the crush.' The duke appeared on one side and Lord Peregrine on the other.

'Thank you, gentlemen. I'd no idea how rough this race was going to be.'

Rufus calmed with the horses beside him and she was able to catch her breath for the first time in several minutes of pandemonium.

'Riding astride was a sensible decision, Miss DuPont, but I fear not everyone will agree with me.'

'But if I have your approval, your grace, I'm sure that no one will have the temerity to comment on my disgraceful behaviour.'

There was no time to say anything else as the starter dropped his flag and all ten horses surged forward. Her intention had been to remain in the first four and therefore gain herself a place in the final race – but something told her Bennett would not allow her to race a second time after seeing how dangerous the first occasion was proving to be.

She crouched lower in the saddle and dug in her heels. Her mount responded magnificently and shot from between his two guardians like a bolt from an arrow. His ears were forward, his nose stretched out and he burst through the leaders and was at the front of the field.

The mud thrown up whilst she'd been trapped in the centre of the pack had all but blinded her and she daren't let go of the reins and use a hand to clear her vision. She would have to rely on her horse to carry her safely around the track. This wasn't going to be as easy as the first race – from the noise close behind her there must be at least two other horses on her tail.

The roar of the crowd as she went past the starting line for the first time seemed to spur her stallion on. He'd never moved so fast even when he'd overtaken Lucifer the other day. She twisted her hands into his mane and sent up a fervent prayer to the Almighty that she'd arrive at the finishing line in one piece. She was no longer bothered about winning – all she wanted to do was remain in the saddle.

The stallion soared over the stream, negotiated the last bend and the finishing post was in sight. She hung on, ignoring the two horses that were less than half a length behind her, and passed the winning post almost too exhausted to sit back and pull on the reins.

The cheering and shouting coming from either side of the track meant her victory must have been popular. Finally she had time to clear her eyes and gulp in a few welcome mouthfuls of air. Then she saw Bennett riding towards her and he didn't look especially happy with her performance.

* * *

There was going to be trouble from a couple of the losers. They weren't pleased at being beaten by a girl. Bennett guided his stallion towards her, determined to reach her side before any unpleasantness took place. He'd watched the race with his heart in his mouth knowing that if Grace fell she would be trampled underfoot.

She looked exhausted, barely able to keep her balance in the saddle. Thank God she'd had the sense to ride astride as she couldn't have survived on a side-saddle. 'Well done, sweetheart – let me lead you back to the stables before you're mobbed by well-wishers.'

'I don't want to do this again. It was quite terrifying.'

'That's fortunate, my dear, as I've no intention of letting you do so.' He reached over and took the reins of her sweating horse – even the animal seemed relieved to be under his charge.

Then his two brothers were there and the three of them made sure none of the disgruntled losers could approach. He led the procession into the stable yard where her groom was waiting.

Bennett lifted Grace down. Her knees buckled and he picked her up, holding her close. 'Come along, sweetheart, I'll take you to your apartment.' He nodded to his brothers. 'Thank you, I appreciate your assistance. I saw how you protected her at the start.'

Beau returned his gesture with a smile. 'Miss DuPont isn't a young lady I'd have chosen for you, but the more I see of her, the better I like her. You have my full support, Bennett. I sincerely believe she's perfect for you despite her not being one of us.'

The house was quiet, everybody must still be outside. Grace, who had had her face pressed close to his shoulder, tugged at his lapel. 'You may put me down now. I'm perfectly capable of walking. Did I hear aright? Have we now got your brother's approval for our nuptials?'

He'd no intention of relinquishing his hold; he was relishing every moment. 'It would seem so, my love, which is fortunate as you're going to need all the support you can muster to weather this latest storm.'

Her gurgle of laughter touched his heart. 'I know, riding astride was quite reprehensible. The duke said that I'd made the right decision. Are you very cross with me?'

They were now outside her sitting room and he shouldered his way in before he put her down. However, he didn't remove his arms from around her waist. 'I'm ambivalent on the subject. I'm suitably appalled that you did something so disgraceful, but thank God that you did as you wouldn't have survived if riding any other way.'

Her fingers crept around his neck and buried themselves in his hair. Despite her mud-streaked face, the pungent smell of horse that surrounded her, he'd never seen anything so beautiful. He wanted to make love to her, throw aside everything he knew to be honourable. She would be his wife in a matter of days – would it really matter if a child was conceived today?

'I beg your pardon, miss, my lord. I didn't mean to intrude.' Her maid had returned and he supposed he must be grateful.

He stepped away, hoping to hide his embarrassment with his coat-tails. 'I'll see you downstairs later, my darling. Shall we meet in the music room before dinner and you can play for me again?'

She nodded, her cheeks flushed and her eyes dark with passion. 'Tonight will be the happiest night of my life, my love. Now I have your brother's support I know our union will be successful.'

* * *

Grace enjoyed a hot bath and then rested for an hour or two before preparing for the evening. Aunt Sarah had decided to remain in her apartment this evening as she didn't feel ready to socialise. She was given the cut direct by all the ladies she passed and was relieved to find the music room deserted. It was all very well Bennett saying that the opinion of his peers was of no importance; she wasn't sure she could endure much more of being ostracised in this way.

She had arrived somewhat earlier than the appointed hour and settled herself on the piano stool in order to lose herself in the music. She was interrupted a short while later by the duke.

'You play exquisitely, Miss DuPont. I've never heard that sonata played so well.'

She couldn't force herself to turn round and face him. His remark had been innocuous enough but he hadn't come here to exchange pleasantries; of that she was quite certain.

'I am as well educated as any of your family, your grace. Being able to play the pianoforte and paint a pretty watercolour is not the sole prerogative of your class.' Her tone was light, taking the sting from her words. She turned and her happiness drained away.

The man standing before her looked incredibly sad – he must be bringing her the most dreadful news. 'Would you mind if I found myself a chair? This is going to be a most distressing meeting for both of us.'

She waved vaguely towards one of the spindly gilt chairs arranged along the far wall and he fetched one and sat down with a sigh.

'Do you love my brother, Miss DuPont?'

This question surprised her and she answered instinctively. 'Of course I do. Do you think I'd join a family who despises me if I didn't?'

His eyes glittered in the candlelight. 'Then you wouldn't want to ruin his life and cause him intolerable unhappiness.' He paused as if expecting her to answer but she had no coherent response to this. He continued. 'If Bennett marries you he will no longer be accepted in society. I've been making enquiries about your family circumstances and have discovered some unpalatable facts about your father.'

Grace bit her lip, knowing something dreadful was coming next. She raised a hand as if by so doing she could prevent his next words from coming.

'I'm sorry to be the one to tell you this, my dear, but once you know you'll understand why this marriage can never take place. Your father is infamous in certain circles in London – he's made it his life's work to acquire the vowels and debts of a dozen or more gentlemen and has then systematically ruined them. Three of these gentlemen have ended their own lives because of his actions.'

She opened her mouth to protest at this horror, but in her heart she knew what he said was true. Like an old woman she pushed herself to her feet and sunk into a deep curtsy. 'Thank you for telling me this, your grace. I'll leave here at dawn and... and... kindly convey my apologies to Lord Sheldon and say that I release him from the betrothal.'

She swayed and he was by her side to offer his assistance. 'Do you have somewhere you can go? I assume that you have no wish to return to your familial home.'

'I intended to win all the races and make enough money from the wagers so that my companion and I could live until I come into my trust fund next year.'

'You never had any intention of trying to ensnare my brother, did you?'

'Of course not – I don't belong here, but my parents gave me no option. My wish was always to be able to live quietly and run my stud successfully.'

'I can see why my brother is besotted with you – if there was any way around this appalling situation I can assure you that I would give you my blessing. Initially I admit that I thought you unsuitable, but as you know, I've changed my mind. But you must see, my dear, that however unfair, you will be forever tainted by your father's actions. My brother would be forced to remain in the country and abandon all his old pastimes and pursuits. However much he loves you, I fear that this canker would grow and eventually he would regret his marriage.'

'I couldn't do that to him, your grace. It will break my heart to leave him, but I must do so. Will you promise to take care of him for me? He'll be devastated by my desertion – don't let him do anything foolish.'

'I give you my word.' He pushed a soft cotton square into her hand and she mopped her eyes. 'Although at the moment this information is not known by my guests, you can be very sure that it won't be long before someone receives a letter from Town. Bennett would ignore this – would insist on marrying you anyway – but we both know we cannot let this happen.'

She blew her nose. 'He'll be here momentarily and however good my intentions, your grace, I'll not be able to turn him away.'

'I understand. Come, I'll take you to your apartment through the servants' route. I'll tell my brother that you were so upset by the treatment you received from the ladies that you've retired. I'll make sure he drinks heavily so he'll not be capable of visiting you this evening.'

Gently he escorted her to a door hidden in the panelling and, holding her candlestick aloft, he guided her expertly along narrow passageways and up staircases until they emerged in her own dressing room.

'I wish things could have been different, Miss DuPont. I would love to have had you as part of my family. Godspeed and take care.'

Annie had been head first in a trunk, placing tissue paper between the gowns. The sudden appearance of her mistress and the duke shocked her into silence. Grace pulled herself together and spoke first.

'We must leave as soon as everyone has retired. I must change into my travelling gown – no, I want to put on my habit. I'll ride Rufus.'

'Will Lord Sheldon be accompanying us? Where are we going?'

'My association with this family is at an end. Miss Newcomb must be told. As soon as you've done here, make sure you have a substantial supper as I've no idea when we will be able to stop for refreshments.'

As if in a dream the remainder of the evening passed. She tensed every time she heard footsteps outside in the corridor, expecting Bennett to burst in and demand to see her. Aunt Sarah hadn't questioned this decision and for that she was grateful.

Her maid returned shortly after midnight carrying a small leather chest. 'I was told to give you this, miss. It's right heavy, I can tell you.'

Grace was too miserable to respond and saw the object being handed to her companion. The sooner they could leave the better. Being in the same house as the man she would love for the rest of her life, but not being able to speak to him, was agony.

Leaving was the right thing to do but it didn't make it any easier. Bennett would be as heartbroken as she, but when his brother explained the circumstances he would eventually realise she'd done the right thing.

She'd written him a brief note breaking off the engagement and wishing him well. This she left on the mantelshelf, knowing it would be the first place he'd come tomorrow morning when she failed to appear.

An hour after the final footsteps had gone by the apartment, she followed her luggage down the servants' staircase and out into the moonlit night. The air smelt fresh and damp, but it failed to raise her spirits.

Rufus was delighted to see her and seemed fully recovered from his exertions earlier. Peterson tossed her into the saddle without comment. The lanterns were lit on each corner of the carriage and they were ready to depart after her three dogs had scrambled in to join Aunt Sarah and Annie in the interior of the carriage. Grace had no idea where they were going, but just knew she had to get as much distance between herself and Silchester Court before Bennett realised she had gone.

'Grace, my dear girl, where do you wish us to go?'

'Lord Sheldon will go to DuPont Manor. He'll soon discover the stud, so we cannot go in that direction.'

Peterson called down from the box. 'Shall we head north, miss? He'll not think to look for us there. If you recall I went to Oxford to collect a mare for breeding two months ago – I saw a lot of likely properties down that way. I reckon we can find somewhere quiet to rest overnight and continue in the morning.'

She was too dispirited to argue. She wasn't altogether sure exactly how far away this city was. All that mattered was that it was in the opposite direction to the one that Bennett would be searching. How they were going to manage for money she'd no idea, but she had no choice. What did it matter how or where she lived in future? If she couldn't be with the man she loved she was going to be unhappy anywhere.

21

Bennett woke up with a mouth like a bear pit and a head to match. He'd drunk far too much last night and mainly at the instigation of his older brother. He yawned and ran his hand around his bristly chin – time to get up and get himself ready to spend the day with his darling girl.

He threw back the covers but didn't jump out of bed with his usual enthusiasm. He smiled ruefully – he was getting too long in the tooth to drink so much. This pastime was better left to his younger brothers. His valet had everything ready for his ablutions and shave, and in less than the usual time he was immaculately dressed in the latest arrival from Westons – a dark blue topcoat that fitted him to perfection. He wasn't a vain man, but today he wanted to look his best.

He glanced at his gold pocket watch and was surprised to find the hour so late. However, after Grace had been obliged to retire because of the behaviour of the ladies she wouldn't take her breakfast downstairs but ask for a tray to be sent to her apartment.

There would be ample to feed him as well. He strode through the house with a light heart and couldn't remember ever being so happy. Having the approval of his older brother was not essential to his happiness, but made things so much more pleasant. Then something occurred to him that gave him pause for thought. Beau didn't approve of overindulgence of any sort and yet last night he'd broken this rule.

There was something wrong. The duke never broke his rules. He increased his pace and was running by the time he skidded a halt outside Grace's apartment. He didn't knock, but charged in. The room was empty. He threw open the door to her bedchamber and reeled against the door frame. She had gone. Left without a word and he knew this was his brother's doing.

As he stepped away from the door his eye was caught by a square of folded white paper propped prominently on the mantelshelf. He snatched it up and ripped it open.

> *My dearest Bennett,*
>
> *When you read this, my love, I shall be gone from your life. I cannot bear to tell you the reason for my leaving – but when you know you will understand that I have done the right thing.*
>
> *You must forget about me and find yourself a suitable bride, one who will not bring disgrace and unhappiness to your family.*
>
> *Our engagement is over. Do not blame your brother for this, as he was right to send me away.*
>
> *I shall never regret knowing you and it breaks my heart to go.*

The page was smudged and blotted from her tears and her signature was indecipherable. What had driven her away? There could be nothing on this earth that would make him give her up – nothing so bad that he would be prepared to live his life without her.

For a moment he was unmanned, unable to think coherently. Then he straightened, carefully folded the note and pushed it into his waistcoat pocket. He would go after her, bring her back – his life here was over.

His breathing steadied and his military brain took charge, pushing his heartbreak to the back of his mind. He knew where she was going, so there was no need to leave precipitously. His man would return with the special licence in a day or two and, with this in his pocket, when he found her they could be married immediately.

Beau would be waiting for him. He would never forgive his brother for interfering. It would take all Bennett's self-control to hide his anger and antipathy and appear to take this hideous separation in his stride. First he must know what she'd been told that would make her abandon him.

The thought of his beloved Grace leaving in the middle of the night, believing that she would never see him again, made him want to smash his fist into the wall. He had never loved her more. She had given up her own happiness in the mistaken belief that he would be better off without her.

He examined his reflection in the mirror. He didn't look like a man whose true love had abandoned him – if he was to remain here until the licence arrived he must endeavour to appear broken-hearted.

The final horse race was tomorrow and he had every intention of participating. This would give him something to occupy his mind until he could leave. Then his optimism faded as the reality of the situation finally registered.

He had no idea where she was going – she wouldn't return to DuPont Manor and had little money. His rapid return to his apartment gave several matrons palpitations, but he ignored them.

His valet, Abbott, was equally surprised. 'Miss DuPont has gone. She'll be heading for Essex but I've no idea exactly where in that county. Find two of my men and send them after her. It shouldn't be hard to track her carriage, as it will be followed by a chestnut stallion. Tell them not to make themselves known, just remain close enough to discover where they stop. Then one of them must return with the information.'

'I'll do so immediately, my lord. I'll pack your overnight bag so you're ready to leave when you have the facts.'

'Send word to my estate and let them know I shall be returning shortly with my wife and wish the house to be made ready for us.'

There was no need to discuss the matter further. Abbott was more than his valet – he was his confidant and had been with him on the Peninsula. 'Make sure they have sufficient blunt – and they must take extra to pay for Miss DuPont's expenses if necessary.'

Satisfied he'd done everything necessary Bennett was ready to speak to his brother and discover exactly what had driven Grace away.

* * *

As the sun rose over the treetops Grace thought it would be safe to allow her stallion to stretch his legs, although she would be careful not to push him too hard after his exertions the previous day. A decent canter and jumping a hedge or two would force her to concentrate and perhaps push her misery aside for a while.

When she rejoined the lane some twenty minutes later, she was obliged to wait until the carriage trundled around the corner. She manoeuvred her horse alongside and spoke through the open window to Aunt Sarah and Annie.

'There's a decent hostelry no more than a mile or two ahead. We must stop there and allow the horses to rest for an hour or so.'

The dogs were barking to be let out and she reached down to undo the door. They tumbled onto the lane and immediately raced into the wood.

'Are you all right, my dear? You must come inside with us if you're feeling at all tired.' She pointed to the small chest that Grace hadn't bothered to investigate earlier. 'His grace has given us almost one hundred guineas. We shall not be destitute and can find ourselves a decent house to rent.'

'He was almost as upset as I when he gave me the dreadful news last night. He's not nearly as arrogant and unpleasant as I'd first thought – I believe that if things had been different I would have been welcome in his family after all.'

Grace swallowed the lump in her throat and brushed the tears from her eyes. She urged Rufus forward, not wishing to discuss the matter further. No doubt one of her grooms would clamber down and close the door of the carriage.

She whistled and the dogs bounded up, delighted to be able to run about after being held captive for so many hours. 'Stay close, boys, we shall be at the inn very soon and I've no wish for you to be trampled on or run over by a cart.'

The Buck and Hunter wasn't a large establishment but quite big enough for her purposes. A relatively clean stable boy rushed out to take the horse's reins after she'd dropped to the cobbles. 'My carriage will be here in a few minutes. My horses will need watering and feeding and somewhere to recuperate for an hour or two. Is it too early to break our fast?'

Why she was enquiring from this urchin she'd no idea, as he was unlikely to know the answer to her question. He tugged his forelock and grinned.

'I'll take care of your horses, miss, and Ma and Pa will set you up with a fine breakfast.' He pointed to the open door and with a cheerful wave led Rufus away. Her stallion followed him without fuss, which was a relief.

The interior of the ancient building was gloomy as the leaded windows let in little light. She glanced around assessing the cleanliness and was pleasantly surprised. A young woman hurried out into the vestibule and curtsied.

'Good morning, madam, how can I be of service?'

'I'm hoping you can supply breakfast for my companion and maid as well as my three grooms. Your son is taking care of my horse and says he is capable of looking after my team.'

'Oh no, madam, he's not running the stables by himself. My older boy and his uncle will be there as well. I expect you would like a chamber in which to refresh yourselves after your journey.' She looked over her shoulder and nodded and a girl, a replica of herself, sidled in and also curtsied. The children had been well brought up.

'Dolly, show this lady up to our best chamber and then come straight down to fetch hot water.' The child smiled shyly and pointed to the stairs. 'We have only two other guests at present and they won't be down for an hour or two. I'll serve breakfast for you and your companions in the parlour. It will be ready in half an hour.'

The sound of carriage wheels outside meant everyone had arrived. 'Thank you, if you'd kindly direct my companion and maid to my chamber I shall go up directly.'

The rooms she was shown to were as spotless as the rest of the place. She removed her gloves and cap and found the necessary arrangements discreetly hidden behind a screen in the bedchamber.

Aunt Sarah and Annie arrived at the same time as a large jug of hot water. 'This is an excellent choice, my dear, exactly what we need. Why don't you complete your ablutions first and then I'll use whatever hot water is left.'

In less than the allotted time Grace led her small party downstairs. There was no need to ask where to go as the doors to the private dining room stood open and there was a table covered with a crisp white cloth laid up and ready for them.

Despite her heavy heart she was hungry. She had not eaten since yesterday morning and it would be foolish to continue without sustenance. After a substantial repast, all three of them returned to the bedchamber.

'You rest on the bed, my dear; I shall be perfectly well on the *chaise longue* and Annie can put her feet up on the footstool.'

'I don't want to sleep for more than two hours, We need to be on our way by eleven o'clock. I don't intend to ride; I'll join you in the carriage for the remainder of the day.'

'I've brought the overnight bag with fresh raiment, miss. You can change after your rest.'

Grace didn't expect to sleep; after all she'd been too wretched to do so during the night. Annie helped her remove her riding habit and boots and then she slipped between the clean sheets in her petticoats.

Two hours later they were back on the road again and this time she travelled inside the carriage with her companion. Grace dozed, as did Aunt Sarah, but still the day seemed interminable.

Peterson sent the groom riding Rufus ahead to book their overnight accommodation and eventually the carriage turned into a substantial coaching inn at five o'clock. Grace was heartily sick of being bounced about on the squabs and was determined to ride again the next day.

'I'm quite exhausted, my dear. I shall ask for a tray to be sent up to my chamber and will retire as soon as I've eaten.'

'I'll send Annie to attend to you first. I must speak to Peterson before I come in.' Grace embraced her friend and was concerned to see she needed the support of her maid in order to negotiate the short distance to the entrance.

Her head groom was waiting for her. 'The horses are done in, miss. They'll not go another day in this heat without having time to rest.'

'I thought the same. I noticed an empty house on the edge of the town as we came past. Would you go and investigate? I think we might be far enough away to be safe from discovery. If this house is to let then you must take it for us and then we don't have to travel any further.'

He beamed. 'I had a good look as we went past, miss, and I reckon it's perfect. I'll make enquiries from the landlord immediately.'

'Whatever the outcome, I think we must remain here for a day or two. Miss Newcomb is not well and I've no wish to make her worse by travelling any further.'

The Goat and Boot was a coaching inn, which meant that it was bigger and far busier than their previous stop. The landlord was waiting to greet her.

'Welcome, madam, your chambers are ready and there's decent accommodation for your men as well. Sally will show you up.'

The maid led her to a fine room at the rear of the building overlooking a paddock. 'There's hot water waiting, madam, and your supper tray will be up as soon as you like.' The girl bobbed and waited to see if there were any further instructions.

'Where is my companion sleeping?'

'Next door, miss, and your maid has a truckle bed she can pull out when she's ready to retire.'

'Thank you, I should like my tray brought up now.'

After a plain but well-cooked meal she was feeling a little more optimistic. The roof of the house she was interested in was visible from the window and she prayed it would be available, at least for a few weeks whilst she came to terms with her change of circumstances.

Traipsing all over the countryside for days no longer appealed to her. Bennett would be searching in Essex not Oxfordshire, and by the time he realised his error her trail would have gone cold. She might as well live here as anywhere else – it made no difference to her. What was important was that her dearest friend was comfortable and her people safe.

There was little point in retiring until Peterson got back from his errand. He was bound to come up to speak to her on his return.

Annie had remained next door taking care of Aunt Sarah and had been told not to return until nine o'clock. Grace was dozing in a chair when she was roused by a sharp knock.

She scrambled to her feet and hurried over to open the door and, as expected, Peterson was outside. From his expression she knew he'd been successful.

'The property belongs to Squire Evans and has been empty for a year or more – it seems the last tenant died and he's not been able to find a replacement until now. He's delighted to let us have it, and for a reasonable rent too. I've paid what's due and he's sending people to give the place a clean and tidy up before we move in.'

'Then we shall remain where we are until that's done. Is the place furnished or do we have to do that for ourselves?'

'Furnished right enough, but I ain't sure how good it'll be.'

'We'll manage with whatever we've got. Is there decent stabling and pasture for the horses?'

'There is. I was able to look at that and it's in good order. There's even hay and straw in the barn. The shutters were closed so I couldn't see inside the house.'

'Never mind, the news is better than I dared to hope. What's the name of our new home?'

'Drummond House, miss, a fine name for a fine house, if you ask me.'

Long after Annie was snoring quietly at the foot of her bed, Grace lay awake considering her future. The outlook was bleak even with the prospect of her funds becoming available next year. She would never marry, never have the joy of holding her own babies, never spend a night in the arms of the man she loved.

Hopefully Bennett would abandon his search after a few months and get on with his life. She prayed he wasn't as miserable as she was and that he understood why she'd had to leave him and break both their hearts.

22

Bennett headed for the study where he knew his brother would be waiting to speak to him. He was greeted with congratulations for both his win yesterday and his engagement – obviously the information his brother had was not yet known by the rest of the company.

'Come in. Do you have the most damnable headache? I apologise for plying you with alcohol last night, but I had no choice.' Beau looked as wretched as he felt.

'Before you tell me why you sent my future wife away, you'd better know that there's nothing in this world that will keep me from marrying her. I've sent my man to get a special licence and as soon as I have that I'll find her and we'll be married.'

His brother gestured to a chair and Bennett took it reluctantly. There was naught he could be told that would change his mind. When the sorry tale was finished he was shocked, but still adamant that it made no difference to his plans.

'How long will it be before this information is known by everyone here?'

'I'm sure others must have made enquiries as I did. I'm only surprised that Lady Peabody and her family don't appear to be privy to this news.' Beau rubbed his eyes and tried to hide his yawn. 'This is a wretched business, Bennett, but you must accept her decision. Marrying Miss DuPont will ruin your life...'

Bennett was on his feet and slammed his hands down on the desk, making his brother recoil. 'What you mean is that you don't want this family name tainted by association. I'll never marry anyone else and neither will she – we will not be parted by your machinations.'

He stormed from the room with eyes blurred. He needed to get out – get away from this place and clear his head.

He set off at a brisk pace into the woods, hoping the tranquillity of the trees would calm his rage. By the time he returned he understood why Grace had believed she had no alternative but to leave him. However, he doubted he would ever forgive his brother for separating them.

Good God! He must stop the DuPonts from turning up expecting to see their daughter married. He raced inside and scribbled a quick note explaining the situation and then sent the letter express. With luck this should overtake the invitation and prevent an embarrassing confrontation.

As he walked past the stables he could hear an unusual amount of hubbub. Damnation! He'd quite forgotten he was to take part in the final race at midday. If he was going to make the start he had no time to change into something less restricting and would have to ride in his smart topcoat.

Lucifer was saddled and waiting and if he raised a few eyebrows by his sartorial splendour he wasn't aware of it. He would win this race for Grace and make sure everyone was aware the betrothal still stood as far as he was concerned.

With luck he'd have word of her whereabouts on the morrow and the licence would also have arrived. As soon as he had this he would set out and, however long it took, he would convince his darling girl that they should be married regardless of the circumstances. He wouldn't give up until she capitulated.

If his powers of persuasion failed to move her then he'd make love to her and she'd be left with no option but to marry him, or risk producing a bastard child. His mood lifted at the thought and he began to feel a little more optimistic that everything could be resolved.

The race was won without difficulty but he got no joy from it. Grace should have been here; she should have been the one to see him receive the winning ribbon and the accolades of the spectators. He didn't wait to be congratulated but rode directly to the stables and handed over his sweating stallion to a groom.

His jacket had split at the seam, and for some reason this mishap enraged him. He returned to his apartment and his valet wisely remained quiet whilst he assisted his master to change.

He should be out looking for Grace himself, not leaving this to his minions. He would leave at first light tomorrow and head for Essex – if he travelled post he could catch up with his men and assist with the search.

There was no need to inform his brother of his plans – from this point forward he would live his life apart from his family. If he'd enjoyed being a member of the *ton* he wouldn't have joined the army and spent the past ten years fighting the French. Did Beau not know him at all?

His younger brothers and sisters revelled in being members of a prestigious family and all that entailed. If they were in his position and discovered the person they'd fallen in love with was beyond the pale they would break the connection immediately. He was certain even the girls would rather be without their chosen partner than without their position in society.

Tonight he wouldn't dine in company but have a tray sent to his sitting room. He intended to be up with the lark and travel without his valet or any other servant. Abbott had already packed a clean shirt and other necessary items in an overnight bag. He checked he had sufficient money for any eventuality, and retired early, confident that by the end of the next day he would be reunited with his beloved.

* * *

Grace was pleased with her new home. It was old-fashioned compared to DuPont Manor, but the furnishings were acceptable and after the spring clean that it had been given she was content she would be as comfortable here as anywhere else.

The thought of spending the remainder of her life apart from the man she loved was almost too much to bear. She had to be strong – she'd made the right decision and must live with the consequences. After all, she'd only known him for two short weeks so putting him from her mind should be easy enough.

Her companion had taken over the organisation of the household and for that she was profoundly grateful, as for some reason she just didn't have the energy to make decisions.

Although it was past midday she was still not up and had been unable to eat her breakfast. When her friend joined her, she barely managed to lift her head from the pillow.

'How are you progressing with our search for indoor staff, Aunt Sarah?'

'As I am to act as your housekeeper, my dear. We only require a cook and scullery maid and two other girls to take care of everything else. I've already appointed the cook and she's bringing the kitchen maid with her. I don't think there'll be any difficulty finding the other servants we need to run this house. Peterson is happy to manage the outside and will employ journeymen when necessary.'

'Good, then I shall leave everything in your capable hands. Have we sufficient funds to tide us over until you receive your money?'

'We have indeed, my dear. There's no need to pay our staff in advance and Peterson has discovered there is an excellent, if a trifle overgrown, kitchen garden with more than enough to feed our small household. Your dogs will be in their element. I'm certain there will be no rodents in the stables or outbuildings by the end of the week.'

'I thought I heard a cockerel crowing this morning – do we have fowl as well?'

'Yes, there are more than a dozen chickens and several cockerels. They have managed to survive on their own for the past year and the pond also has a plentiful supply of plump ducks. We have fresh eggs and meat already available. Our expenses will be minimal.'

This conversation had exhausted Grace and she wanted to be alone. 'Grace, you mustn't lie about in bed like this. You are made of sterner stuff – I've never taken you for a girl who would give up at the first setback.'

'I'm sure I'll feel more the thing in a day or two. Please leave me to grieve in my own way. I give you my word I'll get over this before long.'

'Very well, I'll leave you alone today. However, I'll expect you to be on your feet and downstairs tomorrow morning.'

The door closed quietly and Grace closed her eyes, hoping that sleep would claim her again. At least if she was asleep she didn't feel the weight of her misery pressing her into the bed.

What was Bennett doing at this very moment? Would he be in Essex and have already discovered she hadn't taken that route? Tears seeped from beneath her lids and she didn't have the energy to wipe them away.

She rolled onto her side and drew her knees up so she was curled into a ball. She wanted to howl and scream, to throw things, to let the world know that her heart was breaking, but she couldn't do this. Instead she sobbed quietly into her pillow and prayed that Bennett wasn't feeling as wretched as she was.

* * *

She awoke a few hours later to see the early evening sun filtering in through the closed shutters and making a pattern on the boards. As requested she'd been left on her own and her stomach rumbled loudly. She also needed to relieve herself urgently.

Once she was on her feet she felt a little better and decided to wash in the cold water from the jug in her dressing room and get dressed. There were no bells to ring and she'd no idea where Annie was, so would have to complete this task without assistance.

The trunk had been unpacked and her many garments were carefully hung on hooks or folded onto the shelves in the closet. She selected a simple muslin that required no buttons to be done up. Within a quarter of an hour she was dressed, had put her hair up in a coronet of braids around her head, and was ready to go downstairs in search of something to eat.

The front door stood open and sunlight poured onto the polished floor. There were flowers in a vase and these raised her spirits a little. She'd barely looked in the main reception rooms and hadn't visited the kitchens and other offices at all.

The drawing room was modest compared to what she was used to but perfectly adequate and she was delighted to see a harpsichord in the far corner. There was only one dining room and a study-cum-library on the ground floor and then she discovered a flight of stairs that led to the basement where presumably she would find something to eat.

She was halfway down when Aunt Sarah appeared. 'Well done, my dear girl, we thought if we left you without sustenance you would eventually come here of your own volition. I'll take you to the dining room and a delicious repast will be brought up to you right away.'

'No, I prefer to eat in the kitchen without any fuss. I would like to meet the staff you've appointed. Do we have the other two maids in residence yet?'

'They are already at work. We shall be a small but select company at Drummond House and none the worse for that.'

The kitchen was frighteningly old-fashioned without the modern closed grate that she was used to seeing; however, those working there seemed happy with their situation.

Grace managed only half a slice of bread and a few mouthfuls of soup before her appetite deserted her again. 'I'm going to wander about outside for a while. I want to see how my horses have settled and if the dogs are happy.'

'Do you wish me to come with you, my dear?'

'Thank you, Aunt Sarah, I would prefer to be alone.' She pointed to the back door. 'I presume this leads to the stables?'

'Indeed it does, my dear, the laundry and vegetable store are on your left, the kitchen garden straight ahead and to the right you will find the coach house and stables.'

Rufus was in the meadow behind the stables accompanied by the four carriage horses and he too was content with his lot. There was no sign of her little dogs.

'Peterson, where are they? I expected to have them around my feet as soon as I appeared.'

He scratched his head. 'I don't rightly know, miss. We've not seen them since yesterday when we arrived.'

'You must send someone out to look for them – I couldn't bear it if anything had happened to my pets.'

'The lad has been looking all day but not found them. I've sent him into the village to ask if they've been back to the inn we stayed in.'

Grace was obliged to turn away as she didn't wish her groom to see her tears. She no longer wished to explore outside and almost ran back to the house. There must be a side door she could use and avoid going through the kitchen a second time.

She dashed through the house and stumbled upstairs to her chamber where she flung herself onto the bed. Something terrible had happened to Buster, Ginger and Toby – she just knew it. They hadn't left her side since she'd rescued them two years ago and they would never willingly stay away from her.

Her head was full of catastrophic scenarios. They could have been killed by a diligence, poisoned by a neighbour or abducted by villains who wished to use them as ratters. Her pillow was sodden by the time she fell asleep.

* * *

After a fruitless few days Bennett returned to Silchester Court just before dinner on the third day without having found Grace. She hadn't gone to DuPont Manor or to the farmhouse where the horses were being kept. He was at a loss to know in which direction to search next.

Beau greeted him with an unexpected embrace. 'No luck? I guessed you'd gone in search of her and I don't blame you for trying. You must reconcile yourself to the situation, for it cannot be remedied. Miss DuPont left of her own accord knowing that by marrying you she would ruin your life.'

He shrugged off his brother's arm. 'It's you who has ruined my life, brother. Without your interference we would have been married by now. Do you honestly think I care if I can no longer parade around in fine clothes and mix with the cream of society? I've always hated it – why do you think I joined the army at the earliest possible opportunity?'

His raised voice had attracted attention, but he cared not. 'I intend to find her; I've only returned to collect the special licence and arrange for all my belongings to be transferred to my estate.'

'Please, reconsider your decision. Think what you will be giving up – we are a close family and your leaving will devastate the others.'

'They are welcome to visit me if they wish, but I shall never set foot here again.' He strode off ignoring the shocked expressions of the spectators. As he shouldered his way through, he overheard a gentleman speaking to his crony.

'I don't understand all the fuss. Sheldon should make the DuPont girl his mistress – nobody would object to that.'

Bennett's grief and anger spiralled out of control and he grabbed the man's shoulder, spun him round and punched him squarely in the face. The unfortunate gentleman collapsed in a heap, blood pouring from his nose.

'If you mention my future wife's name in such a way again, I'll kill you.' This was received by everyone in stunned silence. Bennett left the man to be ministered to by his friends and returned to his apartment to organise his immediate departure.

Abbott made no comment about the split knuckles and began to pack his trunks. Bennett regretted his violence and was ashamed that he'd taken out his frustration and misery on a complete stranger. He didn't intend to dine in company, but he would spruce himself up a bit and go down and apologise.

The grand drawing room was empty when he eventually arrived there. He would have to wait until dinner was over before he could find the man he attacked and try and put things right. Now he came to think of it, the man shouldn't have been a stranger to him as he'd already mingled with all the guests who had arrived two weeks ago.

Those three must have arrived in his absence. He would ask the butler who they were and if the injured man had recovered. Peebles would be busy in the dining room for the next couple of hours so he might as well check that his carriage would be ready for him to leave first thing in the morning.

A slight noise behind him made him turn. His eyes widened in shock. The man he'd knocked to the floor was pointing a pistol at his chest.

23

Bennett had seconds to live. The man's finger was tightening on the trigger. He flung himself to his knees and the bullet whistled over his head. He catapulted forward, crashing into his attacker. The man had had a second loaded weapon and this fired as Bennett landed on top of him.

The pain in his shoulder was excruciating. The world faded and for a few moments he was unable to function. The sound of gunfire had attracted men from the stable and from a distance he could hear voices above him.

Then Beau's anguished face swam into his vision. 'Lie still, the physician's on his way. I'm going to press against the wound and try and stem the bleeding.' His brother dropped to his knees and snatched off his neck-cloth to use as a bandage.

For some reason Bennett was unable to respond. His mouth seemed to be full of wool and his vision blurred. He tried to smile but it was a poor attempt. Then the rest of his family were at his side and his brothers carefully lifted him onto a trestle.

He wanted to tell them to leave this to the staff, but he couldn't find his voice. Every jolt and jar as he was transported inside was agony and it took all his control to stop himself from yelling. The thought of being carried up the long staircase to his own apartment filled him with dread.

The next thing he knew he was comfortably ensconced in a bedchamber he didn't recognise and his clothes had been removed. The quack was hovering above him.

'The bullet is still in your shoulder, my lord. I have to get it out.'

Bennett managed a small nod and then someone pushed a leather strip between his teeth. A horrendous five minutes later the job was done and he drifted in and out of consciousness whilst the doctor did his business and sewed up the wound.

When he opened his eyes again he found Beau sitting beside him, his face gaunt and looking years older than his age.

'Don't look so worried. I'm not going to kick the bucket. I'll be up and about in an hour or two.'

His brother smiled. 'Over my dead body – although that's perhaps not the best phrase to use in the circumstances. The man who attacked you is dead.'

This news cleared Bennett's head. 'How did that happen? I know the bastard tried to kill me, but he was in his cups...'

'He was perfectly sober. If he'd not resisted he would be alive still. Whilst you were being seen to he was ignored and had time to reload. The man was insane and determined to finish the job. Abbott shot him.'

'Who the hell was he? How did someone like that come to be here?'

'God knows! He came for the races and somehow insinuated himself into the company. In the confusion after Miss DuPont and you left, nobody realised he had joined the house party.' Beau rubbed his eyes. 'This is all my fault; if I'd not interfered none of this would have happened. I've sent a dozen men to search in other directions. I'll find her and bring her back to you. I don't give a damn what anyone else says about the matter. Grace will be my dearest sister as soon as it can be arranged.'

Bennett pushed himself up the bed, not quite believing what he'd just heard. 'What about the disgrace that will be brought to the family name? You never stop preaching to us about that.'

'I was parroting what our father used to say to me. I'm my own man; in future I'll make my own decisions. Why should the woman you love be tainted by association with her criminal father? Once you're married she will be part of the Silchester family and I defy anyone to cavil at that.'

'It's a great shame you didn't think of this before you sent her away.' He wasn't quite ready to forget and forgive.

'I cannot apologise enough for my part in this disaster. I'll not rest until Grace is restored to you.' He pushed himself upright. 'I shall leave you to rest. I've told the others not to come in until later.'

'Dinner must have been ruined by this fracas. I am sharp-set – can you have a tray sent here – wherever here is?'

His brother grinned looking more himself again. 'You're in the downstairs apartment that was once used by our grandfather. Fortunately the housekeeper had kept the rooms aired. Now, brother, rest until your food arrives.'

* * *

The next morning Bennett felt perfectly well, apart from a sore shoulder. His injury hadn't gone putrid and he had no fever. He swung his feet to the floor and reached out for the brass bell on the side table and rang it loudly.

His valet arrived at his side so speedily he must have slept in the dressing room. 'You're to stay where you are until the doctor has seen you, my lord. You lost a prodigious amount of blood yesterday.'

'And I've drunk a prodigious amount of watered wine to replace it. By the by, thank you, for disposing of the man who tried to assassinate me yesterday.' There was no need to say anything else; they understood each other perfectly.

His left arm was in a sling, which meant appearing correctly dressed would be impossible. Abbott dropped a loose shirt over his shoulders, added a waistcoat and helped him put his good arm through one sleeve of his jacket. With his stock neatly tied he didn't look too ramshackle.

'I'm going to eat in the breakfast room – no doubt there'll be plenty desperate to cut up my food for me.'

'There won't, my lord – his grace has sent everyone packing. They all left first thing – it was chaos for an hour or two but everything's quiet now.'

'It must be later than I think.' Bennett didn't have his pocket watch. Presumably it was still attached to yesterday's garment.

'It's a little after ten o'clock, my lord.'

'Then I'd better get a move on or there'll be no breakfast left.'

He made his way, slightly less briskly than usual, through the house enjoying the peace. Beau's actions would have offended the cream of society – his brother was obviously determined to upset as many people as possible, which was quite unlike him.

'Bennett, you shouldn't be up; you were told to remain where you were for another day at least.' Madeline ran to his side and embraced him.

'As you can see, sweetheart, I'm perfectly fine. It's a relief to have the place to ourselves again. I'm sorry you went to so much trouble...'

'Please don't say another word about it. All the work was worth it as we have a new sister about to join the family. However, there's so much extra food Beau has agreed that the garden party next week will go ahead to celebrate your nuptials. The villagers, our tenants and staff should be sufficient to use it up before it spoils.'

'Then let's hope we find her soon. I'm sure Cook will have stored the perishable items in the ice house.' This was a strange topic of conversation for a gentleman but everything these past two weeks had been out of the ordinary.

They strolled to the small dining room and he was surprised to find his siblings there to greet him.

'Bennett, you shouldn't be up – but we're glad you feel well enough to join us,' Beau said as he put down his fork and prepared to get to his feet.

'No, remain where you are, Beau. Good morning, everyone. Might I enquire why you're all breakfasting so late today?' He sat down and Madeline began to load a plate for him.

Perry answered. 'We had to wait until the kitchen could cook again – they were obliged to feed our departing guests first.'

'Well, I'm glad on all accounts for it. Is there any news from the men about Grace's whereabouts?'

'I've not had anything encouraging so far, but don't despair, brother, the search will continue until we locate her.'

'It's all very well finding her, Beau, but how can you be sure she will agree to return? She's going to need a deal of convincing that marrying Bennett won't still ruin his life.' Aubrey was about to shovel another forkful of food into his mouth, unaware that his thoughtless comment had not been well received.

'For God's sake, think before you speak.' Beau's sharp reprimand caused Aubrey to drop his food onto his immaculate breeches.

His youngest brother glared at Beau. 'Look what you've made me do. I'll have to change.' Then he became aware of the universal opprobrium. 'What did I do to upset you all?' He frowned and then enlightenment dawned and he looked appalled. 'Surely you didn't think...? I meant that Grace gave up Bennett because she loved him too much to risk damaging his reputation and might not accept that this has changed.'

'In which case, Aubrey, you should have made that clear. I apologise for barking at you. Forget your breeches and get on with your breakfast.'

As he devoured a massive breakfast one-handed (Giselle had carefully cut everything into bite-size pieces) Bennett thanked God that he wouldn't have to abandon his family in order to be with Grace. The badinage continued, but it washed over his head; he just continued eating and listening to his siblings.

* * *

Two days passed and still there was no news of Grace. His buoyant mood began to fade and his shoulder hurt like the very devil. The quack was recalled and declared him to be free of infection but recommended that he slowed down and allowed his injury to heal.

'I'm going to look myself if we don't hear anything by the end of the day, Beau. I can't sit around here waiting for news; it's driving me insane. Small wonder my shoulder's sore.'

His brother's attention appeared to be fixed on something outside and Bennett joined him by the window to see what was so interesting.

'Over there, by the trees, I swear I saw one of Grace's little dogs.'

'God's teeth! I believe you're right. How the devil did he get here?' His question was rhetorical and by the time he'd finished speaking Bennett was racing across the hall, almost giving the footman on duty there an apoplexy. The poor fellow barely had time to open the door for him.

Bennett jumped down the steps, shouting to attract the dog's attention. Of course it could be another animal entirely, but it certainly looked like Ginger. Then the beast was hurtling towards him, barking his delight, and moments later the other two appeared and were heading in his direction.

He dropped to his knees and they flung themselves on his lap. They were bedraggled, filthy and footsore but otherwise unharmed. He patted and stroked them with his good hand, knowing that his prayers had been answered. Grace couldn't be that far away if they'd found their way back here on their own.

'Where did you three come from? You must be half-starved and you certainly need a bath. Look at me – I'm as dirty as you are.' The dogs continued to whine, yap and lick but refused to get off his knees.

'Here, let me take them so you can stand up.' Beau reached down and picked Ginger and Buster up, leaving him to stand with Toby tucked under his arm.

'They need to be fed and bathed; the stables are the best place for them. They've come to fetch me, and once they've recovered they'll lead me to Grace.'

'If you'd said such a thing yesterday I would have thought you fit for Bedlam, but now I believe you might be right. I'll accompany you when you leave tomorrow to make sure Grace agrees to return.'

'I'll take the curate with me, and then we can be married immediately, before she has time to change her mind. Her companion can be the other witness.'

The dogs were handed over and were made a great fuss of by the grooms. Bennett arranged to have his carriage ready for the following morning, although he intended to ride despite his injury. He was perfectly capable of managing a horse one-handed; he'd done so many times when serving on the Continent.

Madeline and Giselle were ecstatic at the news that he was to be married and insisted that they come, as they had no intention of missing such an important occasion. 'You will be the first of us to step into parson's mousetrap, Bennett, and we intend to be there to see this momentous occasion,' Perry said firmly and Aubrey agreed.

'We can't all turn up on her doorstep, wherever that might be, and expect to be accommodated. Maybe it would be better to hold the ceremony here,' Beau said.

This wouldn't do at all. He could hardly explain to the girls that he wished to spend the night with Grace with or without the benefit of clergy. 'No, Beau and I will go on our own and you four will remain here. We shall celebrate our nuptials in style on her return. Get started on the arrangements for the garden party and why don't we hold the ball as planned?'

'In all the upset over the past few days I'd quite forgotten to cancel the invitations to our neighbours. Do you think you'll be back by next weekend?'

'We'll make sure we are, Madeline. Beau, I've been considering how best to encourage the dogs to lead us back to her. If we have one dog running free at a time and the other two inside the carriage they shouldn't get overtired. I'm riding and will be able to follow them across country.'

This announcement elicited a storm of protest, which he ignored. 'Abbott and a groom can ride with me; he prefers horseback to a carriage every time. I intend to travel fast, and one or other of them can make sure the carriage follows in the correct direction.'

'I'm damned if I'm being cooped up with a curate – I'll ride too. Now that's settled, I've some estate business to attend to so will see you all at dinner.'

During the afternoon Bennett and Madeline studied the list of those invited to the ball and decided to add a few more names as they no longer had a houseful of guests.

'I heard that Heatherfield has been sold. Shall I send an invite to the new family?'

'Depends who it is. Do you have any idea?'

'I'm reliably informed that it's one Lord and Lady Carshalton. He's only recently inherited the title and used to be a soldier like you.'

'In which case, go ahead. I like the sound of them. Heatherfield is only a few miles from my estate and it would be good to have another military man to talk to. Hopefully Lady Carshalton will become a friend to Grace too.'

His sister smiled. 'I doubt it. She's his grandmother not his wife.'

'How the devil do you know so much about this family?'

'Giselle is bosom bows with Lucinda, daughter of their closest neighbours, Sir James and Lady Bagshot.'

'I take it the Bagshot family are coming next weekend?'

'Of course, there are also two brothers; after all one can't have too many gentlemen at a ball.'

* * *

The next morning they were ready at dawn and Buster frolicked around Lucifer's feet, eager to set off. All three of the dogs had made a full recovery and Bennett was sanguine they would suffer no harm by returning from whence they'd come.

Even the kidnapped curate seemed happy to be accompanying them. It was fortunate there were three of them mounted as the route Buster took was unsuitable for the carriage. The dogs had obviously made a circuitous journey to Silchester Court, but that was hardly surprising. What was amazing was the fact that somehow they'd found their way back at all.

24

Several more dreary days passed at Drummond House and Grace moped about scarcely eating and unable to hold a conversation without dissolving into tears.

'My dear girl, you must pull yourself together. It will do no one any good if you fade away. How would you feel if you heard that Lord Sheldon had died from a broken heart?'

This bracing comment was enough to give her pause. 'You're right, I must put this behind me and start to plan my future life. Knowing that he's alive somewhere in the world will have to be enough.' She sighed and wandered to the window where the sun shone relentlessly – rain would have been more appropriate.

'Good girl. Why don't you change into your habit and take your stallion for some exercise. You never know, you might find your dogs somewhere in the neighbourhood. If they wandered onto somebody else's land they could have been adopted as strays.'

'I'll do that. However, first I'd better have something to eat.'

An hour later she was in the stable yard and Rufus was prancing about in his eagerness to be off. 'I'm glad I decided to ignore convention and ride astride, for I'm sure he'd have me off otherwise.'

Peterson tossed her into the saddle and then mounted Silver Lady.

'There's a grand ride across the fields, no hedges or ditches to jump – just space to gallop.' He gestured with his whip towards the north where, on the horizon, she could see a forest of some sort.

'That's a relief – straight and fast will suit both of us.' They clattered out of the yard and along a narrow track, which led to the fields. 'I should think we'll hear from Collins today and then we can start to make arrangements to bring the horses down here.'

'I think that both mares will foal next year. Too early to know for sure, but Rufus did his duty in the paddock at Silchester Court.'

This was a highly unsuitable conversation for an unmarried lady but one she was accustomed to having. 'Then it's fortunate that two of the team are geldings or we'd have no animals to pull the carriage next spring.'

'If we're staying here, miss, then I reckon you should sell that vehicle and buy something lighter. A gig or barouche would do just fine.'

It became impossible to continue the conversation as an inviting stretch of greensward was sending her mount into a series of bucks and rears. 'All right, my boy, calm down. We shall have our gallop now.'

After a mile or two her horse had settled and the trees were rapidly approaching. She sat deep in the saddle and pulled gently on the reins. The stallion responded immediately and dropped into an extended canter, then a trot and finally to a walk. He was barely hot; the run hadn't put him in a lather.

'Good boy, that was most enjoyable. Shall we investigate the forest before we return?' Peterson arrived and she was pleased to see Silver Lady wasn't sweating either. 'I'd like to go into the trees. It will be cool and pleasant out of the sun. It's the sort of place the dogs liked to be, with plenty of rabbits and squirrels to chase.'

'We looked in here first off, miss, and didn't find hide nor hair of them. But it won't do no harm to have another look, for they might have wandered back.'

Riding under the canopy of green was pleasant, like being underwater, restful after the mad race down the fields. Grace allowed the reins to slip through her fingers so her mount could stretch his neck, knowing he wouldn't do anything untoward now he'd had sufficient exercise.

'Listen, Peterson, I can hear noises in the undergrowth. It must be foxes, as rabbits don't make so much noise.' She leaned forward in the saddle in order to peer beneath the trees and the next thing she knew she was tumbling through the air and fell on her back on the soft leaf mould.

Before she could move a small, wriggling bundle of fur landed on her chest and her face was smothered with sloppy licks. 'Ginger, my darling boy, why have you been hiding in here all this time?' She pushed herself upright just as her groom arrived at her side.

'Well I never! Would you look at that? Where the devil has he been all week?' Belatedly he nodded at Grace. 'You all right after your fall, miss? Rufus saw the dog and stopped dead and you went flying over the side.'

'I'm perfectly fine; in fact, I've never been better. If Ginger is here, then Buster and Toby must be somewhere around too, for they are never far apart.'

She called and they searched for twenty minutes to no avail. 'I'll take this little chap home with us; I'm not letting him out of my sight again. I'm sure the other two will follow his scent up to this point and then they should be able to find their way to Drummond House.'

Somehow she managed to scramble into the saddle with her dog tucked under her arm. She wasn't going to let him run loose in case he disappeared again.

* * *

Bennett turned the air blue. 'What the hell has happened to that wretched animal? I'm sure he headed into this forest but he's nowhere to be seen.'

'We've been looking for an hour. I don't think he's here. Perhaps he's gone back to join his brothers.' Beau was equally frustrated by this setback.

'I have it – we'll fetch the other two and put them down here. With luck they'll pick up Ginger's scent and put us back on the trail.'

'It'll be full dark in an hour. Let's hope we can find somewhere more salubrious than last night's accommodation. No doubt you're accustomed to having crawlers after your stint in the army, but it's not something someone of my elevated status should be obliged to suffer.'

Bennett laughed at his brother and together they retraced their path and rejoined the carriage. They'd sent a groom to find them somewhere to stay and he saw him in the distance. He was approaching at a gallop and waving his hat and shouting something. Although he couldn't hear what was being said, Bennett almost exploded with joy. Grace had been located – there could be no other reason for this demonstration. He kicked Lucifer and raced to meet him.

'We found them, my lord. Miss DuPont has taken a place called Drummond House. It's no more than three miles from here, on the edge of the village.'

Beau reined in beside them and overheard this information. 'It's too late to go there tonight; they will be abed by the time we get there. There's no rush; we'll arrive in good order first thing in the morning.'

He was about to argue the point but decided to hold his peace. 'You're right – I stink of the stable, not conducive to a happy reunion. We can appear spruced up with the curate in tow tomorrow.'

His brother appeared satisfied with his answer and they followed the groom back to a substantial inn where they were given adequate chambers. Fortunately he didn't have to share with Beau and retired early saying his injured shoulder was stiff after a day in the saddle.

As soon as he was alone with his valet he explained his plan. Abbott wasn't entirely convinced, but agreed to assist him in this lunacy. The hostelry was quiet by midnight and he and his man slipped silently, boots in their hands, through the sleeping house and out by a side door. Ten minutes later they were outside Drummond House, Buster and Toby frolicking at their sides.

* * *

Grace took Ginger up to her bedchamber, determined he was going to stay close to her until she could be sure he wasn't going to vanish again. She was woken by him scratching at the door and whining, obviously desperate to relieve himself.

'You're a nuisance. You should have taken care of that matter before you came up. Wait whilst I put on my bedrobe, kindly don't disgrace yourself in here.'

Once she was ready she scooped him up and, with a candlestick in the other hand, made her way down to the side door. Suddenly Ginger shot from her grip and launched himself at the front door, barking loudly enough to wake the dead.

His noise was greeted by more barking from outside. Her beloved pets had found their way to her. She ran to the door and flung back the bolts. The door was scarcely open when two furry bundles wriggled through the gap and launched themselves at her.

She fell to her knees and held them close, tears of joy streaming down her cheeks. She'd dropped her candlestick and the sliver of moonlight coming through the door was the only illumination in the vestibule. 'Shush, shush, boys, you'll wake the household.' She scrambled to her feet and pushed the door shut and shot the bolts home. 'Come along, you must come with me to my room. I know it's unprecedented to have you inside, but I'm not letting you out of my sight ever again.'

They clattered beside her, their claws loud on the uncarpeted boards, but appeared content to be indoors. She halted on the landing to listen, hoping the racket hadn't woken Aunt Sarah, but everywhere was silent.

'In here, boys, you can sleep on the rug by the window tonight. I'll arrange for something more comfortable in the morning.' She led them into her bedroom and pointed to the place she wished them to settle.

For some reason the dogs were ignoring her and were more interested in something in the darkness by the open door. Quickly she ran back and closed the door, then removed her bedrobe and draped it tidily over the end of the bed. As she turned she walked into something solid.

Her bladder almost emptied in shock and she drew breath to scream. Then she knew who it was. 'Bennett, what are you doing in my bedroom? Have you run mad? I thought you understood the situation.'

'Darling, I've just spent the most miserable week of my life. Your dogs came to fetch me and I'm not leaving your side ever again.'

Before she could protest he pulled her close. Only one arm was around her waist. 'You're injured. Tell me at once what happened.'

'Someone tried to kill me, but Abbott shot him. I'm perfectly well apart from the fact that I can't use my left arm at the moment.'

'I'll find the tinderbox. I want to see for myself. I want to know exactly what transpired.' When she tried to move away he prevented her.

'No, sweetheart, the time for talking is over.' He stepped closer to the bed and pushed her gently backwards.

'What are you doing? You must leave at once before anyone knows you're here. I don't want to be your mistress...'

'I should think not, my love. Tomorrow you'll be my wife and my brother's here to witness the event.'

She shot upright, colliding painfully with him as he bent to kiss her. 'The duke is here?' She peered around his shoulder with absolute horror.

His laughter filled the room. 'Good God, darling, he's not here at this precise moment. Do you think I brought him to witness this?'

She rolled away and dropped to the floor on the far side of the bed. Her eyes had become accustomed to the dark and she could see his outline clearly. 'Go away, Bennett, I don't want to marry you, and you being here doesn't change that fact.'

He ignored her protest and she watched in growing agitation as he began to disrobe. By the time he turned his back to remove his breeches she was mesmerised. Her skin burned and her heart was pounding.

He'd made the decision for her. If his brother was here then the family had decided she was a suitable bride after all and who was she to cavil?

Before he could face her she pulled back the sheet and slipped beneath it. The bed dipped as he joined her. 'This garment is superfluous, sweetheart. Allow me to remove it.'

Instead of pulling it over her head, he gripped the opening at the neck and ripped her nightgown in two. When her naked flesh touched his, she forgot her reservations and discovered what the meaning of true love really was.

When she awoke the following morning she was alone and she was grateful for that. Trying to explain to Aunt Sarah why Bennett had pre-empted their marriage vows would have been embarrassing and upsetting for both of them.

She scrambled out of bed and hastily pulled on her bedrobe. She gathered up the ruined nightgown and hid it at the back of her closet. Would the sheets reveal what had taken place? If she spilled water on the covers Annie would put clean linen on and hopefully not examine them too closely.

Her beloved was going to appear at the front door at ten o'clock with the duke and a curate in tow. She must look suitably surprised when he arrived. Although she would like to put on her finest gown, to do so would reveal she'd already spoken to her future husband and knew his plans.

Her morning ablutions were more thorough than usual, but that was the sum of her preparations for her wedding day. When her maid appeared she refused her morning chocolate. 'As you can see my pets have come home. I was obliged to get up in the middle of the night to let them in. I'm going to take them for a walk and require my oldest gown. I'll change into something more respectable on my return.'

The sun was out and the dogs danced around her feet, as happy as she was to be reunited. She was halfway across the lawn when she was hailed. She recognised the voice and turned to see her dearest love striding towards her.

'Sweetheart, I couldn't stay away a moment longer. My brother will be here shortly. We can be married as soon as he arrives,' Bennett said as he gathered her close.

'I can't possibly get married in this gown. You must tell Aunt Sarah whilst I get changed.'

He released her and she sped away, leaving the dogs with him.

Annie must have seen them in the garden, for she was waiting when Grace rushed in. 'I knew Lord Sheldon would arrive to marry you, miss. Quickly – I've put out your prettiest muslin and sent the girl to gather flowers for your hair.'

Grace was almost ready when Aunt Sarah arrived, also dressed in her finest. 'Dearest Grace, I cannot tell you how delighted I am that you are to get your happy ending. His grace is here and I've never seen him so convivial.'

* * *

Bennett was pacing the carpet. 'How much longer is she going to be? Until I have my ring upon her finger I'll not be content.'

Beau smiled. 'We should have given her more warning. She'll only be a bride this once and will want to look her best. Stop fretting, brother, she's hardly going to disappear again.'

Then his wait was over. Grace stood framed in the doorway and she had never looked more lovely. Her glorious russet hair had been threaded with flowers and she was the most beautiful bride there had ever been. As she hesitated Beau strode forward.

'In the absence of your father, would you allow me to escort you, Grace?'

Her smile was radiant. 'Thank you, I should be delighted to accept your kind offer.'

His brother had done the right thing – had made it plain his reservations about their marriage had gone.

Bennett held out his arm and she placed her hand upon it. Together they turned to face the curate and become man and wife.

* * *

MORE FROM FENELLA J MILLER

The next sumptuous Regency romance in this series from Fenella J Miller, *A Dangerous Husband*, is available to order now here:

https://mybook.to/DangerousHusbandBackAd

ABOUT THE AUTHOR

Fenella J. Miller is the bestselling writer of over eighteen historical sagas. She also has a passion for Regency romantic adventures and has published over fifty to great acclaim. Her father was a Yorkshireman and her mother the daughter of a Rajah. She lives in a small village in Essex with her British Shorthair cat.

Sign up to Fenella J. Miller's mailing list for news, competitions and updates on future books.

Visit Fenella's website: www.fenellajmiller.co.uk

Follow Fenella on social media here:

 facebook.com/fenella.miller
 x.com/fenellawriter

ALSO BY FENELLA J MILLER

Goodwill House Series

The War Girls of Goodwill House

New Recruits at Goodwill House

Duty Calls at Goodwill House

The Land Girls of Goodwill House

A Wartime Reunion at Goodwill House

Wedding Bells at Goodwill House

A Christmas Baby at Goodwill House

The Army Girls Series

Army Girls Reporting For Duty

Army Girls: Heartbreak and Hope

Army Girls: Behind the Guns

Army Girls: Operation Winter Wedding

The Pilot's Girl Series

The Pilot's Girl

A Wedding for the Pilot's Girl

A Dilemma for the Pilot's Girl

A Second Chance for the Pilot's Girl

The Nightingale Family Series

A Pocketful of Pennies

A Capful of Courage

A Basket Full of Babies

A Home Full of Hope

At Pemberley Series

Return to Pemberley

Trouble at Pemberley

Scandal at Pemberley

Danger at Pemberley

Harbour House Series

Wartime Arrivals at Harbour House

Stormy Waters at Harbour House

The Duke's Alliance Series

A Suitable Bride

A Dangerous Husband

Standalone Novels

The Land Girl's Secret

The Pilot's Story

Boldwood

Boldwood Books is an award-winning fiction publishing company seeking out the best stories from around the world.

Find out more at www.boldwoodbooks.com

Join our reader community for brilliant books, competitions and offers!

Follow us
@BoldwoodBooks
@TheBoldBookClub

Sign up to our weekly deals newsletter

https://bit.ly/BoldwoodBNewsletter